THE
ARCANUM OF BETH

BY
MARY JANE RUSSELL

THE ARCANUM OF BETH
© 2009 BY MARY JANE RUSSELL

ISBN 10: 1-935216-01-5
ISBN 13: 978-1-935216-01-8

First Printing: 2009

This Trade Paperback Is Published By
Intaglio Publications
Walker, LA USA
WWW.INTAGLIOPUB.COM

CREDITS
EXECUTIVE EDITOR: VERDA FOSTER
COVER DESIGN BY SHERI

DEDICATION

For Joyce Coleman, friend and attorney extraordinaire—you are always there for me.

ACKNOWLEDGMENTS

Many thanks to Sheri Payton and Kate Sweeney for turning down the first draft of this book but giving me another chance to revise and resubmit; to Kate Sweeney for bouncing ideas for the rewrite that led to acceptance for publication; to Verda Foster for graciously wading through the numerous corrections during editing and finding the last loose ends; and to Sheri (artist, not boss) for the cover designs to choose from.

Most of all, I count my blessings for my parents, William and Alma Russell, who instilled in me the love of books and reading and a work ethic that never allowed me to give up on anything. If they could see me now.

Prologue

"How long did it take you to finish the crossword this morning?" Ellen Harris stood before the coffeemaker as though her presence would make the ready beep sound faster. Her partner had already been through a pot brewed from Seville orange-flavored beans. Ellen preferred Folgers from whatever store had it the cheapest.

She wore men's pajama pants with hems dragging on the floor and a thin, faded T-shirt that she considered her most comfortable. She was just back from filling the bird feeders before any of the neighbors were up to see her outside. Buddy, the tri-colored Australian shepherd, stayed on Ellen's heels. His paws were immaculately clean.

"What?" Janet Evans was not aware of the folded newspaper in one hand and the sharpened number two pencil in the other as she finished watching the morning news on the local television station. "It's decaf." She always prepped the coffeemaker for Ellen when she poured the last of hers.

Her eyes never left the small screen. She was draining the last use from an ancient seven-inch television by letting it run continuously on the breakfast table. She had another small TV turned on in her former sewing room that was now her home office. The Singer cabinet worked well for her computer, but she could not remember the last time she had plugged in the sewing machine. It was a holdover from her defunct marriage. Janet had made most of her daughter's clothes until they both started school.

Ellen's hair had turned solid white in the past several years. She kept it cut no more than an inch long. It was easy enough to tell how she had slept by the angle the hair stuck up from which part of her head.

"Comb's good for that." Janet's yogurt sat untouched. She stuck the pencil behind her ear and idly felt her own not-quite-shoulder-length hair—almost long enough for a trim. Janet didn't need a mirror to know it was time for a dye. She refused to allow the presence of a single gray strand in what Ellen referred to as her Ronald Reagan hair.

Ellen ran her hands through her hair to uniformly tousle it. "How's that?" She flipped her partner off.

"Lovely." Without looking down to see if the dog was in his usual spot beside her chair, Janet held the toast crust beside her hip. The bread was gently taken from her fingers.

"Faster or slower today?" Ellen blew on the hot coffee, knowing the sound annoyed Janet almost as much as the decaffeinated grind annoyed her. She smelled the carton of one percent milk beside Janet's cup to decide the likelihood of eating cereal for breakfast.

"It's fresh." Janet read the clue and knew the answer before she finished counting the squares to fill. "What are you talking about?"

"You always time how long it takes you to complete the crossword puzzle." Ellen glanced at the mostly empty grid. "Must have been a good lead story to slow you down enough to actually read the newspaper and watch the television version, which is usually the reporter reading from the newspaper." She glanced at the clock on the wall. "You're running late." She intentionally let her boobs press against Janet's arm as she leaned over the table for the cereal and the neatly folded front section of the newspaper. "Don't get any ideas."

"Oh, please. You wish." Janet pushed Ellen away as she tried to kiss her cheek. "Sorry, fresh makeup. I want to save that article."

"What's it worth to you?" Ellen had not yet opened the

paper.

"Eat your bran flakes. You know all that matters to you in the morning is a good poop." Janet's hand rested on Buddy's head. "We know who the sweetheart in this house is, don't we, Bud?"

"Damn, how long have we been together?" Ellen snapped the paper open as she walked toward the refrigerator.

Janet frowned through her drugstore reading glasses as she was slowed by the double meaning of the next clue. "Just go to the den. I'll talk to you tonight. I'm running late. Some of us still have a job to go to."

Her partner of twenty-one years had not yet decided what to do with her time now that she'd exercised her option to draw a pension after passing her fifty-ninth birthday and having thirty-seven years of service with the local women's college. Ellen leaned toward camping out in the den watching cable television and cruising the Internet all day. Janet kept giving Ellen the ads for art classes offered by the city with the hope that she would discover a new hobby or, heaven forbid, a hidden talent.

Ellen actually had a knack for ceramics but decided after three weeks of classes that it was too girly for her to continue. They were both watching for the announcement of the recreation department's next woodworking class.

Ellen read the opening paragraph and whistled as she looked over her glasses at Janet. "Congratulations, Mrs. Evans. You did it. Both of those damn women in prison, one for twenty years, the other for five. Murder of the first degree, conspiracy to commit murder. Overt act and malice aforethought...those words you love to hear." Ellen whistled again, causing Buddy to bark. "I still can't believe that sorry-ass brother of hers got off scot-free. You must be glad to have that mess over with. I know you learned things about your friend you wish you hadn't."

"Twenty years with the possibility of parole after five, eight years reduced to five...such a small price to pay." Janet rubbed Buddy's head to calm both of them down. She had purposely avoided knowing the sentence before it was pronounced. There weren't enough years left to the two women convicted to make restitution for the death they caused.

"Who always says justice is fleeting at best?" Ellen frowned and continued to read the synopsis of the guilt phase of the trial that had ended almost a month earlier. Ellen missed the bittersweet smile that briefly crossed Janet's face when she heard the quote she usually muttered about most cases. Ellen shuffled into the adjoining den, dripping milk from the cereal bowl. Buddy obligingly trailed her, licking the drops from the floor and knowing he would have the bowl when Ellen was done. "Why you don't want to retire and do want to be involved in agency and family cases is beyond me."

"Some of us lost money in the stock market instead of catching the small tech companies that paid out big. Some of us went to college later in life and have loans to pay off. Some of us had to pull our money out instead of becoming vested in a decent retirement program. Some of us paid child support. Why you get up this early when you don't have to is beyond me." Janet watched Ellen ruefully. "I know you guys have a busy day of television watching planned."

Ellen had been Janet's biggest supporter when she put herself through four years of college and three of law school. Ellen had waited patiently for their time together as Janet figured out she needed to divorce her husband. Ellen hadn't questioned Janet's changing jobs five years before to become partners with a small town lawyer who never turned down a case, instead of staying with the county's commonwealth attorney. Most importantly, Ellen had understood Janet's friendship with a woman young enough to be her daughter.

Ellen's voice trailed off in the other room. "I did like her, you know. She deserved better."

Janet's pencil stopped midway through the next answer. Her mind was not on the puzzle, even though she felt obligated to fill in at least half of the blanks no matter the time it took. She was not willing to take a chance that missing one morning's mental exercise would hasten whatever form of dementia awaited her in a few years. Her mind was on a decision she made shortly after the guilt phase of the trial was over—she would not become involved in the sentencing phase or appeal unless subpoenaed. Her part had been to bring an indictment to trial. Those women killed her dear friend and there was no appropriate restitution.

She stared out the window, taking no notice of the finches jockeying for a perch on the feeder. To think, her true friendship with Beth Candler started only three-and-a-half years earlier over her impersonation of Dolly Parton, yet Beth had become the friend of a lifetime.

Chapter One

"How in the hell did I let myself be talked into doing this?" Janet looked at herself in the full-length mirror, then at the assemblage of outfit strewn across the bed. "That damn Greg must have cleaned out the bottom of his closet for me…literally and figuratively." She chuckled at her own play on words.

Janet was average height. She preferred to admit to five foot six inches, yet knew she was a little shy of that mark; it just had a good sound to it. Her figure was not bad, just solid and a little more in circumference than she preferred. Reality was a hard taskmaster. She had borne a child, she loved food, and her life's work was fairly sedentary. The outcome was inevitable.

Her religion on Sunday mornings was golf, regardless of the weather. She maintained that she had closer interaction with a divine being on the open greens than anyone confined to a hard pew, boring speaker, and off-key choir possibly could. Besides, it gave her and Ellen much needed time together.

"The only place we're the same size is the bust." She stared at the low-cut dress as she adjusted the plunging neckline and wished the lines didn't continue straight down her body. When had her waist disappeared? She twirled, sending the yards of material in the skirt of the dress into motion similar to a descending parachute.

"Here goes nothing." She pulled and tugged the curly long blond wig over her pin-curled hair. "Jesus, this feels like a bizarre B-girl stocking cap." She adjusted the hairline and burst out laughing.

"May I see you yet?" Ellen called to her from the kitchen.

Janet bargained for privacy while dressing by threatening Ellen with a weekend of transcribing boring legal documents. "Absolutely not. You may only see after I'm completely ready. I don't have time to rebut your commentary." Janet looked at the package of glittery fake nails. These she did know what to do with. She used the plain ones on a regular basis, applying polish to match her lipstick despite the crude remarks from Ellen.

She concentrated on the jars of makeup and variety of foam and bristle brushes. Soon she had on twice her normal amount of makeup, as well as the longest false eyelashes she had ever attempted to stick to her eyelids. "Payback is hell, Greg."

Janet stood back from the mirror and stared at herself. A low rumbling laugh began near her ovaries and carried all the way up until she howled with laughter. "Why did I wait until after I was in my fifties to have this much fun?"

Ellen could no longer tolerate the separation. "What in the hell?" Her jaw dropped. She was absolutely speechless and broke out in a laugh that doubled her over. She barely drew enough breath to speak. "You, Ms. Low-key, conservative, don't-call-attention-to-my-personal-life, are going out in public like that?"

Janet nodded, struggling to breathe and speak at the same time. "I most certainly am. I intend to enjoy parading around like this. I've spent more than my fair share of time in those damn stuffy business suits. Don't even try to ruin this for me. It's not going to work." She accentuated the last few words with an accompanying flounce of the four-inch dangling rhinestone earrings that she had spent an entire dollar on at the discount store.

"Ruin it? I'm sorry now I didn't come up with a Porter Wagoner outfit to go with you. You look like Dolly Parton's bimbo grandmother. I love it." Ellen bent over with another burst of cackles.

"Close enough." Janet clapped her hands together, careful of the nails. "Perfect. You couldn't have paid me a better compliment. That's exactly the look I was trying for. No one at the party knows what my costume is except Greg and maybe Andy if Greg can't keep a secret. What delicious fun this will be. You better reconsider."

Ellen shook her head. "As much as you tempt me...and you do in that outfit, by the way...I'll still pass. Too many straights will be there. Too many of the people you work with don't know about me. I'm not much on mixed parties. You wouldn't want me there drinking enough to loosen up around all those strangers."

"Don't hate. You need to be more open-minded." Janet tried a shoulder shimmy to check if her boobs stayed in her dress.

"Damn." Ellen grinned. "Does Beth know about us?" Ellen gestured toward the door and waited for the lady to leave the room first.

Janet frowned. "I've told her I have an ex-husband and a daughter her age. Have I made a big production of coming out to her? No. I just assumed she knew."

"Humph."

"Don't start that. I have no problem telling people I know. I just don't think my personal life is everyone's business. Who cares about an old woman of fifty-three anyway?"

"I sure as hell do." Ellen slapped Janet's butt as she passed.

Janet patted the wig down. "Play your cards right, and you'll sleep with Dolly tonight." She winked as she walked past her and out of the room. It was impossible not to add a little extra swish to her walk.

Janet did remember to take her camera bag from the hall tree—the only safe way for her to survive that night would be as the one taking the photographs. It was a shame she didn't have a more exciting ride than her nondescript Ford sedan. Why hadn't she thought to rent a two-seater of some sort? What a hoot that could have been. One thing for sure, she would drive very carefully and drink very little. The last thing she wanted was to be pulled over and tested by one of the deputies she routinely worked with.

Janet slowly followed the narrow side streets into one of the older subdivisions. It was a perfect Halloween—just chilly enough to know it was fall, warm enough so the children didn't have to be hampered by coats. She loved October in Virginia.

Beth's was the perfect neighborhood for Halloween—a strong middle-class subdivision that had held its value since first built in the early 1920s as a mix of dissimilar frame and brick two- and three-story family homes. She watched the clusters of children approach the houses with parents waiting in the street. She eased to a stop along the curb in front of Beth's house—a Dutch gambrel with the aluminum siding painted a soft cream and maroon shutters as an accent. It so suited Beth.

Beth Candler was one year younger than Janet's daughter. Janet sighed. She had not seen Melody in the twelve years since the child had graduated from college and moved to Chicago.

Beth bought the house when she turned thirty and left the family farm she shared with her parents through her father's illness and death. It had not been an easy decision for her to leave the land and her mother, but both women knew it was past time for Beth to be on her own.

Beth's mother was called by her mother's maiden name, Keith, since they shared the same first name. Keith was involved in the small farm community through church and volunteer work, as well as being a reliable babysitter. Beth knew Keith was fine on her own. She rented the farm acreage as soon as word of its availability went out each year. Beth struggled with guilt over losing her father, leaving her mother to manage the Candler land, and spending so much time building a career as an accountant.

She started keeping the books on the family farm while in high school and taught herself to treat business laws with a Nancy Drew approach, searching for the clues to keep a business profitable and take advantage of tax laws. It was a knack she refined as she slowly rose through the ranks of a local accounting firm.

Janet knew what to expect when the front door opened. The house was neat as a pin, no random dust or cat hair to be found. Keith teased her only daughter about cleaning a clean house. The furniture was early twentieth century mission oak that Beth found and restored piece by piece at minimal cost. Nothing matched exactly, but all blended together to create the impression of a warm country home that, for the night, just happened to be decorated with orange lights, cobwebs, and hanging skeletons. The food was a mix of country cooking and easy hors d'oeuvres. Beer was on ice in what had been a laundry day wash tub used by Beth as a wading pool in the summers on the farm.

Janet pushed the wine coolers into the ice, keeping one to nurse as she made the first round of guests. She and Beth knew a lot of the same people from the business groups that met courtesy of the chamber of commerce. They had begun occasional lunches and dinners about six months before when they discovered that they liked to be irreverent about many of the same things and people.

Janet tugged at her dress to keep her breasts from popping out.

"Need any help with that?" Beth's boss eased up beside her, enjoying the vantage that his height allowed.

Janet rolled her eyes. "Jerry, you had your chance years ago and didn't take it. I don't revisit missed opportunities, and I've changed teams."

He laughed. The feather sticking straight up from his head was firmly held in place by the sweatband around his forehead. He seemed comfortable without a shirt, wearing extremely tight jeans with a loincloth hanging over the crotch and butt. "It pays to have a pool in the backyard. My tan doesn't stop." He laughed again as he caught Janet studying his body.

"I'm just wondering if my friends will still respect me after this display." She tugged at the bodice again, gaining no material to move upward.

"As long as you don't flop one of those free at the wrong time and put someone's eye out." Beth put her arm around Janet's shoulders and hugged the woman. She was several inches taller than Janet and several dress sizes smaller. Janet loved to tease her friend about who had the grayest hair; Beth refused coloring and had inherited her father's premature salt and pepper.

"And just what are you supposed to be?" Janet raised her eyebrows at Beth just as one of the long lashes decided to dangle instead of stick. She squinted as Beth reapplied the lash for her.

"I'm a nerd accountant, buddy." Beth pointed to her outfit as she explained. "Hair in a ponytail, which is actually very comfortable and the way I really do like to wear it, just not slightly sideways. No makeup, which is also a preference. Big glasses from several years ago. Can you believe that I actually thought these looked good? Plus the tape around one earpiece, which needs no explanation. My shirt is a little too tight, but I thought wearing it with the buttons pulling away from the buttonholes, like a lot of the men I work with, has a certain amount of warped humor to it. You'll notice the dollar bill pinned to my sleeve that's for the vending machine. I really like these pants, but either they shrank or I'm a little taller than when I bought them, however, it does help to accentuate my white socks very nicely. And the loafers, what can I say, high school. Voilà. Geek accountant extraordinaire, have to perpetuate the myth."

"Or mythter." Jerry laughed at his own bad joke and finished off the can of beer with a belch. Both women rolled their eyes.

Janet looked at Beth and laughed as she thought about holding onto Jerry Mitchell just for the fun of it. It was Ellen's own fault. She'd been invited and declined. Jerry was safe enough; he had known Janet with Edward and now with Ellen.

"Come on, I want to introduce you." Beth took Janet's arm and nodded toward the far corner of the room. She led Janet to a couple who seemed to be the only ones not in costume. "Janet Evans, this is my brother, Will, and his wife, Patti."

Each held a drink they had not touched and looked too pained to speak.

Janet clapped her hands. "How nice. Are you fans of mine?"

Beth chuckled as Will and Patti gave Janet blank stares.

"I'm sorry?," Will said and raised his eyebrows. He was a taller, ganglier version of Beth with curly black hair and wearing a three-piece suit.

"She means Dolly Parton." Patti was obviously bored and clearly felt none of the partiers was in her league. She dressed high-dollar and had the makeup and hair styling of a woman used to being around money.

"Well, I don't listen to country music." Will stared at his wife.

"For God's sake, you two, lighten up." Beth looked at Janet.

"They just drove in from Knoxville to spend the weekend and obviously didn't pay attention to the e-mail that I was having a costume Halloween party tonight." She rolled her eyes.

"This is what we always wear to instill confidence in clients. I'm a stock broker," Will said.

"Antiques broker, always working, until he starts making more money." Patti looked about as though all the people together couldn't afford one of the pieces she routinely bought and sold at enormous profit.

"Ah, costumes after all." Janet glanced across the room that was filling behind her. "Well, I know your mother will appreciate that you made the trip."

"Oh, we won't see her on this trip. It's the only way Patti would come with me." Will's words stopped abruptly as Patti elbowed him in the ribs.

Beth glared at Patti. Janet idly wondered what would be said after a few more drinks.

"Oh, Lord, who and what are they?" Patti's eyes were on the front door as a pair of under-dressed prostitutes complete with beehives, heavy makeup, and long feather boas gyrated into the living room.

"Good heavens, those guys…engineers by day, queens by night. My nephew, Greg, who's now partners with Beth's ex," Janet said. "Andy Reynolds is the taller one," she said over her shoulder for Will's benefit.

"I didn't realize this was a coming-out party or I would have dressed better." Beth moved toward the front door and hugged the men. "Greg, you have the best legs I've seen on anyone in ages. Andy, you've been holding out on me. Where'd you find that bustier?" She pushed her dollar down his cleavage as he smacked her hand away. "Why didn't you wear this when we were dating?" She watched his face take on a faint red tint to match his normal hair color.

"You could at the very least have worn something different than your usual outfit for your own party." Andy made a face at Beth reminiscent of when they were preteens.

"Auntie!" Greg clapped his hands together and leaned within

a few inches of Janet in a mock hug.

"You look beautiful." Andy grinned at Janet. "I bet Ellen can't wait for you to get home."

Janet glanced at Beth and saw no confusion. "She'll be sound asleep and snoring."

Beth led the boys toward the table of food while asking what they wanted to drink.

"I wouldn't have put Beth with a crowd like this," Jerry whispered in Janet's ear.

"Oh, it's the quiet ones you have to watch." Janet kept Jerry in tow as she worked the room. She watched Will and Patti set their drinks on the radiator cover and ease up the stairs. She wondered if they would use one or both of the guest rooms.

The costumes were indeed wonderful revelations of personalities. The attorney, who had the look of a 1920s flapper as she wore a vintage cream silk dress and Shirley Temple wig. The police officer, who had the perfect Sherlock Holmes outfit, including the Inverness cape, Calabash pipe, plaid Deerstalker hat, and oversized magnifying glass that he used to check out Janet's breasts. The prostitutes, who were a delightful couple at work and at home, and did dress better than most women, herself included. At least Janet could console herself that Greg inherited his sense of style from her. Her sister disowned Greg when he came out, the same as she'd done Janet. The building inspector, who wore his turnout gear to be the firefighter he gladly volunteered his time away from the office for, particularly when sequestered in the corner with Cher in a skintight black leotard and baggy leather jacket. Lara Croft stood in the kitchen doorway with a shot glass and bottle.

"I thought I had nerve." Janet eased over to Marie, who wore her long black hair in a single braid down her back and skintight wife beater tucked into extremely short shorts.

"And I thought I had dropped a few pounds over the summer." She looked down at the outfit. "Evidently not." She set the glass and bottle on the counter for safe keeping before she mingled.

"Baloney. You have all the men in here drooling over you. I had a figure like that before childbirth." Janet shook her head.

"Who am I trying to kid? I never had a figure like yours."

Marie punched Janet on the arm. "Watch, I'm going to have a little fun. I'm going to do the cat thing. I know who in this crowd I can make the most uncomfortable. Have your camera ready." She adjusted the twin pistols she had borrowed from her son.

Marie worked her way across the room toward the half-circle of split bottom chairs. Beth was seated between Andy and Greg, equally fascinated by their outfits and willingness to be so openly gay.

"This isn't the first time we've done this. Most people love it. We're just at the point that we figure what the hell." Greg touched Andy's cheek affectionately. "I knew Auntie would need us more outrageous than her outfit."

Beth shrugged. "To think everyone believed Andy and I were the perfect couple all through high school and college. You two are the ones who are perfect together. I'm just glad hardhead," Beth hugged Andy, "listened to me when I told him I knew the perfect blind date for him."

Janet trailed along so she could listen. Marie could sense a weakness and enjoyed toying with it.

"So is this the dyke accountant keeping company with two over-the-hill ladies of the evening?" Marie made the most of there being no empty chair and sat on Beth's lap uninvited.

"Damn it, Marie." Beth's face immediately flushed. "You interrupted just as I was beginning to understand layering makeup. Now I'll never get it."

"Oh, you'll get it all right." Marie squirmed closer. "Is that your slide rule, or are you happy to see me?"

"Jesus, Marie, how much have you had to drink?" Greg leaned over and slapped her with the end of his boa. "Give the kid a break. It's her first big grownup party. Take it slow with her."

"All the more reason to make it one she'll remember." Marie looked over her shoulder. "Ready, Janet?"

Janet looked at the camera in her hand and nodded—she wasn't sure for what.

"Holy crap." Jerry nudged Janet so the camera came up just as Marie took Beth's face in her hands and kissed her full on the lips, and not as a female friend or family member. What made Marie slip off Beth's lap and onto the floor with a thump was that Beth kissed her back.

Janet snapped the look on Marie's face as her tailbone cracked against the hardwood floor and all she felt was the kiss. It was a photograph that made the round of friends like lightning. The smile on Beth's face in the next frame as she held her hand out to Marie to help her up was captivating. There was so much offered in one simple gesture. Marie clearly enjoyed being bested.

Jerry leaned down to Janet. "I didn't know she was bi."

"That's all right, dear. I don't think she knew, either." Janet laughed as she had when she first saw her costume on herself.

The party was an instant classic that Beth was begged to repeat the next year.

Chapter Two

"You have to explain this to me again." Janet sat before the computer in her office and stared at the brief she'd brought home to work on rather than stay late at the office again. She actually liked working directly on the computer when doing a final edit—it eliminated the need of finding one of the many pairs of inexpensive reading glasses scattered about the house.

Ellen looked into the room. She did not cross the threshold unless invited. She'd decided long ago that the secret to a long-term relationship was privacy. Janet's office with rolltop desk, computer, and case files was her sanctuary. The den with the big-screen television, laptop, bookcase full of mysteries, and recliners was Ellen's. They shared equally the bedroom and seldom used the living room. The kitchen went to whoever gave in to hunger soonest. Yard work and laundry were Ellen's responsibilities; housework and grocery shopping were Janet's.

"Microsoft Office? You've been using that for years." Ellen stood in the doorway. She didn't want to see any of the names on the documents or in the files and waited as Janet covered or turned over papers.

"No, silly. The bonfire next weekend. Just what is it about burning wood in a hole in the ground and sitting around freezing your ass off while your front cooks that lesbians love so?" Janet did not break her line of sight from the monitor.

"Turd." Ellen laughed. "I'm just ready for spring. I don't care if it's early. We haven't seen most of the girls since all of the

Christmas parties. Besides, it's easy to host a bonfire. Everyone stays outside...most of them even pee in the bushes...and brings their own coolers of beer. It's that whole outdoor howl-at-the-moon thing."

Janet glanced over her shoulder. "Thank you for that image."

"You won't have to do any of the work. I'll take care of everything." Ellen eased into the room and rubbed Janet's shoulders. "Bless your heart, lots of knots."

Janet took deep breaths to help the knots release. "Okay, you win. It will be good to see everyone. I'll invite Beth."

Ellen continued kneading. "Do you think she's ready for an all girl party?"

"Seems to be. I haven't talked to her since middle of the month. She was working late on Valentine's Day. I think she needs one of our gatherings."

"You know the single ones, and some of the committed ones, will be standing in line to hit on her. Fresh meat, not to mention pretty, drama-free, and financially solvent."

"You know who I'm concerned about."

Ellen sighed. "Lou."

Janet turned and frowned.

"Lou is with Stephanie. Last time I stopped by campus, Lou said they were thinking about a child."

"Uh-huh."

Ellen exerted a little more pressure.

"Ouch! Okay, okay. I know you two are buddies. I just don't like her reputation."

"Just because you and I had the longest and most chaste courtship on record doesn't mean everyone else should."

"You just keep an eye on Lou, please."

Ellen leaned down to whisper in Janet's ear. "Beth can take care of herself. She's not Melody nor your responsibility."

Janet stiffened. "I know that. Could I talk you into bringing me a Diet Coke?"

"You bet. I'll do anything for you that I can."

Ellen was as good as her word. As the weekend approached,

she cleaned the house and stacked the dry wood next to the fire pit in the backyard. She brought all of their lawn chairs out and hosed them off. She went to Sam's Club and stocked up on party appetizers.

Janet was pleasantly surprised to arrive home Friday afternoon and find everything ready. There was even a tomato stake in the ground near the heaviest shrubbery ready for a roll of toilet paper. Saturday morning was relaxed with a late breakfast and midday shower. Ellen strung the stereo speakers outside just before the first couple arrived at 4:15. The other dozen women drove in two or four to a car within the next hour and parked at angles to the driveway.

Janet watched the crowd gather. Ages ranged from late fifties to early twenties. Most of the women were in couples, whether casually dating or committed.

Beth arrived among the last. She was dressed in tight dark jeans and a medium blue cowl neck sweater. She made her way directly to Janet.

"I almost changed my mind and didn't come." She touched the neck of her sweater. "It's a bit of a throwback, but it's warm with two shirts underneath. We'll be outside the entire time?"

Janet chuckled. "Lord, you sound like me when I went to my first of these twenty-five years ago. I was twenty-nine and a senior at the women's college that Ellen worked at. She'd organized the gay students and staff for a party. No one would dare do that these days, having faculty and students drinking beer at the same place."

"I have to tell you." Beth looked around at the group of women openly in couples. "This strikes me as very cool."

Janet hugged her. "Just remember all wolves don't have penises."

Beth laughed.

Janet waved Ellen over. "My partner of twenty-one years, Ellen Harris. Beth Candler."

"Just call me R-E-T-I-R-E-D." Ellen ducked the backhand thrown by Janet and hugged the young woman. "I feel as though I already know you. Come on, let me introduce you around. This is a good group."

Janet kept the food flowing from kitchen to picnic table while watching over Beth. Beth met all the women and easily engaged each of the groups in conversation before finding an empty chair and sitting down to watch the fire.

A short version of Amelia Earhart dressed in faded jeans and a suede bomber jacket walked over to Beth and handed her a Sam Adams. Beth smiled and thanked her, then listened intently. Without warning, the woman leaned down and kissed her on the lips.

Janet crossed the yard to her friend as the woman walked away.

"You saw?"

Janet nodded.

"She didn't tell me her name, only that she didn't want to miss the opportunity of being the first woman here to kiss me." Beth's cheeks were pink from more than the bonfire.

Janet watched the woman saunter back to two chairs pulled side by side, motioning another woman to bring her cooler over.

"That's Lou Stephens, a friend of Ellen's from the college. The woman beside her is her girlfriend of two years, Stephanie."

Beth nodded. "I hear what you're saying." She grinned. "But that was a good kiss."

Janet shook her head and looked across the fire to see Ellen shrug her shoulders.

Chapter Three

Janet glanced about the Japanese restaurant as she waited for the hostess to return from seating the couple before her. She didn't see Beth anywhere. The restaurant was locally owned and authentically operated by a Taiwanese immigrant and her two daughters who had the patience to teach local girls the intricacies of the menu. The room was equally divided between traditional tatami floor booths and Western tables with chairs separated by bamboo screens. Prints that looked as though taken from ancient Chinese mah-jongg tiles lined the walls.

"Two, please, non-smoking, a corner if one is free, and a table unless all of you want to help me off the floor when we're done." Janet followed the giggling young woman, taking note of the faces they passed. Good, no one she recognized. Beth had called that morning and asked about dinner, not the usual week or two out but within a few days. Janet decided to forgo her exercise class at the new gym just for women. From the sound of Beth's voice, something was going on that she needed to talk about as soon as possible.

Janet was comfortably seated and scanning the menu when Beth entered the restaurant. Janet watched her cross the room to join her. Beth was noticeable in a very subtle fashion. She wore a minimal amount of makeup—the dark brows and eyelashes that accentuated her hazel eyes needed little help. Her clothes fit well and were always muted colors. That night was no different—a pale gray wool suit and lavender tailored shirt. Her shoulder-length hair was soft against her collar with a hint of gray brought out by her suit. She was average height and size—the farm had toned her body and she rode her bike every chance she could steal away from the office, resorting to a treadmill when necessary. There was just an easy elegance to her. When she talked, people listened. She only spoke when she had something of relevance to say. She had the innate ability to stay calm no matter what the circumstances and assuage other's emotions at the same time. Janet knew thoughts raged inside Beth, but on the outside, she was very soothing to eyes and ears.

Beth leaned down and hugged Janet, brushing her cheek against the other woman's and teasing her with a formal greeting. "Mrs. Evans, you are the best for doing this tonight. I hope it was as easy for you to change your plans as you said."

"Stretch and grunt or have a nice relaxing meal with a dear friend. Let me think about that." She glanced at her watch. "Maybe I can still make the end of class."

Beth bumped her shoulder into Janet's as she slid into the chair next to her.

"Forgive Ellen for not joining us. Lazy bum didn't want to change clothes and drive across town. What can I say, I love her."

"That says it all and no explanation is needed. I'll guilt her into it the next time." Beth looked up and smiled as their waitress approached the table with steaming hand cloths.

"I'm Kathy. I'll be taking care of you two tonight. Am I going to have to separate the two of you?" She waited for them to stop laughing before using tongs to give each a towel. "What may I start you ladies off with?" She moved closer to Beth, letting the hem of her short black dress touch Beth's arm. Kathy's ash blond hair was bobbed, reminiscent of Doris Day in her heyday, giving the twenty-something waitress an uncanny resemblance to an actress she likely had not heard of.

"Beer, anything but the cheap domestic," Janet answered for both of them. "This feels so good. I'd put it over my face if the makeup wouldn't wash out." She surrendered the cloth to the bamboo tray beside her water glass.

Kathy looked to Beth.

"What can I say other than she knows my weaknesses very well. Sapporo? The tall one?" Beth was on a kick of Japanese beer. She folded the cloth and centered it in the small tray.

"I'll be right back." Kathy cleared the table of the trays.

"That way, we can honestly say we only had one beer. It just happens to come in a twenty-two-ounce can." Beth glanced down at the menu. "Andy and Greg have me hooked on sushi. We drive all over the state on weekends deciding who has genuine sushi and who has leftover bait."

"You have loosened up."

Kathy set the serving tray on the table beside theirs and poured the first glass for each of the women.

"A woman who knows how to pour beer without two inches of foam on top. Your tip just increased." Beth raised her glass to Kathy before she tasted the beer.

"It could be a night to remember." Kathy winked as she tucked the tray under her arm. "Are you ladies ready to order?"

They both ordered sushi, staying with tuna and salmon rolls they could share.

Beth exhaled slowly. "Thank you so much, Janet. I need to talk."

"I know." Janet shook her head slowly. "How else do we keep our sanity?"

"You know I love my mother dearly." Beth took a long swallow from the glass and refilled the drink. "Keith is nuts over this child she's keeping every day. Don't get me wrong, he's a sweetheart, but now she's on a mission for me to be married and producing grandchildren. She even asked me if I'd consider artificial insemination." Beth waited for her friend to stop laughing. "Janet, it's just not going to happen."

"I know. She means well." Janet savored the beer. "Mine is on a kick for me to move back to the coast. My sister and her husband, God love them, live in the house just down the street from her."

Beth interrupted. "The sister who won't speak to you or Greg because of her homophobia?"

"One and the same. Mom is clueless. She wants Ellen and me to pack up and sell everything here to be close to her. She thinks it would be perfect for us to move to Williamsburg and retire. Hell, I haven't worked enough years to pay back my student loans yet. I don't want to do any more than visit Williamsburg for the shopping several times a year. I sure as hell don't want to retire there or anyplace else. Ellen and I would be plotting each other's demise in short order."

Beth raised her glass toward Janet. "Mothers." They toasted.

"Will is not helping any. He and Patti have been married for almost nine years and have no children. My guess is they won't have kids. They're too much into each other. That's not meant as a cut, just an observation. Besides the fact that as best I can surmise, Patti is in her early forties...she refuses to tell her age and has sworn Will to secrecy. Mom was so disappointed when he married someone older. They were smart enough to go to Tennessee so they could make a completely fresh start when their divorces came through. Sheesh...take me away."

"Do you need a distraction, sweetheart?" Kathy eased the trays of sushi between them. "Try this. I guarantee it will take your mind off everything. Are you ladies good with the beer?"

"One's a plenty. Any more and I'll be asleep in the corner with you trying to figure out what to do with me," Beth said.

"Honey, that wouldn't be a problem. I'll check back on you later." She squeezed Beth's shoulder.

Janet leaned closer to tease her friend. "You're blushing."

"And you're enjoying this way too much. She is cute." Beth looked over her shoulder at the waitress.

"Are you trying to tell me something?" Janet waited. It was up to Beth.

"Hell, yes. You know what it is. You've probably known as long as I have. You were at the Halloween party. Why do you think all of this with Keith is bothering me so much?" Beth emptied the can in her glass. "I've tried relationships with men, Janet. Men don't do anything for me, other than trying to convince Andy and Greg to adopt me."

"I know. I've watched you struggle with it and wondered how

long it would take you to admit it to yourself, much less anyone else." Janet reached across the table for Beth's hand. She knew this wasn't easy. "From one late bloomer to another, welcome to enlightenment. Coming out is the best thing in the world for you. I ought to put that on the billboard my firm uses."

"You're shitting me."

"That's an awful expression, dear. No, I'm not. It's tough, Beth, personally and professionally, to admit anything outside of what is perceived as normal. You have to think about family and career." Janet shook her head. "I did it. I knew I had to divorce Edward for my sanity, as well as his, and it still just about ruined me, as my mother would say. Losing custody of Melody to Edward was the hardest thing I've ever been through."

"I know." Beth hesitated. "You know, I never would have said anything like this aloud, much less thought about acting on it while my father was alive. I would rather be miserable than hurt or disappoint him."

"You think he would have been?" Janet swirled the last of the beer around in her glass.

"I honestly don't know. He was never around anyone homosexual that I'm aware of. It just wasn't in his realm of understanding. Other than when he was in the service, he lived a very sheltered life. Yet he was always very understanding about our shortcomings. Not that being gay is any kind of shortcoming. You know what I mean."

"What about Keith?" Janet flinched at the thought of the other woman's reaction, particularly one who wanted grandchildren.

"It's not going to be pretty." Beth almost waved Kathy over for another beer but caught herself just in time. She was driving.

Janet leaned forward and lowered her voice. "Have you said anything at all to her?"

Beth shook her head. "Not even a hint. That's part of why I needed to talk to you or explode. I must have the conversation most daughters dread. I won't sneak around."

Janet raised her eyebrows questioningly.

"I met someone at your bonfire." Beth smiled. "Someone I'm really attracted to. I don't know if anything will come of it or not, but it finally made me admit that I want to try a relationship with another woman, something more than one night. There's more than occasional curiosity on my part."

"Tell me who. Do I know her?"

"Yes." Beth braced herself. "Lou Stephens."

Janet felt like a heel as she prepared to quell the animation that had taken over her usually calm and collected friend. "I know her well enough. Honey, you're going to hate me for saying this, but she's way out of your league. She's a player who only settles down until the next conquest comes along. Let me introduce you to someone nice and single. Has she actually asked you out?"

"Just to lunch, but as lunch not as a date. She's breaking up with someone. I'm being very tentative. She's been sending the greatest e-mails, has flowers delivered to the office and my house, and sometimes leaves things in my car."

"Honey, she made a move on you the night she met you with her girlfriend there to watch." Janet couldn't stop the words. "It sounds more like stalking to me."

Kathy cleared her throat. "Are you ladies doing all right? Need anything?" She let her hand slide along Beth's arm as she reached around her for the empty plate; the other hand was on Beth's lower back.

"Coffee." Janet again spoke for them as Beth nodded agreement.

"Irish?" Kathy asked.

"Plain, nothing fancy. Pleasure from a good bean." Beth looked the woman in the eye and smiled.

They waited as Kathy walked away and heard her final comment to herself. "Mmm, mmm, mmm."

"Well, you do seem to attract women." Janet raised her glass to toast with the last swallow of beer. "Just, please, let me find you someone else."

Beth thought it over but made no answer. "Mom is going to freak, but I have to tell her. The first thing she'll do is call Will, then he'll freak. He and Patti are so into church these days, even though I think it's a front for business connections. Thank God, they didn't witness anything at the party. I feel as though they've been lured into a cult. He reads his Bible morning and night. Hell, Mom's been a strong churchgoer since high school. I just fell by the wayside as soon as I could get away with refusing to go. My dad put his foot down and said it was my decision. Sheesh, I must be the abnormal one, the deviant personality, in the family."

"Don't even try to go there." Janet dismissed the concept.

"Do you have any idea what it means to me to be able to talk to someone about this, even if we do disagree on Lou? Greg and Andy have been giving me hell, threatening to stage a date for me and just lock me in with someone." Beth sighed. "I wanted to tell you myself before it hits the rumor mill."

"You know there are things I'm obligated to say. I am your legal counsel after all. The boys will tell you this, too. I had the same conversation with Greg." Janet tried to set up taller to make the words more effective.

Beth rolled her eyes. "Go ahead."

"I would say this regardless of either party's gender. Okay?" Beth nodded.

"Take it slow. Get to know whoever you date before you rush into anything. Enjoy dating for a while, date several women at once. This is a big step to even think about. It's much easier to get into something than get out of it. Don't be seduced by the forbidden or secretive nature of this. Act like two adults trying to figure out if there's a connection that could amount to something."

Beth waited.

"That's it. I'm done with that part. Now as your friend and someone who's been concerned over how much you work and how little you socialize…" Janet smiled.

Beth waited again.

"I'm so glad for you. I only want you to find the right someone. For crying out loud, allow yourself to have a little fun." She clapped her hands together.

Beth smiled and nodded. "That's kind of where I'm at with all of this. I know I work too much. I do want someone to share a life with. I would very much like to have a relationship. Won't it be fun to try? If not Lou, someone else," she finally conceded. "It amazes me that there's an entire sub-culture out there that I've been oblivious to. How did I miss all of this until now?"

"You're asking someone who married out of high school and had a baby a year later. Six years after that, I started college and just happened to discover, as part of my undergraduate education, that I preferred women."

Beth held up her hands for a double high-five. "Even I can't top that."

"You're damn right. See, I almost said straight and caught myself."

They both laughed as they slapped palms.

"Ladies, it's been a pleasure serving you." Kathy placed the small tray with the check on the table.

Janet beat Beth's reach. "My treat. We're celebrating your official coming out."

"Janet, what am I going to do with you?"

"Say thank you. Are you ready?"

Beth looked over her shoulder again. "I may stay for a bit."

"Good heavens, you're not wasting any time, are you?"

"Not anymore. It's time for a little fun in my life. What does work get me but an empty house and bags under my eyes? Thank you, sweetie. You know I love you."

The two women embraced.

"And you know if you need to talk about anything, any time, I'm here for you. I do care about you." Janet touched Beth with her index finger. "I promise not to overreact or lecture any more than I already have."

Janet looked over her shoulder as she reached the door just in time to see Beth catch Kathy's eye as she walked over to the bar.

Chapter Four

Ellen sighed. She honestly believed that there was no place anywhere on Earth more beautiful than the campus of Fletcher Women's College. She had in all seriousness asked the chancellor during her retirement party if her ashes could be scattered in the nature sanctuary separating the Gatehouse and Faculty Row. The chancellor had agreed and confided that she planned on doing the same.

Ellen took a deep breath and felt renewed. What better time than early April to visit the campus. Daffodils and azaleas were in full bloom with rhododendron and laurel ready to burst open in the coming weeks. Dogwood and redbud trees were starting to show their brightest colors. Leaves were full on all the towering hardwood trees.

The board of trustees had accumulated over three thousand acres for the campus since its founding before World War I. Half of the brick buildings around the quad had recently been designated as a historic district by the National Register of Historic Places. It was more than that, though. The college's reason for being was strictly to nurture women, and no one involved with the campus had lost sight of that over the years.

The college was world renowned for its equestrian and dance programs. Some of the most cutting-edge female writers visited the English program rotating in and out each semester. The only concession to the times was the addition of an engineering program in the science center. Ellen wished that curriculum had been available when she was a student.

She had come to the campus at eighteen from her small hometown in upstate New York and fallen in love with Virginia, the campus, the philosophy, and quite a few of the women she met. She chuckled to herself. She'd been sent by Janet on a mission to talk to Lou Stephens. It didn't occur to Janet that it was a matter of the pot calling the kettle black.

"But I was young and finding my way as most of us on campus were at that time. It was 1966, for crying out loud. I had no idea women's college was code for girls who thought they were lesbians or were planning to be for four years anyway. I didn't make a lifetime calling out of changing partners."

She decided to loop around campus before stopping at the physical plant. She slowed in the semicircle around the front dell and felt pride in the stately brick buildings off the quad that she had served her tenure of maintaining. She cut through the parking lots to the back service road and drove all the way to the lake and boathouse. The boathouse was a two-story wooden fire trap, but the great room over the boat slips had hosted some of the best parties and fondest memories of her life. She decided against driving to the opposite back corner of the campus that was the riding center—she had never developed an affinity for horses.

Ellen returned to the building tucked inconspicuously behind the girls' laundry and bistro. She followed the asphalt drive to the lower lot where employees left their vehicles when taking off on the fleet of tractors and riding mowers necessary to maintain the campus as though a fairway.

She glanced at her watch; she should be early enough to catch everyone finishing coffee if the routine had not changed. Janet had been incredulous that Ellen was up, dressed, and almost out the door when she came in for breakfast.

"James, Sam, you guys are slowing down." She grinned at the two local black men just a few years younger than her and tapped the face of her watch.

"Ellen, baby! Hey, should I leave my money in that mutual fund you put me onto last year?" James flipped his baseball cap around backward and held his hands up as though a rookie catcher.

She wound up and threw him an air baseball. "Absolutely."

Sam waved them both off and climbed onto the Kubota tractor with mid-mount mower. "I'll take my money to Atlantic City and come out better."

"That's the right idea. Investing is a gamble that you should never put more into than you can afford to lose."

Sam mimed shooting craps and waved as he drove away.

Ellen entered the building through the center of the five bays. She gave the new facility director his due—none of the equipment was more than ten years old and all of it was kept clean and maintained by an employee-signed checklist hanging on the wall near each machine. The checklist had been one of the first paper tools she had implemented.

Ellen went to the far right corner of the building and stood at the rated door in the firewall to the office that was Lou's as grounds manager. There was an office in each back corner separated by a parts room and a shop. All had solid glass windows with fire curtains that looked out into the bays.

Lou faced her computer on the side wall with her back to the door. She was intently working on a lengthy text message in her personal e-mail.

Ellen studied the woman. She was undeniably attractive—5'4" tall, 120 pounds, muscular, brown hair and brown eyes, and deeply tanned by outdoor work. Ellen had always teased Lou about having the appearance, energy, and demeanor of a pixie.

"You need to rotate your desk ninety degrees so someone walking in doesn't see what's on your screen." Ellen stopped in the doorway, waiting for Lou to minimize the window.

Lou held up one hand while she finished the line. "Can you believe I have to resort to this to write well enough to impress this woman?" She pointed to a thick dictionary beside the keyboard. "The guys love the e-mails. They beg me to read them out loud for pointers to use at home."

"Lou!"

"Just the ones I write. I have a little respect for others." She grinned.

Ellen shook her head in disagreement.

"Hey, old woman." She hit the send button, then bounced out of her chair and met Ellen with a hug. "Look," she pointed to a ring binder on her desk. "The male shit they hired to fill your job still uses your work plan. He just changed the binder. Do you believe it? They ought to pay you commission. God help them when they have to upgrade computers and lose all the macros you set up. Plus, he's moved his office into the same building with the chancellor and can't be bothered with us more than once a day, if that."

"And that's a good thing." Ellen took several steps back and looked into the shop. "Aren't you supposed to store all tools and clean surfaces before you leave here each day? How many times did I write you up?"

Lou dismissed her with a wave. "Then get it all back out the next morning. I put a stop to that after you left and no one's said a thing. We find everything eventually, and we stay on the mowing schedule. No one cares." She whispered the last. "You just have to let that neat thing go."

Ellen frowned. "Speaking of letting things go." She knew Lou well enough to know what was coming. "Don't do that."

Lou rolled her eyes anyway.

Ellen continued. "What's the deal with you and Stephanie? I thought all was well after two years, and she was going to have a kid for you two to raise."

Lou shook her head. "She couldn't get pregnant, and I didn't want to. A baby is fine, but count me out of gestating for nine months. We've been spending more and more nights apart, any excuse will do. You know how it goes. The relationship has played itself out, no bad on either of us." Lou shrugged.

"And Stephanie would give me the same answer?"

Lou grinned. "She's programmed as two. Call her yourself." She held out her cell phone.

Ellen waved it off. "Beth Candler is special. Don't do your usual to her, and I say that with love and affection. She could be the one to settle your ass down, Lou. Treat this one right."

Lou stared at her. "I know. That happens to be my plan."

Ellen hugged her. "I do love you, kid, but your reputation sucks. Don't let me down or my life will be hell to pay."

Lou grinned her cockiest. "Really? Well, I might just have to rethink it then. Split up you and Janet and finally have a chance with you." She appeared to ponder the possibility.

Ellen gave her a push back into her office. "Dream on. Now play nice. How about letting me mow this morning for old time's sake?"

"Give up my four hours of hemorrhoid development on the tractor seat and stay in my office on the computer?" Lou wasted no time tossing her the key. "Knock yourself out."

"You behave, or I'll knock you out."

"How did you know I liked it rough?" Lou called as Ellen walked away.

Ellen checked the oil and gas levels and switched on the ignition. The tractor roared, then settled into a smooth rhythm. She had to give the devil her due—Lou was a topnotch mechanic who kept all the mowing equipment in perfect condition. Lou could work at any of the auto shops in town but chose the college campus for the two-legged scenery and slow pace. Ellen looked at Lou's complete focus on the computer and didn't feel reassured about Beth.

Chapter Five

Ellen listened intently to her BlackBerry, unused to talking into it. "Greg says the door is open, come on in, make ourselves at home, they can't leave the Viking right now, whatever the hell that means." She shrugged.

"It's their commercial range." Janet looked at Ellen as they walked in the front door of Greg and Andy's house. "Damn, I feel badly that we didn't at least bring a bottle of wine."

Ellen leaned toward Janet. "I don't. They don't like the wine we pick out because we won't spend over ten dollars for one bottle. Besides, they like to fuss about with the food and drinks." She looked around the foyer.

The boys had purchased the house directly from the contractor before a Realtor ever listed the property. Both had worked on the plans—Andy for the heating and cooling system, Greg for the electrical circuits. They fell in love with the house on paper, only to learn that the contractor had to have a quick turnaround and would sell it practically for cost to get out from under the construction loan.

The exterior was faux English Tudor, borderline tacky, but the boys liked to think of it as campy. A ten-foot-diameter turret rose above the roof line at both front corners. The main level was four large rooms for living, dining, library, and kitchen. The master suite was upstairs using two dormers to span the midsection of the house for a bedroom with fireplace, walk-in closets, and bathroom complete with a corner whirlpool tub for two. The two guest rooms were on the ground level along with a two-car garage. Everything about the house was constructed to a larger scale from the ten-foot ceilings to the bidets in each of the three baths. Andy referred to it as their English-country-comes-to-town house.

A knock sounded on the door behind them. Ellen beat Janet to the handle. "Welcome to Tudorville."

Beth and Lou stood on the front stoop, ending a long kiss while waiting for the door to open.

"Don't mind us, but you rang the bell," Ellen said.

"But you weren't supposed to be so close to the door." Lou motioned for Ellen to leave them alone.

Ellen obligingly pushed the heavy mahogany door toward its frame.

"Just kidding. Where are Batman and Robin?" Lou bounded into the house as Beth adjusted her hair and clothing from the quick grope.

"We seem to have arrived at a critical time with something going on in the kitchen so they asked us to entertain ourselves for a few minutes." Janet pointed to each room visible from the foyer. "Lovely rooms. If I could decorate like this, no one would ever recognize our house as a simple ranch built about the time we were born."

They all looked into the dining room that appeared as though furnished from a medieval castle with traditional heavy English table and sideboard, then into the library just enough to see the huge partners' desk that filled the room and walls covered with bookcases, then into the living room that had the decor of a California white room with an L-shaped sofa positioned with its vertex across from the fireplace.

Lou whistled. "Damn."

Greg slid across the hardwood floor in his sock feet. "You called?" He hugged each of the women.

"Where's the cute one?" Lou asked him.

Greg looked duly offended. "Now don't be jealous. He and Beth were an item a long time ago...no need to be bitchy any more so than you usually are."

Ellen looked at Janet. "Ouch, I felt that one."

"Serves her right. No one had better say anything derogatory about my favorite nephew in my presence." Janet pointed to her face.

Greg kissed her cheek. "Auntie, I'm your only nephew."

"Exactly, dear."

They all laughed and walked into the living room to enjoy the large, well-padded sofa and the gently blazing fire.

"I almost had to turn the air conditioning on this afternoon to have the fire. I wanted crackling logs to add to the atmosphere tonight for the love bugs." Greg added chemically treated pine cones to the fire to create sparkles of blue and green. He poured wine for all of them. "Not that your palate can taste the difference," he said to Ellen, "but this is a very good Riesling we found at a winery in Nelson County."

"Not that we'll ever find the same route to it again," Beth said. "That was a fun Saturday."

Lou looked at Beth questioningly.

"The boys and I used to go exploring on weekends. Just guessing whether to turn right or left and seeing where we ended up."

"We'll have to try that some time." Lou put her arm around Beth.

"You have to leave the house first. We know where you two always end up." Greg sighed. "Young love, I remember it well."

"Old love isn't so bad, either." Andy came into the room wearing a red apron and sat on the arm of the sofa next to Greg. "Ladies." He held up his hands to show off his gay pride oven mitts. He looked to the center of the room at the large flat-screen television mounted above the fireplace. "I can't believe he doesn't have HGTV on."

"Thanks for reminding me." Greg reached for the remote and they all groaned. "It's a healthy addiction."

"And you, young lady, never answer your telephone at home anymore." Andy looked at Beth and lost his stern expression to a grin. "How are we supposed to find out all the details about this grand love affair?"

Beth blushed as she pulled a cell phone from her jeans pocket.

"Modern technology is a wonderful thing."

"For some of us anyway. Do you two ever listen to your messages?" Greg stared down his nose at Janet and Ellen. "I tried to catch you all afternoon to pick up garlic cloves for me on the way here. But, no, I had to run out to the store myself."

"You just had to bring that up. You can always e-mail me." Ellen held up the new BlackBerry.

"She's attached to that thing and only uses e-mail anymore. I don't even try to call her," Janet said.

"I hate talking on the telephone." Ellen shrugged. "Of course, some of us can't hear the clicks on the line that mean a message is waiting because of those big-ass throwbacks to the 1960s earrings." She pointed to Janet's ear lobes.

"I remember my mother wearing those when I was a kid," Andy said as he noticed Janet's jewelry.

"They're my trademark. The guys wear flashy ties to court. I needed something to show my personality when wearing those drab suits. I became hooked on collecting them." She held her ear out so they could admire the tight circles of tiny purple beads that made her earring about the size of a thick silver dollar.

"So…" Greg crossed his legs and leaned against Andy. "Have you two called Acme Moving Company yet?" His face was the picture of innocence.

Beth looked puzzled. "There's no Acme Moving in our area." She turned to Lou.

Ellen made the roadrunner beep. "You know, every service on those cartoons was provided by Acme something or other."

Janet studied the two young women. "I think he's asking when you two are doing the traditional second date and moving in with each other."

Beth glanced at Lou. "Well, now that you mention it, what are you guys doing two weeks from today?"

Greg held out his hand to Andy and wiggled his fingers. "I bet him it would be within a month of your first real date."

Andy handed Greg a twenty-dollar bill. "I need some help in the kitchen…Beth, Ellen."

"That was subtle," Lou said as they left the room.

Andy turned to Beth as soon as they entered the kitchen. "Have you lost your mind? Tell me you're at least going to rent your house so you can move back if you need to."

"The Realtor's sign goes up this weekend. She already has other agents calling her wanting to see the house for clients."

"Beth!" Andy went to the Viking range and turned down the gas on all the burners. He threw off his oven mitts. "It's too soon."

"You're being overprotective. How long did it take you and Greg?"

He wouldn't answer.

She walked over to him and made him hug her. "Be happy for me." They fit together like an old pair of gloves.

Ellen spoke when Andy turned to her for support. "I said my piece to Lou several weeks ago. Janet lectured this one. They're already in too deep." She sighed with resignation. "What can we do to help?"

"I have a big favor to ask of Janet. I'll wait until she has more to drink." Beth pulled them toward the others. "Come on, buddies."

And they did.

Chapter Six

Janet tried not to frown as she mused to herself about how she managed to be talked into some of the things she did, being a reasonably intelligent and independent woman. Just how had Beth maneuvered her into driving Keith into the mountains to the house she had just moved into with Lou? She didn't even know Keith that well—a few minutes in the office to go over wills and powers of attorney and a few lunches with her and Beth. Seeing her daughter for the first time as half of a lesbian couple should be something Keith would do with one of her closest friends.

Janet had already loaded boxes and locked the doors at Beth's by the time Keith had driven the twenty miles from the Candler farm southeast of the city. Andy, Greg, and Ellen had wished Janet well as she waited and headed out, each driving a pickup truck and following Beth's Subaru—they had packed the trucks the afternoon before, covered the loads with tarps, and tied everything down tight.

"Keith, how are you? Please, make yourself comfortable." Janet spoke to her through the open window on the passenger's side as she leaned across the seat and opened the door. "Adjust the seat and the window as needed. If the music is too loud, please turn it down." Janet hoped that music might deter conversation. She watched the other woman settle in beside her.

There was a grim set to Keith Candler's features—the usual twinkle in her blue eyes and easy smile were nowhere to be found. She was clearly not pleased with today's trip, but she was also not ready to disavow herself from her only daughter. She had to see for herself what Beth had gotten into. Keith was in her mid-sixties, about ten years older than Janet, as well as a little shorter and much heavier. Gray mixed with the brown of her hair.

"I'm as well as can be expected, Mrs. Evans. If this doesn't trigger a heart attack or stroke, nothing will." Keith drew her sweater around her and crossed her arms. "Have you been to the house before?" It sounded like an accusation.

"Please call me Janet." She was determined not to rise to any provocation. "No. But you know Beth...she drew us a map, doesn't look too difficult to find." Janet handed her the neatly drawn map on grid-ruled paper.

"Out in the middle of nowhere." Keith glanced at her watch. "I'm timing how long her drive will be back into town to work. I thought she left the farm so she wouldn't have a long commute to the office."

This was going to be a long afternoon, Janet knew. She could understand Keith's disappointment. She just hoped Keith could move past imposing her own values on her daughter—a near impossible task for any parent.

"How well do you know this Lou person?" Again, the sound of an accusation. Keith glanced at Janet before resuming her straight-ahead stare.

"We've met a time or two for dinner. My partner, Ellen, worked with her for about a year before she retired. I don't know her that well. The girls are about the same age and both like being outdoors. Beth seems very happy." Janet tried the last statement tentatively.

"Beth has no idea what she's doing. It must be some sort of a midlife crisis or depression. I can't believe she sold her house the first weekend it was listed." Keith's hands were clenched into tight fists.

"Beth is a grown woman, Keith." Janet glanced at the map. "We stay on the main highway another mile?"

"Yes." Keith snapped the piece of paper. "I know she's grown. She's also intelligent, attractive, and makes good money. What did I do wrong for this to happen to my daughter?" Keith was on the verge of tears.

"You didn't do anything wrong. Neither has Beth. It's life. It's her life. It's unexpected, not planned. Beth didn't just make this huge, life-altering decision. Haven't you seen it coming?" Janet kept her eyes on the road for fear of wrecking her car.

"What?" Keith's answer was very soft.

"Keith," Janet sighed, "it's not the end of the world. It's not a fatal disease. It's a lifestyle, widely practiced. It's the way she is. It doesn't change anything about the daughter you've loved all these years. My guess is that when you think about this later, after it all calms down a bit, you'll see the indicators that have been there since she was a child. It's the way she was born." Janet tried the obvious logic.

"It's a sin. It's a defiance of church and God. It will keep her out of heaven. You too." Keith whispered the last.

Janet didn't respond until she eased the car into the next parking lot they came to. "Surely, you can't believe that. How is your daughter possibly sinning? I'm another story." She tried to make a joke. "Beth is in love with and loving another human being. Why is that so horrible? Isn't the love what truly matters?" She turned and faced the other woman.

"It's not natural. One man and one woman is the natural order. It's how all of her family, generations before her, have lived their lives. How can she turn her back on all of them, on how her father and I raised her? This would kill her daddy. It's illegal in the commonwealth of Virginia. You're an attorney. How can you practice it?" For different reasons, this was the last straw for both women.

"Don't do this, Keith. Should I take you back to your car? I'm not going to Beth and Lou's like this." Janet waited.

"What if she's making a terrible mistake?" Keith's face reddened.

"What if she is?"

"How does she go back? Her house is sold. People will know. Her colleagues know. What about her reputation?" Keith was honestly beside herself with worry about her youngest child.

"If she can get herself into this, she can get herself out of it. We'll drive out and help her pack up again." Janet smiled at

Keith. "Don't make yourself ill over this. It is what it is. Have you ever been able to make Beth's decisions for her? Would you really want to?"

Tears rolled down Keith's cheeks. "I have to go, but I can't acknowledge how they're living. If Beth wants a roommate, if she wants to be back in the country, I can accept that...nothing else." She took a deep breath and pulled a handkerchief out of her sleeve to wipe her face.

Janet stared out of the car. "If that's the best you can do for now, fine. I will not be part of some huge drama. If that's why you're going today, I will not be a party to it."

"I didn't want to go by myself, and I haven't told any of my friends." It was that simple for Keith. "I don't want to make trouble for anyone. That will happen soon enough on its own accord. I can't acknowledge anything but friendship. Can you understand that?"

Janet nodded as she returned to the highway. "Yes."

Keith was silent for only a few moments, it went against her nature. "You mentioned your partner."

"Ellen, that's right."

"Yet you were married and had a child. I knew Eddie when he was a tagalong kid."

"Really?" Janet had difficulty with that image of the homophobic man she had gone from loving to dreading. She was convinced his anger with her had tainted their daughter during her formative years.

"When did you...change?"

Janet chuckled. "I was a little younger than Beth, late twenties, when I realized being married to Edward was not good for any of us. I would have only made him and me miserable, and that would have carried over to Melody."

"So you divorced him, gave up your daughter, and took up with this Ellen."

"Yes. As much as I regret the estrangement from Melody, I wouldn't do any of it differently when I look back at it." She didn't say that she had not cheated on her husband; she had just decided she didn't want to be with a man. Ellen had been nothing more than a good friend during all of those changes in her life.

"Hmm." Keith pondered this. "Well, I hope this Lou person is neat."

Janet glanced at the older woman and waited, knowing there was more to come.

"Beth can't stand things not being put back where they came from."

They drove the last few miles in silence.

Janet spoke as they slowed to turn onto the gravel road of the large lot private subdivision. "Here we are."

"Thirty-five minutes, not including when we pulled off the road." Keith stared straight ahead. "Eight miles farther than the homeplace to downtown. I did the odometer numbers in my head."

Janet drove slowly so as to disturb as little gravel dust as possible. Of course, she had just washed her car the day before. "Oh, Lord."

They slowed before the ruins of an early nineteenth century home at the mailbox reading Stephens. "Surely, that's not it." Keith stared forlornly out the window.

They saw that the house was abandoned and empty as they followed the driveway. They passed two log barns. "Beth said it was on fifteen acres." Janet mentally crossed her fingers.

They left the dense stand of trees and emerged in a clearing before a story and a half Cape Cod. "That's...nice." Keith sounded surprised.

Granted, few improvements had been made to the house since original construction in the 1940s, Janet thought, but knew better than to say. She also knew better than to tell Keith that she had just filed the deed in the courthouse in which Lou gave Beth half interest in the property. Her silence had nothing to do with attorney-client confidentiality.

"Yes, it is." Janet was relieved. Her CPR training was a little rusty. She pulled in behind the three pickup trucks Ellen and the boys had driven out of town packed full.

Beth came out of the front door to meet them. "Did you have any trouble finding us?"

Lou was behind her. She wore overalls with holes and paint stains over an undershirt. Beth wore a crisply ironed oxford shirt and spotless jeans. Andy and Greg were in blue jean cutoffs and tank tops already soaked through with unloading the trucks on a typical June day.

Keith stepped out of the car and hugged Beth as though it had been years since they'd last seen each other. She forced the smile on her face. "It's so nice. You must be Lou. I'm always glad to meet Beth's friends." She hugged the other woman. "Andrew." Keith held her arms open and waited.

"I'm sweaty."

"I don't care. Give an old woman a hug." Keith beamed at him as he did as asked.

"I stink, but I feel like such a man, driving a pickup truck." Greg approached Keith.

"I've smelled much worse." She embraced Greg as fondly as Andy.

Janet shook her head. Keith had accepted Greg because she loved Andy like a son. Greg had come along several years after Beth and Andy broke up, so there was no association of blame. She knew Keith would come around to Beth and Lou.

Keith hugged Lou again.

Lou looked over Keith's shoulder to Beth questioningly. "Mom?"

Janet caught Beth's eye and shook her head. "It was a beautiful drive out. And we have boxes of breakables." She gestured to the car. The boys groaned.

Keith took Beth's hand. "How about a tour? Look at that view of the mountains. You girls have your own little paradise here."

Janet frantically shook her head at Lou not to go there.

"The house is great, Mom, a little smaller than mine. It needs some work, but we'll get to it. Nothing paint and new appliances can't take care of and maybe an addition. We've already found a contractor. It just needs a little attention." Beth held onto her mother's hand.

"Don't we all." Lou winked at Janet as they followed mother and daughter inside and left the unloading of the car to the boys.

Chapter Seven

"You're kidding, right?" Ellen looked at Beth in the rearview mirror as she drove east on Route 460.

"You can stop saying that any time." Lou smacked Ellen on the shoulder from the backseat of Janet's Ford Taurus.

"I'm not kidding. What can I say? I've been deprived. I've never been to the ocean." Beth shrugged.

"I thought everyone did a beach trip after finishing high school as a rite of passage." Janet studied the state map. She liked to track their progress and anticipate the next turns. Her reading glasses from the glove compartment had bright pink frames.

"Well, I didn't. I'm not a water person. The most water we played in as kids was a creek that came up to our shins." Beth stared at the huge frame houses along the main street of the small railroad town.

Lou chuckled. "Water has nothing to do with going to the beach when you've just turned eighteen or twenty-one."

Beth looked at her, clearly confused.

"She means all the bars." Ellen imitated throwing back a shot. "Some of the kids don't see the ocean because they drink all night and sleep all day. Personally, I love walking in the sand and looking for shells or glass while watching for dolphins. Usually, all I get wet are my shoe soles if it's too cold for bare feet," Ellen said.

"So what's the deal with your house?" Lou asked.

Ellen grinned. "You'll see. I think it's funny as hell. My tiny little cottage has weathered the hurricanes with minimal damage over the years. I bought the house thirty years ago as an investment when I was living in free campus housing. Cost me little or nothing. Most people had never heard of North Carolina's Outer Banks at that time. My parents used to drive down the coast from Norfolk when I was a kid and my dad was stationed in Virginia. We camped on the beach before it was regulated. It's a three-room house, oceanfront now…six blocks back when I bought it. All around it are these big-ass houses with five or six bedrooms and baths that are leased out for thousands a week in season."

"And she just jumps in her ten-year-old Toyota pickup and putters to the beach house when the mood strikes her to fish and walk and make fun of all the rich tourists," Janet said.

"Sweet." Lou nodded.

"You bet. It's my ultimate retirement plan. I can sell the lot for hundreds of thousands of dollars any time it suits me and invest the money while some schlemiel builds a million-dollar house and is in debt out the wazoo."

"And have a better investment in the long run the way she knows the stock market," Janet added.

"Exactly. I figure to hold onto it as long as the cottage is standing, sell after the next big hurricane instead of rebuilding."

"I've never seen the ocean," Beth reminded them as she snuggled against Lou.

"Well, you'll love it in October, not as crowded and not as hot as in summer. As far as I'm concerned…perfect conditions," Janet said.

True to its description, the white frame house was a tiny three-room cottage.

Janet truly loved the place and enjoyed its simplicity. They all became too carried away with buying houses bigger than needed and acquiring more possessions than used. Stepping into Ellen's cottage felt as though a huge load had been lifted from her shoulders. Janet knew during their years together the cottage had given Ellen a much needed break and refuge when things were too intense between them, usually because of a complicated case she was engrossed in. Sometimes, and they both admitted this, they just needed a break from each other. There was nothing wrong with acknowledging a need, quite the contrary as far as Janet was concerned.

From the small front porch with white frame railing, entrance was to one large room that served as living, dining, and kitchen. Off of the kitchen was a bathroom. Straight through from the bathroom was the bedroom Ellen used since it looked out to the ocean. Off of the living room area was the guest bedroom that looked out to the street. A screened porch ran the width of the back of the house and overlooked the beach; high tide during a storm brought waves to the pilings the house rested on.

Janet stood on the back porch gazing at the ocean. She sighed with contentment.

Ellen walked up beside her and put her arm around her.

"It still takes my breath away," Janet looked out across the Atlantic, "just as you do. I was so lucky to find someone to love who was patient enough to understand my need to be an attorney and the hours that takes even now."

Ellen hugged and kissed her. "I knew you were the one. There are a lot of crazy women out there who live for drama and confrontations. I saw you just plugging away, determined to earn a degree and pass the bar while struggling with a bad marriage but dealing with it. You just made up your mind and took it all one step at a time. To think we started as friends because we were the same generation amidst teenagers." Ellen chuckled. "All the while, I was wondering if there could be more."

"Yet you put no pressure on me."

Ellen nodded. "That wouldn't have been fair to you, Edward, or Melody."

"I'll never regret having Melody, but thank goodness girls don't feel the need to marry right out of high school anymore."

"Amen to that." Ellen looked over her shoulder. "You think they'll be okay in a small room and sharing a bath with us?"

"It has a bed, doesn't it?" Janet rubbed Ellen's thigh.

Ellen chuckled. "And I made sure the springs don't squeak in either room."

Janet laughed. "I feel like cooking. Let's make a run to the fish market and see what was caught today. I love being able to do that. I'll cook us a nice dinner tonight."

Ellen nodded. "I always enjoy that after the long drive. We'll take the girls to Lucky's tomorrow night."

Lucky's was the landmark lesbian bar in Nags Head owned by an old friend of Ellen's who had bought the fishermen's hangout about the same time Ellen purchased the cottage in Salvo. Delores liked to break the ice with a new customer by asking what her name rhymed with. She was tall and trim and gave the impression of easily being able to vault the bar and kick butt if necessary.

Of course, Lou shouted, "Clitoris," in response to the question as Beth turned three shades of red. Lou hopped on the bar stool and gave Delores a kiss full on the lips. She was rewarded with a free shot for her and Beth. "Now this is my kind of place. I was afraid this was going to be one of those yawner vacations." Lou looked about the dimly lit bar, full of twenty-somethings dancing, drinking, and shooting pool. She was clearly in her element.

Beth elbowed Lou before speaking. "Tonight is on us, for inviting us to stay at your cottage to celebrate our contractor finally finishing his part of the remodel and addition."

As a retiree, Ellen was quick to say, "Thank you. Fair enough. You needed a break before all the painting and unpacking."

Janet and Ellen sat side by side in a booth and watched the women at the pool tables. Lou was already on her next round. Beth whispered in Lou's ear, was given a kiss, and joined Janet and Ellen, refusing a dance as she crossed the open floor.

"She's a character." Janet looked at Lou as she nursed a beer. "Why does this taste so much better here on tap than out of bottles at home?"

"It's the ocean and the company." Ellen said.

"And the lack of work." Beth raised her glass in a toast, then sipped carefully. "I'm learning to enjoy time away from the office. I don't always have to be doing half-again as much work as everyone else to prove myself."

Ellen raised her mug. She caught Delores's eye and raised three fingers and pointed to the beer. She looked at Beth. "Take my advice and get off the hard stuff so you can go for a walk with us in the morning instead of hugging the toilet bowl."

Janet nodded. "We have a ritual of drinking coffee outside as we walk along the beach to see the sun rise over the horizon."

Beth smiled. "I'd love to if it's not intruding on something special between you two." She left her first shot half drunk on the table.

Janet sighed and glanced about the packed room. "Nowadays, we're always the oldest couple here, but coming to Lucky's is part of our beach ritual just like the morning walk." She grinned. "I like the energy even if I don't have it anymore. I enjoy watching the girls, vicarious as it may be."

"You have energy when it counts, honey," Ellen said. She nodded toward the open floor. "Look at her."

They all turned and watched Lou coax a young blonde out on the dance floor. Lou danced as she did everything else, no holds barred.

Janet studied Lou's behavior. "That doesn't bother you?"

The expression on Beth's face was bittersweet. "That's part of Lou. She's going to flirt with every woman she encounters. I've talked to her about it. She assures me it's all harmless."

"Is the honeymoon over?" Janet asked.

Beth looked at them and nodded. "But the marriage is just beginning."

Chapter Eight

"Well, I guess I should be grateful to be alive and here while you all are doing this." Keith stood in the middle of her dining room, hands on hips, while looking at the crystal, china, and glassware pulled out of the sideboard and divvied up on the dining room table for each to take home.

"It could be worse. We could be getting ready for a yard sale." Patti eyed the stacks of antique dessert plates going to Beth.

Beth motioned Janet into the kitchen and lowered her voice. "Patti is pissed because we're stepping on her stilettoed toes."

Janet raised her eyebrows.

"Breaking up households of the elderly is how she makes her money. She befriends someone having to downsize their life, pays them a pittance for the belongings they no longer have room for, and sells it all to dealers or on eBay. She makes a huge profit with no more overhead than temporary storage. She uses the cleaning guys from Will's firm as movers. My guess is she doesn't report a third of her income. The people she cheats think she is sweet to help them." Beth rolled her eyes.

Janet began a question. "How—"

"I checked her out with a fellow accountant in Knoxville. Don't belittle my nerd grapevine." Beth stared at her sister-in-law. "She thought she and Will were going to swoop in here and do that to my mother." Beth shook off her anger. "Be-ach."

"Don't worry. I'll stay close to Keith." She squeezed Beth's arm and left the kitchen. "Keith, here, please sit down. You're making me tired." Janet pulled a chair out from the dining room table and motioned Keith toward it.

Keith pulled the chair closer to the boxwood inlaid middle door of the sideboard. "Luke's mother had this brought over from England…top is in one of the outbuildings since it was too massive to put together in this room. What would I have done with a wine cellar?" She ran her hand along the dark mahogany with affection. "I have to see it all on its way. You all have to know where and who each piece came from or it won't really mean anything to you. I just hope I can remember all of it."

Janet was incensed as she watched Patti cross her eyes at Will. Janet was a collector of antique glass—daisy and button pattern was her favorite. She felt privileged that Keith had asked her to be present to help identify and value the family heirlooms as needed. They were to sort and label everything that day; movers had been hired to take the heavy pieces in a few weeks.

Will offered no opinion on any of it. He just lifted as directed by one of the women in the room. He raised the double windows and looked out to the driveway and cornfield beyond that stretched to the county road. It was a false spring day in late January that made the low ceiling room unbearably warm with the wood fire burning as Keith preferred.

Ellen stamped her feet on the mat at the back door into the kitchen. She walked around the small round table used for everyday meals and into the formal dining room. "Damn, Keith. Based on what little I know about tools, you have a treasure trove in your basement. Will, why aren't you down there with me?" Ellen brushed a cobweb off the top of her head and reached after it wafting to the hardwood floor. Majority willing, she was to photograph, pack, and list much of Luke's tool collection on eBay. Keith insisted on paying her a commission.

"Oh, he never took any interest in anything his father did." Keith's eyes did not leave Beth as she knelt on the floor and reached onto the far back of the shelf.

"And he's not going to fill our garage up with dirty old tools that he's never going to touch." Patti dared her husband to contradict her.

"Or know what they are." Lou clapped Will on the shoulder. "It's okay. I'll save all the pencils for you." Lou grinned at Patti.

"You two are awful. Will, what do you want from home?" Beth looked to her brother.

Janet watched the siblings, whose roles had reversed long ago. While Beth had blossomed with the responsibility of her parents and her job, Will had become furtive, as though caught at something and now treading water. Everything he did seemed tentative and needing the approval of his wife.

Will glanced at Patti as though to prove Janet's point. Patti nodded slightly. "We'd love the low-post spool bed for our guest room. Patti is crazy about the original Jenny Linde beds." He corrected himself as soon as he saw Patti's frown—it had to be called by its 1860s reference to make it valuable to her.

"Is that so you can have a comfortable bed to sleep on instead of the couch?" Lou baited the man.

Will Candler was easily recognizable as Beth's brother. His hair was short and curly as opposed to her shoulder length, but with the same salt and pepper shading and texture. His hazel eyes and freckles matched Beth's. Beth's eyes had the twinkle of her mother's; Will's were flat. He was four inches taller than his sister and had the appearance of being stretched thin while Beth looked compact and muscular. He had played no sports in school. Beth had consistently beaten him playing twenty-one at the hoop set on the end of the log outbuilding in the barn lot when she could get him to venture outside. Beth had gone to college on a softball scholarship and worked for her pocket money; Will had recently finished paying off his student loan.

"Daisy and button salt cellars. Look, Janet, you'll have to take these. I knew they were tucked in here somewhere." Keith held out a stack of two-inch square, shallow-cut crystal bowls. "They belonged to Luke's grandmother." She looked to Beth. "You don't mind, do you, sweetie?"

"Heavens, no. I can always shame her into giving them back to me later." Beth grinned at Janet.

"I think we ought to convert our basement into a shop," Lou said. "I've wanted to properly waterproof and finish it off, just didn't know as what." She nudged Beth. "Don't you want to keep some of your father's woodworking equipment? I know I do." Lou was already starting toward the basement with pad and pencil in hand. "I'll make a list and a rough sketch of how he set it up so we'll know what to do with it. We can always extend the equity line just a little more, can't we, honey? Hands off the basement, Ellen, until I can talk her into it."

"Lou!" Beth swallowed the rest of what she was going to say. "There's enough to keep some of the tools we might actually use and sell the rest so Mom can have the money. Daddy had two and three of most everything. I used to tease him about stamping his initials on each piece. He loaned tools to anyone who worked for him or stopped by to ask a favor. Sometimes he bought a replacement before his was returned. He told me that all eventually came back. He never lost one hand tool." Beth shook off the memory of her father. "Ellen, make it worth your while for helping us today. I know you're interested in woodworking, so keep some things for yourself, as well. Mom?"

"I agree. I can't thank all of you enough for giving up your Saturday. It is what it is. I can't keep this place or all these things. I have to consolidate. Might as well do this now while I can be here and see what happens with everything."

"Oh, we're glad to help." Patti's tone said the opposite of her words.

"We have to head back in a little while, Ma. Four hours on the road is difficult on Patti's back."

"Do you have any balls left?" Lou mumbled to Will as she passed him on the way out of the kitchen. Patti actually snorted.

"Ellen, don't let the girls take everything from downstairs. If you and Beth split the tools between you, that's fine by me. Please keep an eye on Lou. I swear, that child is more like my own than my own." Keith pushed Ellen after Lou.

Ellen looked to Beth and her mother. "I say we inventory, research an approximate value, and definitely sell duplicates. Beth has first choice of what to keep. I'd like to trade a cash commission for a few things. All will be properly accounted for. Keith, what you do with the profit is your call."

"Shit fire and save matches. Do it." Keith waved her hand.

Janet stared at Keith as Ellen chuckled her way out the back door.

"I like her. She's a good match for you, Janet. What? An old dog can't learn new tricks? Don't you believe it. Depends on the old dog." Keith held up two hand-edged linen dinner napkins. "Hmm. Were these my grandmother's or Luke's grandmother's? I can't remember for the life of me."

"Who is Beth like in the family?" Janet asked.

Keith's expression glowed with pride. "Her father. He was so easygoing and smart."

"Tell her, Ma." Beth ignored Will.

"Two years after I graduated high school, while I was working for the telephone company, I saw Luke walking past my office window downtown. First thing I noticed about him was how shiny his shoes were. I was on eye level with the sidewalk. When I saw the rest of him, I knew he was the man I was going to marry."

"That suddenly?" Janet asked, even as Patti shook her head not to encourage Keith to reminisce.

"Oh, yes. He was the one. I watched which store he went into, then asked the owner's wife to introduce me. We started dating and married six months later. Then these two." Keith pointed to the framed baby portraits of Beth and Will hanging over the sideboard.

"Amazing." Janet looked at the smile on Beth's face. She knew if her friend had heard the story once, she'd heard it a hundred times.

"She is her father's daughter." Keith inclined her head toward Beth. "Two peas in a pod. All I did was carry her nine months. She was Luke's the rest of his life."

"What about William here?" Patti looked at her husband and didn't bother to mask her disdain as she used his full name.

"I don't know where Will got his bookishness from. Both of them know figures and finances like I never even thought about. Must have come from their father's uncle who was an attorney and land developer when Luke was a child. Difference was that I had to stay on Beth to do her schoolwork instead of being outside with her father. Will always had his done not long after the bus dropped him off. He'd then work on something beyond what the teacher was doing or be glued to the television. He used to love to follow along with the old movie musicals, singing and dancing."

Beth burst out laughing. "I'd forgotten that. You loved the King Family, Lawrence Welk, and anything by Rodgers and Hammerstein. What a dork. No one else our age would even admit knowing about any of that, much less watching them or buying the original albums." Beth rolled over on the floor and stretched out as she tried to get her breath from laughing so hard. "Do you need to come out of the closet, too, big brother?"

"I'm going to start breaking down the furniture upstairs if no one minds," Will said. "I didn't pull the trailer up here on the back of the Mercedes for nothing. What is it that you and Lou came in, little sister?"

"Why, Lou's Nissan pickup, of course, with a rainbow windsock on the antennae. The Subaru couldn't quite haul enough." Beth howled as she struggled to finish her answer. "It's what the Lesbian Handbook requires us to drive. Such good gas mileage." She was laughing so hard that tears streamed down her face.

Keith let out a long sigh that made Beth laugh that much harder.

"You're killing me," Beth choked out.

"Right family, wrong member," Patti whispered softly before forcing a laugh.

Janet shivered unexpectedly, then laughed along with Beth and ignored Patti's comment. It was good to see them settling Keith's affairs openly and with humor, even if too much humor, if there was such a thing.

Will remained expressionless as he started up the stairs with a small toolbox that looked brand new.

"Try not to scratch any of it." Patti raised her voice. "I guess I'll help him while Lou is in the basement. Smells too musty down there. My allergies can't take any mold or mildew." She followed Will as though taking the last steps on death row.

Janet watched the obviously unhappy couple. "Oh, my."

Beth managed to take a breath before she burst out laughing again. "And we want the right to do that to ourselves."

Keith looked at Janet. "She's losing it, isn't she?"

Janet smiled and shook her head. "I thought this would be sad. Silly me. Come on, giggle box, help me carry your mother's generosity out to my plain old Ford sedan."

Beth passed Janet with a box. "You're so lipstick."

Janet cupped her hand and swatted Beth on the behind.

"What did she mean about your lipstick?" Keith frowned at her daughter. "And thank you, someone needed to do that."

"Do what?" Lou walked into the room carrying a wooden toolbox packed with hand tools. She grinned from ear to ear. "I love your father by the way."

"Smack me. We can talk about it later. Mom is encouraging exploration of the dominatrix thing." Beth started laughing again as she left the house.

"Oh, Lord, there goes the Model-T. You had to get her wound up, didn't you?" Lou looked to Janet. "I'll have to listen to that giggling all the way home. She amuses herself so." Lou rolled her eyes and grinned.

Janet hugged her. "Poor you."

"Is there really a Lesbian Handbook?" Keith looked puzzled.

They heard Beth hoot from the driveway.

"What...never mind, I don't want to know." Lou followed the sound of her partner.

"Those girls are always pulling my leg. What would I do without them?" A tear came to Keith's eye that she quickly blinked away. "I can't wait to be settled in my new place."

Beth had known she needed to prepare for being Keith's caretaker and had rolled it into remodeling their house. Keith would have nothing to do with assisted living or an apartment amongst strangers.

"Life is good," Janet said quietly.

Keith Candler nodded in agreement and without hesitation.

Chapter Nine

"I hate to sound like Keith, but I wouldn't want to make this trek five days a week," Janet said to Ellen as she drove along the county road at a blistering thirty miles per hour. She was following a heavily loaded pulpwood truck. "Look at the size of those damn logs." The diameter of the tree trunks was about the same as the tire on her car.

"Imagine if that load breaks loose on the highway." Ellen was in rare form. Her white hair stuck straight out from her head, prompting her to jam on a New York Yankees cap.

Janet backed off the truck a little farther, not at all reassured by the small corner stakes forming the sides that kept the logs in position. She could see the end of a chain dangling beneath the rear axle.

"Can you believe that it was a year ago that we moved Beth in with Lou?" Ellen whistled. "I would have put even money on them breaking up by now if not for Keith." Ellen leaned back against the headrest and yawned. It wasn't long before she was gently snoring.

Janet thought about the last time she had made this drive with Keith beside her. Where had the time gone? She occasionally saw Beth in town; they relied on e-mail more often than telephone. Beth and Lou had withdrawn into a world of their own during their newlywed period, and Janet had respected that. She had visited Keith each time she was in the hospital and helped Beth temporarily move her mother to skilled care for rehab. Once again, Janet sensed something else behind Beth's invitation a few days earlier to come to the country for the day to see what they'd done to their place.

Janet pulled into the driveway, trying to figure out what was different. She tapped the brakes and sent Ellen forward against her shoulder restraint.

Ellen looked at her. "What the hell...?"

"Stay up too late watching Cinemax, Ms. R-E-T-I-R-E-D?" Janet smiled sweetly as she spelled her status as Ellen did when she wanted to rub it in. "We're here. Take a look. It's unreal."

The ruins of the original house were gone, the site leveled and grassed. All the kudzu had been pulled off the log barns and the tin roofs painted dark green. The woods had been thinned out gradually, like a disappearing hairline, as the final approach to the house was made. The remodeled house had charcoal architectural roof shingles, gray vinyl siding, vinyl replacement windows, and an addition out the back that Janet knew was for the expanded kitchen and new den downstairs and Beth's home office and master suite upstairs. There was also a landscaped walkway connecting the back door of the house to the small guesthouse that was a scaled-down version of the main house. The driveway had been extended down the slope to stop before the steps to the front door.

"Holy shit." Ellen unhooked her seat belt and looked at Janet in wonderment. "Are you sure this is the same place? How in the hell did those two do all of this in a year?"

Janet turned off the ignition and stared. "They did most of the finish work themselves with Greg and Andy's help. Beth showed me drawings as they evolved the remodeling, but I had no idea it was all of this. The remodeling was Beth's buy-in for being put on the deed."

"Beth must have maxed out her equity in her first home to have this work done. She won't move again any time soon if she expects Lou to buy her out," Ellen said softly.

"Fools rush in..." Janet grimaced and nodded. "Keith's share went to building the cottage and paying medical bills. I only heard one reference to Will's share being invested in jewelry for Patti."

Janet shuddered as she climbed out of the car.

"Just saying that woman's name will do that to you." Ellen chuckled as she watched Janet dig in her tote bag for her digital camera.

Keith had moved into the cottage two months earlier. She'd gone through a series of surgeries for her heart and could no longer be alone on the family farm. There was still enough agricultural business in the south side community so that as soon as Keith's situation was known, an offer had been made to buy the Candler farm.

Janet's ears rang as she heard a motor louder than in a car or truck. She glanced about and saw the trademark green of a John Deere tractor approaching around the contour of the steep hillside that sloped from the house down to the woods. The figure on the tractor waved a baseball cap at her while standing on the brake to roll the tractor to a stop beside the car. A tri-color dog followed, running in a zigzag pattern back and forth to compensate for the slow-moving tractor.

Janet smiled, held up the camera for permission, and snapped a photograph.

"What do you think?" Beth jumped down from the tractor. She was as tan as Janet had ever seen her and appeared as though she had toned down ten pounds. She wore hemmed denim shorts and a sleeveless knit shirt. The dog bounced as she rubbed his head and back. Janet had never seen her look better.

Beth immediately hugged Ellen, then gave her cheek a kiss for the benefit of the photograph Janet snapped.

"I hear an adult beverage calling me. Lou promised to have Heineken in the freezer and not give me a hard time that it wasn't yet noon. R-E-T-I-R-E-D," she spelled over her shoulder as she walked toward the house calling out to Lou.

"I think that's one damn big tractor." Janet held her hand up to shield the sun from her eyes. "It seems you have a new best friend. One more and I'll put it away. I know you don't like having your picture taken."

"My weekend toy and my playmate." Beth posed by patting the fender and kissing the dog's head as he placed his front paws on her chest. She was slightly taller than the rear tire. "I'd forgotten how much fun it is to get out on a tractor and just drag the bush hog through the fields to clean everything up. I'm going to seed for hay next year and check on a used baler, might as well make something off all this land. I'd forgotten how much I loved having a farm dog around. This is Buddy. He belongs on the neighbor's place but stays here all the time." She adjusted her cap from the college softball championship year that she'd played catcher. "Mom likes to be able to see in all directions, makes her a little more comfortable in her new place. Mowing is also a great way to work through all the crap that's gone on during the week at the office."

"I'll take your word for it. That looks like a little more than I want to maneuver while my mind is on something else. But I do like that you can carry your makeup kit on the front."

"What are you talking about?" Beth followed her friend's line of sight. "Doofus. That's the box filled with weights to keep the front end of the tractor down and all four tires on the ground to compensate for the bush hog attached to the power take-off on the back. If I maximize the tire pressure, it really makes a difference with the way she handles but makes her a little too light on a slope unless weights are added. Without the weights, I'd have to go up and down the slope instead of being able to loop around. I'd end up down there," she pointed to the woods, "and not in a good way. Lou rigged it from an old toolbox, adding bolts to keep the lid closed tight and filling it with the old cast iron window weights we took out of the casings, adds well over two hundred pounds. We had about half what we needed, the guys at the college found the rest for Lou when she told them how she was using them. That way, it's easy to remove the weights if we're skimming a light snow off the driveway."

Janet feigned a yawn.

"Okay, I get it. I forget you're a city kid."

"Thank God. I don't understand you or Andy. He'd be fighting you to get in the seat and take a turn on this thing."

Beth giggled. "I know. I'm too comfortable on a tractor. My farming methods make Lou crazy. I tend to think that I can get this machine to do anything I can visualize in my head as though I'm connected to it. Lou thinks I'm too reckless. I have all the respect in the world for farm equipment, but it was my playground as a kid. You should've seen Andy and I race tractors before we were allowed on the highway in pickup trucks."

"Neither of you have changed a bit." Janet hugged her. "Mmm, you smell good, like a piña colada."

"Sunscreen. Better safe than sorry. I hate sunburn." Beth climbed up the step to the small seat. "Let me roll this in the shed, and I'll be right back. The only tricky part about running the tractor is dodging Lou's projects. I've learned that she's great at starting something and usually years in finishing. That's one." She nodded to the shed and a pile of new roofing panels on the ground that had rusted the same as the old attached ones. The pile was partially covered in weeds. "I clipped that with the bush hog, talk about a cheap thrill. Her latest is extending the downspouts underground and not telling me how far she made it toward the creek with the underdrain. Soft spots in the earth are not good to find by accident on one of these. Go on in the house. I'll be right behind you." Beth started the tractor, backed up from the car, and slowly made the turn toward the equipment shed that housed another smaller tractor and a riding mower. Buddy followed along.

"Hello," Janet called out as she entered through the front door. If nothing else, she would alert the cats to scatter instead of waking one up unexpectedly.

"We're in the back," Lou answered.

"With the cold beer," Ellen added.

Janet blinked as she walked into the kitchen. Stainless steel appliances and Birdseye maple cabinets popped against the dark red paint of the walls. The original red oak flooring had been restored and refinished. A sunroom off the kitchen held the formal dining table and chairs Beth had grown up with.

"Wow."

"I know. Sometimes I don't think I'm in the same house that I've lived in for ten years. No more 1970s avocado appliances and boxy little cabinets. If we had a toilet in here, I'd never leave the kitchen." Lou sat on a stool at the island with the newspaper and a cup of coffee. She wore her usual paint-stained shorts and shirt that appeared to have legs and sleeves trimmed by dull scissors. "Miss Crack-of-Dawn had to get up early and finish the mowing before you got here so it would look nice."

Ellen sat across from Lou, already settled in with the sports page. "I hate to drink alone but not that much." She raised the dark green bottle and her eyebrows.

"I'll wait until after I see Keith." Janet walked over to the large oval wooden bowl on the counter beside the stove.

"Her grandmother's dough tray, she also made bread this morning." Lou returned to the newspaper. "I tried to tell her to mix it last night, but she doesn't listen to me."

Janet glanced out the window and watched Beth walk across the yard from the equipment shed. She slowed by the cottage and walked over to the open window. "They're here, Mom. We'll come over in ten minutes or so. Take your time getting dressed, you're doing great."

"It must be so much easier having Keith here." Janet's eyes stayed on Beth.

"Easier. I don't know. At least Beth is driving less. Her getting home so late after checking on her mother each day was getting old and made dinner too close to bedtime. We have to get up early to commute into town for work." Lou skimmed the newspaper as she spoke.

Janet remained silent for a moment and tried to convince herself that she was not hearing what she thought she was. "Your households have blended together well. This place is wonderful."

The newspaper didn't move. "You bet. I keep telling Beth what's mine is mine and what's hers is mine." Lou peeked around the paper. "It's a joke. Beth is a catch. I'd help her with most anything. Look at what's been added to the property value. I couldn't afford all this. Who needs to throw parties or play the stereo full blast? Keith living here is a small sacrifice on my part."

"Or none," Janet said to herself as Ellen coughed to hide the comment she knew Janet would make.

Beth came through the back door talking to the Australian shepherd on her heels. "I'll be back in just a few minutes. You know I'll bring you something. Keep an eye on Mom. Good boy."

Lou glanced over the top of the paper. "Don't encourage him."

"The neighbors don't love him, and we do. He just has that annoying habit of barking at Mom every time she tries to leave the cottage." Beth chuckled as she washed her hands at the kitchen sink. She raised the corner of the towel over the dough tray. "Cool. Almost doubled, never know with yeast bread." She walked over to Janet and hugged her.

"Don't mind me, I know you love her more." Lou topped off her coffee.

"Whiney butt." Beth stepped closer to Lou and hugged her. "Oh, don't look like an abandoned puppy." She hugged Ellen again, then looked at Janet. "Don't pay any attention to her. She hasn't absorbed enough caffeine yet. What may I get you? Hot coffee or iced tea?"

Janet shook her head. "I'm an early riser, too. I've already had my quota of caffeine for the day, drank my usual pot of coffee before I left home. Ask my sweetie how many times I had to stop to pee. I swear my bladder is shrinking."

"How about a tour?" Beth took Janet's hand.

"I'll wait for you here." Lou didn't budge.

"You'll show me the shop in the basement." Ellen emptied her bottle and took the newspaper from Lou's hands.

"I'll show Ellen the shop." Lou led the way to the stairs to the basement.

Janet and Beth toured the house. Every room was freshly painted. Beth's furniture mixed with Lou's to give the look of an antique store. "We didn't have to buy any furniture. What little extra space we had filled up when Mom sold. It's so good to see you." Beth hugged her again.

"You're happy?" Janet stopped at the head of the stairs.

"Hell, yes. I know you don't want details, but the physical relationship is the best I've ever experienced. I love being back in the country without the baggage of the home I grew up in and watched my father die in. I can work fifteen acres. I worried about three hundred. Lou is just fun in so many ways. We went to Virginia Beach for my birthday. You and Ellen have me hooked on the ocean. It's as though we have the best of all worlds. She's great with Mom. Keith actually tells everyone that Lou is now officially her adopted daughter."

"How is Keith?" Janet held onto Beth's shoulder as she led the way down the steps to the living room.

Beth sighed. "She's holding her own. I pray that the operations she went through repaired everything. I just function day by day and try to spend as much time with her as I can. I alternate between feeling guilty that I'm either with Lou too much or Mom too much."

They returned to the kitchen. They could hear muffled voices from the basement.

"Come on, take a look at Mom's cottage. Those two will be down there all day if we let them."

"Ellen and I are next in line for the cottage, you know. We've decided to adopt you so you have to take care of us in our old age."

Lou called from the basement. "You mean you aren't there already?" They heard Ellen punch her. "Just kidding. We're staying down here. I may even share the location of the treasure trove some refer to as a fifty-year-old trash dump."

"She has a shop and a pool table," Ellen called. "I'm seriously jealous."

"Gee, thanks." Janet looked at Beth.

"Well, there was room, and I knew a guy selling a table cheap." She shrugged and called down to the basement. "You girls play nice." Beth took Janet's hand. "She's like a kid at Christmas going through the stuff we brought from the farm. Will can't do anything with any of it. Lou is always tinkering with something here or at the college."

Janet nodded. "I should pay Keith for the entertainment value Ellen has had with eBay and selling the surplus tools. She's just about decided she could make a business out of selling secondhand castoffs if she needs the extra money."

Beth pointed to the woods at the low side of the property. "People will buy anything. Can you believe that Lou sells what the people before us filled in the swale in the woods with as trash? Lou loves digging through the pile for old medicine bottles. She's found newspapers in perfect condition from way back in 1950."

"Damn, that old? That's the year I was born."

"Oops."

They followed the walkway to the bungalow. Buddy was stretched out on the small front deck. He moved only his eyebrows as he watched them approach, tap on the door, and enter the house.

Janet felt as though she'd entered a time warp. The cottage had the look and feel of a World War II-era movie set. Overstuffed furniture with large floral upholstery and crocheted antimacassars on arms and backs filled the small living room. Mats were on every tabletop. Beth had carefully arranged the best of the Candler antiques so that her mother could maneuver yet still have her favorite furniture. Framed photographs of young men in uniform were interspersed with those of Will and Beth all the way from infants to teenagers.

Keith came out of the bedroom slowly, using a walker to guide her. She breathed heavily. The customary sparkle in her eyes and easy smile on her face drew Janet to her.

Janet leaned over and carefully hugged Keith. The older woman seemed to be shrinking.

"Look at what these girls did for me. Isn't it beautiful? All I own on one floor and with central air conditioning. No grass to mow or snow to shovel. Beth picks up my mail each night and brings my paper to me every morning. I never thought I'd have it so easy." She lowered herself carefully into the nearest chair and looked at Janet. "It seems so long ago since you drove me here the first time." She plucked at the hem of her knit shirt. "How is your better half?" She grinned at her own joke.

Janet smiled. "Fine, she'll be out to see you later. She took a detour by the girls' shop and we can't get her back upstairs yet."

"Have you had meds and breakfast?" Beth watched her

mother's every move.

"Oh, yes." She looked at Janet. "She does all my grocery shopping and won't let me pay her back. We go to the doctor every three weeks, and I do my errands then. My monthly check just goes to the drug store. I don't miss driving at all with such good chauffeurs."

"The neighbors are great. Several of them take turns coming by to pick up Mom and take her to church. They couldn't be any nicer to her if she'd lived here all her life."

"Kindness of strangers." Keith nodded. "Will may come this weekend. Depends on how busy he is with clients."

Beth rolled her eyes. "Or how many plans Princess Patti has already made. She gets so bored at home by herself all week."

"Beth." Keith frowned at her daughter. "You know Will would help if he could. He has other obligations."

"Meaning Patti can spend money faster than Will can make or inherit it, and all from the comfort of home."

"Now," Keith scolded. "You must promise me you'll look after your brother. He's going to need your help, and yours, too," she looked at Janet, "when he realizes he has to get rid of that wife."

"Ma!"

"We all know it and avoid talking about her. She's awful and awful to him." Keith gave way to a deep rumbling cough.

"And if he could find his backbone..." Beth handed her mother a tissue.

"Bitter?" Janet looked at her friend.

"I'll stop. I promise, Ma." Beth walked over and kissed her mother on the cheek. "We'll be back with lunch in a little while. I'm baking bread."

"Bring honey," Keith reminded her.

"I'll tell Ellen what her new nickname is." Beth giggled. "You bet. Love you, Mom." She nudged Janet toward the door and lowered her voice. "If you don't keep moving, an hour will go by listening to Mom and you would swear only five minutes have passed." They walked toward the main house.

"Follow me." Janet guided Beth away from the back door.

Beth sighed.

"What's with this super woman routine? Are you trying to go before Keith does?" Janet held onto Beth by the shirttail.

"Her health was fine until I moved in with Lou."

"Don't even try to go there. Look at your mother's age and lifestyle…no regular exercise and country cooking." Janet lightly smacked the side of Beth's head. "Lighten up."

Beth nodded. "Mom wasn't part of the deal when Lou and I got together. Lou's been great about bringing Keith here and helps out as much as I ask her."

"It's all part of the deal. Mates do come with families. Lou had to be aware of that."

"She was, at least she tells me she was."

"And she knows Keith being here will keep you here."

"What?" Beth stopped and looked at Janet.

"Face it. All the work on the house and your mother moved in makes it that much more certain that you'll stay."

"Who said I wouldn't stay anyway?"

"You know what I mean."

Beth was silent for a moment. "Yes, but I don't like where your thoughts are taking us."

"Remember, I am your attorney." Janet pointed to the dog running across the field. "Your friend's back."

Beth embraced her. "Yes, she is."

The five women spent an afternoon to remember together.

Chapter Ten

Janet stopped in the hallway outside the room and took a deep breath. She hadn't been able to get away from the office until shortly before noon. Lou had called her just before she left home that morning.

The curtains were drawn across the glass wall that enabled the nurses to see inside of the unit. Janet saw everyone's feet but not the rest of him or her. She recognized Beth's hiking boots near the head of the bed. She assumed the wingtips in the far corner belonged to Will, the pointed toe stiletto heels to Patti, and the scuffed New Balances to Lou. She knew by the number of people allowed in the unit and by how quiet they were that the prognosis wasn't good.

She walked through the center opening and stared at Keith. There was little color and no animation to her face. The brilliant blue of her eyes appeared glazed. There was a ventilator tube in her mouth. An IV bag slowly dripped morphine through a line into her arm. A clip on her index finger and cuff on her upper arm attached her to the monitor tracking oxygen level and blood pressure. The catheter bag hung on the side rail. She looked very small in the hospital bed and resigned to knowing this day had been inevitable.

Beth stood next to the head of the bed with her hand resting on her mother's shoulder. She appeared as dazed as Keith. There were dark circles beneath her eyes. She looked blankly at Janet.

"I'm so sorry." Janet was at a loss for words.

"She can't talk." Beth's eyes filled with tears that she barely held in check.

"Imagine that," Lou mumbled.

Janet glanced at the corner as Patti smacked Lou on the back of the head and a stricken look passed across Will's face. They filled the recliner, Will in the seat and the women on either arm of the chair.

Patti was her usual meticulously groomed self—not a salon set hair out of place, makeup and nails perfect. She wore a sleeveless dress that fit her slim body perfectly and showcased her hours at the gym. Will's tie was askew from his unbuttoned collar. He wore a sport coat that matched the cream pinstripe in his slacks instead of his usual three-piece suit. Lou wore khakis and polo shirt with the college's logo. Beth looked as though she had not changed clothes in days. Her jeans and oxford shirt were as crumpled as her spirits. She had tired of her hair hanging about her shoulders and pulled it back in a ponytail.

Lou met Beth's stare. "It was just a joke."

"An extremely poor one." Beth frowned toward the corner.

Janet hoped she didn't hear Patti snicker. "Will, it's been a while. Patti, you're looking well." She crossed the room and held out her hand. "Lou, smart-ass." She placed her hand on Lou's shoulder and squeezed until the woman winced.

"Our good friend, Janet Evans, attorney extraordinaire." Lou looked from Will to Patti.

"My best friend." Beth held her arms out to Janet and waited for the woman to come to her.

"Why don't you sit down, sweetie?"

"I found an extra chair and put it at the head of the bed for her. She refuses to leave Mom's side." Will tried to put his arm around Patti. Patti's eyes stayed on Lou as she pushed him away.

Beth shook her head. "I've sat around this hospital for days, following Mom around through testing and unit changes until I ache. Standing feels better."

"Walk with me." Janet tried to gently pull her away from the bed.

"Will's right. I'm afraid to leave her."

"We're here." Will stared at his sister.

Beth shook her head.

"Well, we'll walk around so the room isn't so crowded." Patti left the arm of the chair and grabbed Lou's sleeve.

Will watched them leave. "Beth, you must stop thinking that you're the only one who cares about Mom." He paused, watching the two men who approached the room.

Beth followed her brother's stare. Her face brightened. "You guys." She almost smiled as she crossed the distance to meet Andy and Greg.

Janet had a quick flashback of the two men in sequined dresses, wigs, and feather boas at Beth's first Halloween party—Will's last encounter with them. Both men were sandy-haired and dressed this time in pressed jeans and crisp polo shirts. They were engineers who worked in a business casual office necessitated by the hours they spent on construction sites.

"We've been so worried about you." Andy leaned down to hug Beth. He was four inches taller than Greg and almost six inches taller than Beth.

"We kept calling your office to find out where you were. Amber is a piece of work, by the way. I thought I was going to have to leave my passport with her just to find out which hospital." Greg pushed Andy aside to embrace Beth. "Your faithful companion won't call us back."

Janet placed a hand on either man. "Just check with me next time. I keep as close tabs on her as she will let anyone. I swear I'm better about taking my earring off and listening for the message beep." The men giggled. "Just where have you been, Junior?" She hugged her nephew a second time.

"Andrew has been needy and controlling lately."

"You wish." Andy pulled Greg against him.

As Will watched the two men, his face became tighter, eyes narrower.

Beth stared toward the corner of the room, watching her brother. "You remember my old high school boyfriend, Andy Reynolds. Will, you've not met his partner, Greg Davis. You and Patti avoided them at my Halloween party." She caught her friends' eyes. "My brother, Will."

They turned to him. Andy extended his hand as he closed the distance to the corner but stopped himself as he saw that Will was neither going to stand nor uncross his arms. They spoke as Will nodded in their direction.

"Ouch," Greg muttered behind his hand to Janet.

"Do you need anything at all, sweetie?" Andy took Beth's hand in his. "From the office, from home? Pets okay?"

"Everything's fine. Lou is back and forth at home while I stay here with Keith. I call in at the office once a day. The others are covering my clients. Thank goodness it's not tax season." Beth stretched.

"You sit right down. I can at least get the knots out of your shoulders. I know how you are." Greg motioned to the chair.

"Showoff. You just enjoy the one opportunity you have to make a woman scream." Beth did as told.

"I heard that." Greg laughed as Beth grunted.

"Will, are you okay, need a cup of coffee or a soda?" Andy kept his distance from the other man.

"No, thank you. I don't need anything from you." Will caught himself. "I don't need anything. We just came back from lunch."

"And I'm guessing she didn't go with you." Greg squeezed Beth's neck.

"No, ouch, I didn't." Beth tried to pull away from him.

"Well, that settles it. We know your favorites. We'll be back shortly with food. You need to eat. Janet, how about you?" Andy moved toward the door.

"I'm good. Munched on the way, didn't think to bring her something, damn it."

"Don't even try to talk us out of it." Greg patted Beth's shoulders. "We'll be right back, sweetie." They nodded and left the room.

Janet sat in the chair as Beth stood and flexed her shoulders.

"That hurts so good. I love those guys…what good friends. You ought to be ashamed of yourself, Will. When did you become so narrow-minded?" Beth frowned at him.

"We're not having that discussion here or now." Will would

not look her in the eye. "Other things are more important."

Beth sighed and motioned Janet to follow her to the far side of the room from the bed. Beth turned her back to Keith. "Mom's kidneys have failed. Her liver is losing function. At least one heart valve is leaking and filling her lungs with fluid. She's miserable. The doctors are talking to us about another operation."

"And I'm for it." Will leaned forward in the chair and whispered.

"Ruth caught me in the hall early this morning and told me I could request the removal of the ventilator and addition of a morphine pump to the IV line. I swear if it weren't for the nurses, I wouldn't know what the hell is going on with Mom. Ruth Dunn is the best she's had." Beth glanced over her shoulder as a tech entered the room to check vitals. "Ruth's advice makes the most sense to me. I've already requested no resuscitation."

"We can't facilitate her passing." Will joined them.

"Janet, I want you to be a witness." Beth cleared her throat as she returned to the bedside. "Mom, can you hear me?"

Keith nodded slightly.

"Do you want another operation?"

Keith tried to focus her eyes on Beth.

"It may help you to be more comfortable." Will spoke louder than was needed.

Keith's head moved enough to look at her son.

"It won't make you any better, Mom. It will make you stay like this longer." Beth gently took her mother's hand in her own.

Keith's eyes closed.

"I'm not agreeing to anything until she gives us some direction." Will returned to the overstuffed chair. "I don't care what piece of paper you have that she signed."

Beth looked at Janet. "Remember what Mom said so often because of the way my father died? You weren't around to hear it, Will."

Janet nodded.

"I don't want to outlive my usefulness." Beth looked away from her mother. "I can't stay here right now."

Janet took Beth by the arm and led her out of the room and

along the hallway. "How long have they been here?"

"Since the weekend. They're at the house with Lou. I want Will here." Beth hesitated. "What is Patti turning my brother into? There was a time when he would have hung out with Andy and Greg. He only tolerates Lou because of me. Hell, he barely tolerates me. I just save him from being responsible for the farm and Mom."

"Well, at least Lou doesn't seem to mind keeping her entertained."

"They're like two teenagers getting on my every last nerve. I feel like Mom used to with Will and me." Beth stopped and leaned against the wall. "Oh, Lord, Janet, we need to let her go, don't we?"

Janet nodded. "I'm afraid so."

"I'll make the decision if Keith can't. Hell with Will, he's been no part of either of our parents' illnesses. I can love him and not particularly like him." Beth took a deep breath and stood up straight. She walked back toward the unit.

"I see someone who needs a decent coffee." Lou caught up to Beth and handed her a cup topped with foam.

"I have a milkshake for Will. What a sweet tooth that man has yet doesn't gain weight." Patti held up the tall glass.

"Our two little peas in a pod," Lou did her imitation of Keith. "Have you ever seen a brother and sister more alike?" She fell in step with Janet. "Responsible, dependable, focused, and calm even when something like this is going on. They don't need anyone but themselves to reason through it all."

"Watch when I hand him this. He'll thank me and tell me I shouldn't have gone to any trouble." Patti laughed.

Beth sipped the coffee in silence. She wouldn't meet Janet's eyes.

Patti entered the room. Will reacted exactly as predicted.

Even Beth chuckled at her brother and at herself. "Okay, you have us pegged. If you wanted excitement, you chose the wrong partners." She punched her brother.

"What?" He looked completely confused.

This made the women laugh more.

"This has made me realize how truly important family is." Patti nodded as she handed Will a napkin.

"We've talked it over and decided to move back to Virginia. We really like the area just west of you guys and love the houses on the lake lots. We explored a little as we drove through. Patti's parents would only be thirty minutes away." Will dabbed at the chocolate on his tie.

"You're kidding." Beth looked first at Will, then Patti. She stared at her mother and lowered her voice. "Why in the hell didn't you move back when she could have enjoyed it? You're only doing it because of Patti's parents," she whispered.

"Fantastic." Lou hugged Patti, then Will. "Shouldn't show favoritism."

"Family is what matters. You're right, I should have done it sooner for her sake. I tried." Will spoke only to his sister.

"It's always about her, isn't it?" Beth sighed. "It's okay, Will, I would like you back in my life." She hugged him.

"Beth." Janet inclined her head in Keith's direction.

Beth returned to her mother's side. Keith moved her hand with effort and reached for the ventilator. Beth caught her mother's hand.

"What is it, Mom?" Beth leaned down closer to her mother.

Keith shook her head slowly and touched the tubing going to her mouth.

"Take this off?"

Keith nodded slightly.

"You don't want surgery?"

Keith shook her head.

"You do want control of the morphine?"

Keith nodded again. Tears ran from the corners of her eyes.

"I love you, Mom." Beth hugged her as best she was able. "I'm so proud of you for making this decision. It's the right thing to do. I haven't forgotten my promise to you about Will." Her voice faltered as she whispered the last.

Janet guided Lou and Patti out of the room. "Give them time alone with their mother."

Lou nodded.

"He's going to take it hard."

"So is she." Lou looked at Janet.

"They're both going to need you two now." Janet hoped that the women heard and understood her.

Chapter Eleven

Beth stared at the portrait of her mother, then glanced over her shoulder at Janet. "This has always been my favorite."

Janet nodded. She stayed close to Beth in case she was as weak as she appeared. Janet insisted on driving her friend to the funeral home. Ellen would come later to manage the register at the front door. It would be her first time wearing slacks and jacket since her retirement, which spoke volumes for her respect of Beth and Keith.

"Mom had not turned twenty-one yet. It was just after Daddy proposed. Look at how pretty her hair was, such a beautiful chestnut brown. I love the way she wore the clips to pull it back from her face. Look at those eyes, what a beautiful blue."

Janet smiled fondly. "I like the way she's looking to the side so that it's not quite a profile shot but you have a better sense of her face and how she really looked. And that expression…not quite a smile, but you can feel the happiness and joy in her."

Beth nodded. She looked at the other portrait on the second easel. "Church photograph taken a year ago. Lord, look at the change. I didn't realize how hard her illness had been on her. You don't see it when you live with someone day in and day out."

"That's true for all of us."

"Mom was sixty-four in this. She looks a little confused. Look at that complexion, though. She had the best skin of anyone I've ever known."

Beth took a deep breath and made her feet take the steps that brought her before the open coffin. She forced herself to look down at her mother. "She looks empty. She really isn't there anymore."

Keith Candler wore her favorite purple gingham church dress with the beads she had strung to go with it. On her left hand were her wedding and engagement rings on her third finger and Luke's wedding ring on her middle finger.

"I never knew about the promise she and Daddy had made that the one left behind would wear the other's ring, then keep them both on at their time. I don't know where that came from, but Mom insisted it was my father's idea." Beth allowed the tears to trickle down her face. She reached in and touched her mother's hand. "I love you, Mom. Tell Daddy I miss him."

Beth turned slightly and nodded to the man waiting patiently just outside the room. "It's okay to close it now." She stepped back and watched the lid as it was brought slowly down. "Will doesn't want to see her."

Janet stepped beside Beth and put her arm around her. Beth leaned against the woman and coughed.

"Can you believe I picked up a bronchial infection being in the room with Mom when she first tried to come off the ventilator?" Beth shook her head and coughed again. "I feel like crap."

"Well, you look even worse. Come over here and sit before you collapse. The choices for lying down around here are not the best."

Beth chuckled. She did as told, a sure sign that she was sick. Her cell phone vibrated. She flipped the phone open.

"Hey, Will." She listened.

"Yes, it's closed now. Everything is ready for tonight…No, I'm just going to sit here with her until the others start coming in…Because I don't want to be anywhere else…Janet…Stop it, Will. I'm not listening to you about this." She snapped the phone shut, ending the call.

Beth looked at Janet. "Don't you just love hearing one side of a conversation?" She cautiously took a deep breath, trying not to set off another bout of coughing. "They're going to dinner and will try to be here when the visitation starts." She closed her eyes and concentrated on calming down. "I don't like Will, Patti, or

Lou very much at this point. Reminds me of when Mom would tell Will and me that she was going to line us up and knock our heads together. We knew we'd gotten on her last nerve and to tread lightly for a while." Beth chuckled tiredly.

Janet slid a chair close to her. "You're exhausted. No wonder everything anyone says or does is trying your patience. Give it time. Just concentrate on one thing at a time and get through tonight. The rest will settle down and return to some normalcy in a few weeks."

"I know." Beth nodded in agreement. "You know I don't mean this the wrong way, but would you leave me alone for a few minutes? I want her just to myself one last time."

"I understand. Open the door when you want anyone else in here, or call me." Janet patted the cell phone in her pocket. She left the room and shook her head at the funeral director lingering in the hallway. "Don't bother her, please."

He bobbed his head and went through the door to the back of the building.

Janet stood in the wide front hall of the house—double doors opened into viewing rooms in the four corners of the building with a closed door to the back offices. It had been a rambling farmhouse until ten years before when taken over and remodeled for funeral home use. She glanced out the front door sidelights at the adjoining pastureland. It made sense to have a funeral home in the country to save the long drive into the closest city. They did a steady business supplemented by farming, Beth had explained to her. Of course, Beth kept their books.

Janet sat in the overstuffed chair and leaned her head back. They could all use a little rest. Keith had passed two days before. Arrangements had already been made according to Keith's own choices. That night was the visitation before the interment the next day. It would be a very long evening.

Janet looked up in time to whistle softly as Ellen entered the building. Her hair was smoothed into a respectable pixie, black pants suit and shirt were immaculate, and lips showed just a hint of gloss. Janet was so used to seeing Ellen in baggy shorts and shirts she was taken aback to see how attractive she looked. "You cleaned up nice, sweetie. Thank you."

Ellen's eyes filled. "She was a classy woman and her daughter takes after her." She went to the lectern and placed her Montblanc pen on the guest book. "Only the best."

The four viewing rooms in the funeral home filled quickly. As each room became crowded with the growing line waiting to see the family, the noise level rose. It was hard not to visit with one another as the line slowly advanced to the family.

Lou looked behind Beth and across the length of the coffin at Patti. She silently formed the word, "Moo."

Patti allowed a fleeting smile.

Will and Beth flanked the coffin—Will and Patti to the left, Beth and Lou to the right—in an attempt to spread the family out and keep the line moving. Janet worked the room, keeping people moving and an eye on the family.

Janet frowned at Lou, then Patti. Both women ignored her.

Everyone stopped to hug Beth and tell her a favorite story of her parents. Beth had found a reserve of strength none of them knew she possessed. She smiled at each person, remembered their name and that of their significant family members, angled her head as she listened intently to each reminisce, and hugged the teller to make him or her feel better.

Janet watched her proudly. She'd never seen anyone any more gracious. She had to agree with Beth about lining the others up and knocking their heads together.

"I'm glad we had a drink with dinner," Patti mouthed the words to Lou behind Will's back.

"If one more old man asks me who I am, then says 'that Lou,' I'm not responsible for my actions."

Will cleared his throat.

"I was in your mother's Sunday School class for twenty years," the woman said as she held onto Beth's hand. "Best teacher I ever had. She never ran out of ideas to make the lessons interesting."

Beth nodded.

"I just have to tell you. She was so proud of you. She never failed to praise how you looked after her and how the two of you had looked after your father. That meant the world to her. She loved you dearly."

"And I, her. I was so fortunate to have the parents I did." Beth hugged the woman.

"Florence-fucking-Nightingale. How do you live with her?" Patti whispered to Lou.

"Enough," Will said to his wife.

"I know you didn't just try to tell me what I may say, Will Candler. We didn't have to be here tonight. These people are coming in for Beth. We could have waited until the funeral tomorrow to make an appearance."

"Are you the son?" The man grasped Will with a gnarled hand the color of cured tobacco. He wore crisply laundered overalls and a starched white shirt. He tugged at the tight collar against his neck.

"Yes, sir."

"Uh-huh. Heard about you. Shame you didn't take over the farm. Beautiful land. Your father and his before had a gift with crops. Guess it wasn't your calling." The man looked at the suit with vest that Will wore as comfortably as most men did jeans and a T-shirt and moved into his place before Beth.

"Hiram." She smiled and hugged him.

He blushed. "If you want a summer job again, there'll always be a place for you dropping tobacco plants. Never saw anyone with a better eye for spacing those seedlings. Your father won my grocery money one week, betting that the majority in the row you set was equally spaced. Then he gave me the money back because he said the pleasure was in watching me pull the string line between each plant and seeing the expression on my face."

"You're lucky he gave your money back. He always kept mine. You'd think I'd have learned not to bet with him." Beth chuckled.

"You did right by both of them, girl. That's all any of us can hope for."

She hugged him again.

"And who are you?" The man stopped in front of Lou.

"Keith's adopted daughter, Lou Stephens."

"Oh, well, glad you're here for Beth." The man shifted his

weight from one foot to the other, couldn't think of anything else to say, and moved on.

"I'm Will's wife," Patti spoke first to get the question over with when the next person stopped in front of her.

"Who's Will?" The woman glanced along the line.

It was all Janet could do not to laugh. She hovered behind the family line, making sure Beth had something to drink and catching people's eyes to encourage them to move along.

She looked across the room. Ellen had not moved from her post and made sure everyone signed the registry. Beth would need help later to remember all who came through the receiving line. Ellen knew some of the people from her years at the college. She slipped back into effortless chatter with strangers.

"They never talk about any of this." Greg glanced about the room of plain, country people as he spoke to Lou. "It's a whole different life that she and Andy were supposed to be a part of." Lou had decided to stand with Will and Patti so they could all three be politely ignored at once. "It's as though she was another person on her parents' farm. Andy's the same. Sometimes I forget he and Beth were a couple."

Andy left the line when he reached Beth and now stood beside her. They looked as though they had been comfortably married for years as Beth leaned against him for support.

"She never says much about the past or her father," Lou said. "I knew she helped care for him before he died, but I didn't realize it was for years." She looked at Will as though he should have explained it better to her.

"And you wouldn't have known that unless you heard it from her mother or some of the others." Greg leaned closer to Lou. "She barely told Auntie about any of it until Keith launched into it in front of Janet. Most people had no idea what Beth did with her twenties, being a co-caregiver to her bedridden father. She never complained except to say she should have handled it better. She did once say that if she had the decision to make all over again, she would have done the same but with more patience."

Will sighed.

Greg looked at Will. "She wasn't even bitter about doing it

alone."

The couple in front of Beth and Andy stalled the movement of the line.

"Everyone knows about you two. They don't pretend to understand, but they know both of you too well to be critical of who you live with." The man was Andy's age but with black hair and heavy mustache and the deep tan of farming.

His wife hugged Beth again. "They're still disappointed you two aren't married and living on the farm. Don't bother to try and tell them that you're married to someone of the same sex. It just doesn't connect with their image of you two."

"I tell them when they ask my opinion that anyone who wants to suffer through marriage ought to be able to, regardless of sex, same or nonexistent." With that, his wife pulled him away to join their set of friends in the corner.

"And to think we went through school with all of them." Andy watched his former friends and teammates who had turned into their own parents.

"Thank God, we're not normal." Beth giggled and sagged against Andy. "I could use a stiff drink if I didn't think it would put me out cold."

"Are you sure that would be a bad thing?" Andy held onto her as he watched Greg slip behind the line to his aunt.

Beth nodded. "Thank you so much for being here and for that huge tray of cold cuts at the house. You guys have fed us for a week at least. Mom thought the world of you and never forgave me for letting you get away. She told me I should have married you anyway." She chuckled. "Maybe she was right."

"She was always decent to me even after she saw me with Greg. I appreciated that. She didn't miss a beat speaking to both of us and wanting to know how we were doing."

"Mom struggled with her faith but never stopped loving me even after I upset her entire world." Beth glanced at the church photograph again.

"She accepted all of us. She just couldn't talk about it." Janet had her arm around Greg's waist as they joined Beth and Andy.

"More than she accepted that." Andy stared at Patti who had

eased out of line and found a chair in the corner so that she could listen to her iPod. Will made no attempt to carry on a conversation with any of the locals he should have remembered from his childhood.

Chapter Twelve

The drive to the Outer Banks was painfully subdued. Janet and Ellen talked quietly in the front while Beth propped herself up with pillows in one corner of the backseat and slept, waking only when they stopped to eat lunch. Lou sat in the opposite corner and occupied herself with a CD player from Patti.

"I'm glad we finally talked Beth into this," Janet said quietly to Ellen as they crossed the state line into North Carolina. "She hasn't rested since Keith's death, between playing catch-up at the office and handling Keith's estate."

"I know. I remember acting as my mother's executrix. It's a major pain sorting out all the hospital bills and Medicare statements while trying to settle life insurance policies and close out bank accounts and credit cards." Ellen looked over her shoulder to make sure Beth was still asleep. "Beth told me that Keith still had policies taken out by her parents and converted when Keith came of age with companies that have been gone for decades. She has to track the buyouts."

"Good heavens. Good thing she's a CPA." Janet glanced in the rearview mirror. "Wild child doesn't seem too concerned about anything."

Lou nodded in beat with the music and stared out the window.

"That's what worries me." Ellen reached for Janet's hand. "Here I go again. We brought them here the first time October a year ago. Can you believe the change in them?" She looked at

Janet.

"What a difference a year makes," Janet said ruefully. "Except in us." She grinned at her partner.

Ellen nodded.

They pulled into the driveway of the cottage by mid-afternoon. Ellen couldn't wait to be out of the car and smell the salt air. "Home sweet away from home."

Janet popped the trunk open to unload bags.

"Need any help?" A woman's voice carried across the sand from the four thousand-square-foot house next door.

Janet hit her head on the trunk latch trying to see who was talking to them. She heard Ellen before she saw the source.

"Fuck!"

Janet stepped around the car. Ellen pointed to the crow's nest atop the roof ridge next door.

Patti was dressed in a pink jogging suit and waving to them. She pushed Will toward the steps.

Lou stretched as she left the car and immediately looked to the house across the sand and waved.

"Damn her, she knew!" Ellen dropped the bag she had pulled out of the trunk and prepared to go at Lou.

Janet grabbed her arm. "Wait."

Ellen's face turned a bright red. She held her tongue as Beth emerged from the backseat, looking groggy from napping. She smiled at Janet and Ellen. "We're here. I had forgotten how much I love this place. I can't think of anywhere else I'd rather be. Thank you so much, Ellen."

"You might reconsider that." Janet pointed to Lou jogging toward the house next door. Lou kicked sand at Will in passing. Patti started down the steps to meet her.

Beth's face fell. "Oh, no."

"Oh, yes. You're not having a nightmare, sweetheart," Janet said, watching Lou and Patti hug.

"Are you too tired to drive us back?" Beth looked at Janet. "Just kidding." Her smile was as wan as her complexion.

"Hey, little sister." Will stopped in front of Beth, hands in the pockets of his baggy knee-length shorts. He wore a Fletcher

Women's College sweatshirt.

"Will, what the hell did she talk you into? You don't have the money to throw away on that place for a week." All hope Beth had of relaxing disappeared with her question.

"Her parents treated us." He shrugged. "We told them how stressed we were with Mom's death and the move to Virginia to be closer to them, and they offered."

Ellen tried but could not stop herself. "How stressed you and Patti are? What kind of bullshit is that?"

"I don't know, Ms. Harris, how many kinds are there?" Will was in no better mood than Ellen.

"You didn't want to come, did you, but you couldn't let her come alone?" Beth asked her brother.

He wouldn't answer.

"She made you because of Lou."

He stared at Beth blankly. "Do you want help with your bags or not? Or do you have enough old bags?" His attempt at humor was not well received.

"Not," Beth said quickly and picked up her two duffels and started toward the cottage.

"Fine." He turned and walked back toward the big house.

Lou waved from the crow's nest as she twirled Patti in a dance step. Lou's bags were left sitting in the driveway.

"You're welcome to stay with us," Will said over his shoulder to Beth. "You know where Lou will be most of the time."

Beth continued into Ellen's cottage without responding. She dropped her bags in the front bedroom and continued through the house and out the back door. She was soon walking north on the beach, away from Lou and Patti and Will.

They settled into a routine of Janet and Ellen's early morning walk with Beth accompanying them in silence as Lou slept. Beth then went for mid-morning and mid-afternoon walks alone as Lou slept in each morning and hung out or shopped with Patti in the afternoon. Lunch was catch as catch can. Dinner was open for whoever was in a mood to go out. Lou spent her evenings with Patti and Will; Beth with Janet and Ellen. Beth went to bed at

10:00 just before Janet and Ellen; Lou usually wandered in about 1:00 to sleep part of the night with Beth. They all studied what one another was doing.

Ellen waited up for Lou on their third night in Salvo. She was sitting on the back porch in the dark when Lou tiptoed up the steps to the house at 1:15 a.m.

"What in the hell are you doing?"

Lou jumped as though shot at. "Are you crazy? You scared the crap out of me."

"Someone needs to."

"Mind your own damn business."

"Not when it's going on under my own roof."

"Then we'll move out."

"Beth won't."

This stopped Lou. "What do you mean?"

"You can go wherever the hell you want to. In fact, we don't want you in the car with us for the drive home."

Lou's face hardened. "Fine."

"Beth is no fool."

"I didn't say she was."

"That bitch Patti is married, for Christ's sake."

"So?"

Ellen threw up her hands. "Beth watches you and Patti. She knows something's going on."

"But she doesn't want to believe it. That's the beauty of it."

"She can't allow herself to believe it…it's her friggin' sister-in-law."

Lou shrugged.

"You little shit."

"Well, I'm not the first to break up a marriage. At least there's no child involved."

Ellen forced herself not to throw her 160 pounds at Lou. "If you're implying I did, you've been told the wrong story."

"I'm not accusing anyone of anything. Live and let live. We're all grownups."

"Yes, but we don't all have the innate honor that Beth does. This will destroy her. Don't do this to her so soon after losing her mother."

"It's out of my hands." Lou started toward the door. "I'll go back if you don't want me in your doll house."

"Get out of my sight. Beth still wants you here. Find an excuse to go home separately."

"Not a problem." Lou entered the house.

Ellen didn't move.

"Honey," Janet whispered to her from the bedroom, using the window that opened onto the porch, "come to bed."

"You heard?"

"Yes."

"I hate her."

"I always did. Come inside." Janet met her in the kitchen and grabbed two beers from the refrigerator, hoping the lager would help them fall asleep.

An uneasy silence settled over the cottage whenever Lou checked in with Beth. Beth said nothing about what she observed until their last night. Will had decided to stay at the cottage to watch college football while Patti and Lou went to dinner. Janet and Ellen were civil to him for Beth's sake.

"Will, walk with me." Beth held out her hand to her brother and led him out the back door.

"I think I need to stretch out." Janet looked at Ellen and started for their room.

"Janet," Ellen said as she stood from the sofa, "wait for me."

They eased open the bedroom windows.

Beth and Will stopped on the beach directly out from the cottage. Will had almost tripped over a half-buried bottle he wanted to see the rest of—it looked like a fairly old whiskey decanter with the bottom sticking out of the sand three inches.

"Wonder if the top is still on this. That would be a pretty good find to take home. Better than any of that crap Lou digs up in the old trash dump at the house."

"Did you enjoy the trip, big brother?" Beth sounded older than Keith.

Janet reached for Ellen's hand.

"Some of it." Will was intent on moving sand with his Cross pen.

"Will…" Beth waited for him to look up at her. She stared until he stood and faced her. "Will, it's time. Patti needs to leave this family."

"Go on."

"What is her hold on you? Money? I'll give you all I have if that's what it takes for you to be rid of her. Even Mom saw how bad it was between you two."

He didn't respond.

"She's throwing herself at Lou. Lou keeps telling Patti that she's not an experiment and not interested in anything but friendship."

Janet audibly sucked in her breath.

"What did you say?" Will finally showed some emotion— amusement.

"Patti won't leave Lou alone."

Will looked around as though he wanted someone else to hear this. "You've got it backward, baby sister. Your Lou has been coming after my Patti ever since they met. Patti has never been interested in other women that way until Lou."

Ellen whispered to Janet. "Yeah, right."

"What are you saying?" Beth's voice trembled.

"Lou is done with you and has moved on to Patti. You and I are just supposed to tolerate what they're doing until they decide who they want to live with. Patti will never leave me. She won't give up her social connections from a heterosexual marriage, which also happen to be her business connections. Whether you want to salvage something with Lou is your call. I don't give a shit."

A wail escaped from Beth that made the hairs on Ellen's head stand on end.

"I suggest you get a grip on yourself. What did you think… that I was in denial because I love my wife? Get real. I've despised her for years."

Beth fought her emotions as Ellen held Janet in the room.

"If what you say is true, then that's all the more reason for you to be rid of Patti. You have to let me help you."

"You are so out of your league. There's much more to it than that, or I would've been long gone from her by now." He shook his head. "I'll talk this over with my wife on the drive back to Virginia and get back to you." He turned and walked away. "Better yet, the three of us will discuss it—me, Patti, and Lou—on the way home. See you in the commonwealth, little sister."

Beth stood stock-still, unable to move. She finally sank down to her knees.

Ellen released her grip of Janet.

Beth didn't respond as Janet knelt beside her.

"Sweet baby." Janet caught her breath. "You would be the Marine in battle who would throw your body on a live grenade to save everyone else."

"And what a dumbass I would be to do it for that bunch."

Janet pulled Beth to her. She didn't have the heart to agree with her.

Chapter Thirteen

Janet was totally engrossed in proofreading and highlighting the paper draft of the interrogatory she had dictated earlier when she heard a slight tap on her office door.

Lou peeked around the door at her and raised her eyebrows. "There was no one out front."

"Wanda must have left for lunch without telling me, or I didn't hear her. Care to guess which?" She marked the last paragraph read with a penciled check and removed her reading glasses. "Come on in." Janet took one last look at the document and wondered how long it would take her to recover her frame of reference. She sighed.

"Are you sure? I could come back later. I can tell I've caught you at a bad time, Janet." Lou stuck her hands in the back pockets of her jeans as she apologized. Her cotton sweater was a size too large for her.

"My concentration is not what it used to be. I find I have to read most things twice now to retain as much as I should." Janet walked around the end of her desk. "Come in. I've stopped now." She studied the woman. "Is everything all right?" She leaned against the front edge of her desk.

"That's why I'm here. I do apologize for not calling first. It was a last-minute decision, and I didn't have your number with me. I thought I'd take a chance on finding you or your secretary here and just make an appointment if nothing else. I was afraid to put this off any longer." Lou paced back and forth in front of the sofa.

Janet couldn't help but think that Lou was smart enough to know that if she'd called for an appointment it would have been made for sometime in the next decade. "Alight somewhere. You're making my neck hurt. Start from the beginning." Janet returned to her chair. Lou sat on the middle cushion of the sofa.

"First of all, I want to apologize, and I will offer the same to Ellen when I see her." Lou perched on the edge of the cushion.

"Go on." Janet sat back in her chair and frowned—this was turning into quite a performance.

"What I did, what Patti did, is inexcusable." She took a deep breath. "We had both become bored with good, decent spouses, and we took the easy out of an affair. I was flattered, and Patti was curious. We were wrong to act on it." Lou watched for a reaction from Janet.

"I assume you've said this to Beth." Janet was surprised by Lou's frankness.

Lou nodded. "Will, Patti, and I talked it all out on the way back from the beach. Patti and Will have done much soul searching and have agreed to try and work things out."

"How about you and Beth?"

Lou looked briefly away from Janet, then back to meet her eyes. "I don't think there is a better person on this earth than Beth Candler. I screwed up big-time. She's forgiven me, which I know is far more than I deserve, but she can't let go of what happened. She's deeply upset, and she has every right to be. We agreed to try counseling after tax season. It's just that...I'm worried about her, and I don't know what to do."

"How so?" Janet hated that she found herself believing Lou's sincerity.

"She shuts down at night. She doesn't want to watch television...it either makes her fidget or puts her to sleep. She doesn't want to go out. She just doesn't enjoy our friends that much anymore. Most times, she goes to the guest bedroom, lies down on the bed with the television on, and just stares out the window toward the cottage. Sometimes, she goes to the cottage to sleep in Keith's bed. Sometimes, she's awake all night. We don't talk much anymore. We don't do anything together anymore. She has no interest in a physical relationship with me. She just doesn't want to be around any of us." Lou let it all out in a rush.

"Us, as in Will and Patti?" Janet asked.

Lou nodded. "She first began by making excuses. Now she just gets on the phone with Will and tells him she doesn't know what I'm going to do, but she's tired and going to bed, for the rest of us to have a good time and she'll catch us another time. I swear to you, Patti and I do not spend any time alone together anymore. We promised Beth and Will."

"Will doesn't argue with her?"

"Will doesn't argue with anyone."

"Have Beth and Will talked since the beach? Just the two of them?"

"I don't think so. Beth hasn't withdrawn from just one thing. She has withdrawn from everything and everyone that's familiar to her."

"Is it work, bringing too much of the office home?" Janet idly thumped a wooden pencil against the legal pad on her desk.

"Just the opposite. Remember how she used to be in a routine of working half days on weekends? Even after they bought her a laptop?"

Janet nodded.

Lou shook her head. "She doesn't set foot in the building during weekends now. She struggles to make herself go to the office and pull eight hours. I can almost set my watch by how she leaves every morning at 7:30 to barely make it through the door when the office opens. She's at home every night by 5:30, which means she's shooting out of the door the second the hand is near quitting time. She takes walks at lunch, lunches that run long because she forgets to time herself so she can get back within an hour. If they call her at home, she won't answer the telephone. If I do, she won't take the call. I wouldn't be surprised if they fire her, probably would have by now if it were anyone but her."

"This is not good." Janet glanced at her calendar for the week—booked solid.

"She won't talk to Andy and Greg, either. I've asked them

to try. She just won't open up. She barely stayed at dinner with them a half hour. Greg cooked so they could stay in and not have to face a crowded restaurant. Andy told me they tried to talk to her about Patti and me, and she walked out." In answer to Janet's unspoken question, Lou continued. "I asked Andy face to face what happened. He and Greg are furious with me."

Janet had debated with herself, and she and Ellen had a long talk about it before they told the boys what happened at the cottage in October. They had to all but restrain Andy and make him promise not to do anything foolish. He had finally calmed down when Greg suggested cooking dinner just for Beth and giving her a chance to bring it up with them. So much for that plan. Janet looked at her calendar for the following week. Wednesday night was open if she canceled a business dinner with several other local attorneys.

"She has no interest in any of the projects we had started on the house. Most of the remodeling is done except for the last finishing touches. She will go outside and clear brush with the tractor, but I think that's as much to get away from me as anything. It takes her back to farming with her father. She gives the dog more attention lately than me."

"Would she see a counselor now on her own?" Janet watched Lou closely.

"I've suggested it with no luck. Frankly, I think she's putting me off by agreeing to couple's counseling in the spring. It's no secret that I went through therapy when I split with my first partner, and it does help. She refuses."

"Keith's pastor?"

Lou shrugged. "Maybe. She liked the way he helped Keith. She came to know him fairly well through all the time at the hospital. I've been reluctant to involve him because our community is so small and most of his members have a strong, traditional view of relationships. He was only comfortable around us in crowds at the hospital."

"What about her doctor?"

Lou shrugged again. "She won't set foot near a doctor after all those months taking care of her mother. We better hope she doesn't become ill any time soon." Lou hesitated.

"So what are you thinking?"

"You're my last hope. Would you talk with her?" Lou stood and walked over to the desk. "I know it's a lot to ask. I know you're extremely busy. I know I'm the last person you want to do a favor for. If you don't have time, you don't have time. Forget that I was here or that I asked you."

"I didn't say that." Janet was not surprised by the request. She had intervened not long after she met Beth when she realized the younger woman was in over her head with a double workload and on the verge of a major crash and burn. Lou knew about it.

Lou leaned on Janet's desk. "I know you mean the world to her. If anyone can get her to open up, it's you. Would you please think about it and let me know? I have to do something. I can't believe she hasn't said something to you herself."

Janet shook her head. "No, I've not heard from her. Now I feel guilty. I knew she was extremely upset, but she usually does better if she has time to process things, then talk when she decides she's ready. I should have checked in with her. We've exchanged a few e-mails but nothing with any substance to it."

Lou walked to the door of the office. "Thank you so much."

"I'll try, but we still may have to approach this through her doctor."

Lou nodded. "I'm gone. I've taken enough of your time. I need to get back to work. They've been lenient with me ducking out at odd times, knowing my partner is having problems. Let me know if you have any luck talking with her. If there's something I should be doing that I'm not, all she has to do is tell me, talk to me. I can't read her mind."

"I'm not sure I'd want to." Janet caught Lou and gave her a hug.

"Isn't that the truth?" Lou closed the door behind herself.

Janet glanced at her calendar again and jotted Lou Stephens's name as a drop-in. It was interesting that Lou had confided in a boss she neither liked nor respected about her personal problems.

Chapter Fourteen

"Beth Candler, I know you didn't just walk past me without speaking." Janet raised her voice and quickened her pace. She couldn't believe her luck. She was at the courthouse to file a suit on behalf of a client and just happened to glance across the clerk's office and spot her friend. She didn't care how quiet the room normally was or who she disturbed. The clerks could frown at her all they wanted if it meant she had a chance to chat with Beth.

"Janet Evans." Beth turned and smiled as she recognized the voice. She left the pile of paperwork on the appraiser's desk and met her friend.

Janet caught herself before she blurted out her concern. Beth appeared to have lost weight and sleep, but it was more than that. Beth no longer appeared young—she looked ten years older in the three months since the beach.

"I didn't see you, but I certainly heard you. Are you trying to get us banned from the place that we do the majority of our work? Nut." The two women hugged each other.

"What are you doing here?" Janet glanced at the mound of papers.

"We're working through probate on three large estates. I have my fingers crossed that I don't get something mixed up. What about you?"

"Usual messy divorce." Janet shook her head, dismissing the routine case. "How are you, really?"

Beth smiled and took a deep breath. "Missing my mom

more every day and it's been five months. Her death has been an epiphany to me. I always thought I was such a daddy's girl and that I was crushed by watching him waste away and die." She hesitated. "Losing Keith is as though having a physical part of me removed. I was just so used to her in my life. We went through the usual love-hate thing when I was a teenager. I respected her so for how she looked after my father. Then the fact that she weighed her chances and quality of life and chose to die."

"Which she couldn't have done without your support…all of that, so hard to witness." Janet placed her hand on Beth's arm and led her to the side of the room where senior staff earned the use of highly coveted offices with windows to the outside, as well as to the records room.

Denise Baker had been responsible for tracking land transfers since before Beth was born. She approached the two women, touching each of them on the shoulder as a way to interrupt politely. She motioned them into the tiny room. The glass window kept them visible, but closing the door would keep their conversation private. "I'm going to lunch early, you're welcome to use my office."

"Thank you, sweetie." Janet waited for the woman to grab her tote bag and leave. She looked to Beth to continue.

"I respected Keith for the way she stood by my dad. She never lost patience with him, never criticized him, and never betrayed him. She might burst into tears washing their wedding china, but she didn't play her emotions out on him."

Janet nodded. "It was hard on all three of you."

Beth shook her head. "That's not my point. It was a bad time, but we loved each other and dug our heels in to do what we needed to. We tried to understand what each other was going through. I wouldn't change being part of that for anything, even if I didn't spend my twenties as most people do."

Janet nodded again.

"After that, I started calling mom Keith." Beth smiled. "She didn't mind. It was as though we had been through a rite of passage. We were no longer mother and child. We were two grown women building a good relationship as adults. I don't know how else to explain it."

"Then you bought your house," Janet said.

Beth nodded. "Mom was great about that. She helped me with the down payment and with decorating. She knew I'd just throw up a set of blinds and consider the window treated."

They laughed at Beth's minimalism.

"Then the relationship with Lou." Janet waited.

Beth sighed. "It nearly broke her heart, but she stayed involved. She came to like Lou even if she couldn't completely accept the relationship. I understood and didn't push her."

"Then her heart problems." Janet waited again.

Beth's eyes filled with tears. "The health issues were there, undoubtedly, waiting to catch up with her. I can't help but believe that my relationship with Lou exacerbated the situation." Beth held her hand up. "Don't try to talk me out of it. We've had this conversation before, and I don't think either of us has changed our minds."

Janet held her hands up in mock surrender.

"I miss her. I can hardly draw a breath without thinking about her. Every direction I turn, I see something that she made or gave me or helped me with. She's always going to be close by. I know that's hard to accept or understand if you've never had that kind of closeness with another person."

"Lou's estrangement with her parents?" Janet suspected that Lou lacked understanding for the sense of loss Beth was experiencing.

Beth nodded. "Just because I was frustrated with Mom's worsening health and growing dependency on me didn't change the depth of my love for her. Lou heard my whining about the little things and decided I had no better relationship than she does with her parents, so how could I possibly be that upset over losing Mom. It's what I like to think of as perverse logic. She has no clue as to what I'm going through other than seeing what I'm physically doing or not doing. I have little patience with having to explain myself to her."

"You'll have to eventually if you intend to stay in the relationship. Are you going to stay in the relationship?"

"I've agreed to try." Beth looked away.

"It's a hard road, knowing what you know. We have room for you any time you need it. You know you can use the cottage if you need to get away from all of us." Janet repeated her original question. "So how are you doing really?"

Beth shrugged. "All those boxes we moved from the farm and stored for Mom," Beth rolled her eyes, "are everything that Will and I ever touched as kids that Mom saved. I could kick him in the butt for not helping me go through this stuff. I'm talking baby teeth, my first ponytail, all our school papers, and the clothes Mom made us that we didn't wear to rags. It's unreal."

"What are you doing with it?"

"I feel guilty as hell. I save a little of it, but most of it is going in the trash or to Goodwill. I hate it but don't know what else to do with it." Beth leaned against the door.

Janet was worried about how weak Beth looked and at how she was telling her everything except what she asked her. "Do you need to sit?"

Beth shook her head. "Mom's finances are surprisingly good. I've settled all her bills and have begun on the charitable donations she wanted made if there was anything left over. I never realized how many churches she belonged to over the years." Beth sighed. "I wish I had her faith or that church gave me the satisfaction it did her. It just feels like one more client base that I'm supposed to work."

"Beth…"

"Just what she and I kept of the crystal and antique glassware she collected is overwhelming." Beth shuddered. "I'm enjoying dropping in on some of her friends and giving them something to remember Mom by. I can't keep all of it. Will doesn't care about it. I refuse to sell it for the money as Lou and Patti want me to. Mom would want it to go to her friends," Beth said.

"So you're pretty much going at all of this nonstop?" Janet was determined to have her admit she was in trouble.

"Books…I hope I'm not wearing out my welcome with the local library. I thought I was bad about collecting. I actually made a deal with the jail to start a lending library for the prisoners with some of the book club editions that don't hold up as well for public lending. I'd love to see some of those guys get hooked on Christian romance novels. Is that a hoot? Keith would love it." Beth smiled.

"Sounds like a full-time job." Janet studied her friend. Beth had to be constantly engaged, mentally and physically, to avoid her biggest dilemma.

"I know. The guys at the office have been great. Jerry told me to lighten my client load for a while and get this done, then be prepared to make up for it later in the year. That's more than fair."

Janet nodded. "That's a good way to work it out."

"Have to get it done. The longer it waits, the more emotional I'll be about it. It's closure for me, Janet. Does that make any sense?"

"Absolutely."

"I'm taking an online class toward my master's." Beth smiled at Janet's surprise. "I've tried to keep it low key. It's so much easier by computer and my own schedule than trying to make a set time in a classroom. I've kept Mom's telephone line in so I can dial-up from her house. Lou is always IMing on ours."

"That's wonderful. I had no idea."

"Will is pissed. He has no intention of getting his advanced degree, and of course, everything is competition with him. I finally had to tell him that I needed time to myself. That and the fact that I need a little distance from him and Patti. Lou swears she spends no time alone with Patti. They have apologized profusely, even Will." Beth sighed. "I remember hearing my dad say that sometimes people got too thick with each other. I never understood that until recently. Now Lou, Will, and Patti are all pissed at me. We were just spending too much time together. Will and I enabled what happened between Patti and Lou, not that they weren't dead wrong for cheating. I've also realized that I want my time back with other friends once I wind down on all of this with Mom's estate." Beth paused and thought about her next statement. "I have to be sure that there's something left between Lou and I, between Will and I, before I can begin to forgive either of them. Will was so awful at the beach. Can I ever really trust or believe Lou again? I'm just angry with Patti. I never really liked her anyway."

Janet nodded.

"Lou and I had a quiet Christmas at home, no parties, no Will and Patti. I kept looking for Keith. But you know what?"

Janet waited.

"I'm going to get through this." Beth chuckled as she thought about what she was going to say next. "I remember Keith never missing a chance to remind me what my first sentence was."

Janet raised her eyebrows.

"I can do it myself."

"And you haven't changed."

"No, Janet, I haven't, and I see no reason to. Life can be hard, but doesn't it make you appreciate the good things all the more? I've actually agreed to counseling in the spring."

"Lou told me."

"What?"

Janet could not believe the huge blunder she'd just made.

"What did you say?"

"I ran into Lou."

Beth waited.

"At my office."

Beth's face hardened into an expression Janet had never seen on her before. "Is that why you tracked me down here? So what do you think? Is she sincere about staying together and being sorry for what she did? Or is she just sorry that she was found out? Does she still love me?" There was an uncharacteristic sarcasm in Beth's voice. "Never mind. Rhetorical questions. Welcome to my world."

"She seemed sincerely concerned about you."

"Was she alone?"

"As far as I know."

Beth stopped herself from saying more. "God, what is wrong with me? I see double or triple meaning in everything. I don't trust any of them or myself," she finished quietly.

"Are you trying to stay so busy that there's no time to think about them?" Janet held her hand up, asking Denise to wait another moment before reclaiming her office.

Beth nodded. "I...I don't love any of them anymore. I can't stand feeling that way. Family has always been my foundation and my reason for everything else."

"I'm probably going to regret saying this, so feel free to kick me later. Honey, give Lou a chance to make it up to you. She went to the trouble of asking me to talk to you to make sure you're all right. She must care about you. Think what a twisted mess Will has lived in for years. Give it all time. You don't have to do anything. Talk to Ellen and me. Talk to Greg and Andy. We all love you. We're your extended family."

Beth was silent as she walked out of the courthouse with Janet and blinked at the bright sunlight. "Won't be long now. An early spring is forecast. The pastures will be growing soon."

"Woohoo. Tractor time."

Beth smiled faintly as she walked away. "You know how I enjoy bush hogging. See you later." She waved over her shoulder.

Janet watched her go. There was something else different about Beth—she now had a measure of Will's furtiveness.

Chapter Fifteen

Janet glanced at her watch again as she climbed out of the car. "Crap!" Beth had finally called her for lunch, and she was running late. She caught the strap of her shoulder bag in the door of the car. Of course, the door had locked. She fumbled with the oversize key and punched the unlock button.

Janet glanced about the parking lot. Beth's blue Subaru was easy enough to spot in the midst of all the company cars and pickup trucks. It looked to be a slow day at the small restaurant just outside the city limits. Janet wondered why Beth had given them both such a long drive when there were restaurants downtown that were middle ground for them. It didn't matter. She was just relieved to hear from Beth. As many hours as both of them worked, no one gave a thought to an occasional long lunch; rather the opposite, it was encouraged.

Janet entered the restaurant and turned to the non-smoking side away from the bar. She told the hostess that she was meeting someone already there. She stepped into the dining room and spotted Beth in the corner booth. Beth was not alone. Lou sat opposite her. Both women were silent; Lou was stacking toothpicks. "That's not a good sign," Janet mumbled to herself.

Beth looked up as she approached. Janet had not thought it possible that in a matter of a few days her friend would look worse than at the courthouse. Beth's eyes were dull with dark semicircles beneath. Her face was pale and her hair lank. Her suit looked as though it needed a trip to the dry cleaners.

"Oh, shit," Janet whispered as she braced herself for what she knew was going to be an unpleasant hour.

Beth slid over so that Janet could sit beside her. Janet leaned in and pecked her on the cheek, then looked at Lou. Lou was dressed in her college logo fleece crewneck and loose carpenter jeans. It looked as though she was letting her hair grow out. She appeared relaxed yet concerned. She looked at Janet as though they were co-conspirators about Beth's welfare.

Beth placed both hands on the table. "Lou, since you went to Janet about your concerns regarding my mental stability, I thought we should have this conversation with her present."

Lou looked as though she had been hit across the back with a two-by-six.

Beth waited as they glanced at menus and ordered food they would barely touch.

"What's your involvement with Patti?"

Lou rolled her eyes. "Oh, God. Do we have to do this again?" She held up her hands in mock surrender. "Okay, if that's what it takes, let's do it." She folded her hands and looked from Beth to Janet. "Patti and I were bored. We had an affair from shortly after Keith's death until the trip to the beach. We both knew how wrong we were and how lucky we are to have you and Will. We want to reconcile if you and Will can forgive us. Will has agreed. You have agreed. Patti and I have not been alone together since the beach." She drank half of her glass of water and waited.

Beth looked at Janet. "What do you think, counselor?"

Janet was beyond uncomfortable. There was much more going on here than she or Lou realized. "I think she's contrite. I hope she's being honest."

"Completely," Lou interjected.

Beth nodded. "Patti has sent such caring e-mails. She really seems to want everything to go back to the way it was."

Lou nodded. "We both do. If there was any way to take it all back, we would."

"Beth..." Janet began as their food was set before them.

Beth held up her hand to stall Janet.

"Let her talk, honey. We're all so worried about you." Lou

leaned back as the waitress refilled her water.

"Don't include yourself with Janet. Janet is my best friend and lawyer, don't forget." Beth looked at the food as though it was a foreign substance.

"Try to eat something. You never eat a full meal anymore. God knows you aren't sleeping worth shit." Lou cut up her chicken.

"I'd be careful about bringing God into this. I've talked with him quite a bit lately."

Janet felt an uncommon sensation—fear. What in the hell was going on in Beth's mind?

"You see, this is exactly what I told you about." Lou looked at Janet, pointing at Beth with her fork. "She needs help."

Janet was almost ready to agree with Lou. She looked up and was grateful she had no food in her mouth. Patti Candler walked purposely into the dining area, carrying a drink. She must have been biding her time in the bar. Her appearance was perfect as usual.

Patti slid onto the bench seat next to Lou. She nodded to Janet and spoke to Beth. "See how early in the day you have me drinking because my guilt is so fierce."

Beth stiffened. Janet felt the change in Beth's body.

"I know I wasn't invited today. I'll say my piece and leave. You haven't given me an opportunity to talk to you face to face." Patti finished her highball. "I'm sorry. I'll say it every way possible. I was wrong. We were wrong." She glanced at Lou, who nodded agreement. "I should never have crossed that line. I realize now how much I care for you and Will and how poorly I've treated both of you. It will never, never happen again. I only want to be your sister-in-law again and Lou's prissy friend." She tried unsuccessfully to lighten the mood that had settled on the women in the booth. "Can't we go back to how we all started out?"

All eyes turned to Beth.

Beth spoke as though with someone else's voice. "I would like to feel all of that again. The sensation of holding your breath as you wait to see the one you love. The feeling of wanting to be in the same room to just see each other. The pain of being apart. Having your own language. Feeling as though you've found your home and refuge in another person. Dealing with the obstacles to being together. Making plans together."

Patti glared at Lou and abruptly stood from the bench seat.

Beth looked at Lou and said softly, "At least I have time on the tractor to look forward to."

Patti left the restaurant without a word to anyone. Lou stared at Beth and followed Patti's example.

Janet grasped Beth's ice cold hand.

"I certainly know how to clear a table." Beth stared out of the window. "You know what I wish, Janet?"

"What, sweetie?" Janet was amazed to hear her own voice. She wasn't sure what she'd just witnessed, but her brain felt numb.

"I wish there was more violence in my nature. I wish I could just beat the crap out of them and walk away. But with me, everything goes on here." She touched her temple. "And it's ceaseless."

"Beth—"

"Don't. Not here, not now. Later. I'll come to you and Ellen later." She pulled cash out of her jacket pocket to cover all of them and placed it on the table. "I need to go."

"Let me drive you somewhere." Janet stayed close to Beth as they left the restaurant. Outside there was no sign of Lou or Patti.

Beth shook her head and felt in her pocket for her keys. She looked at Janet. "Give me a little time to think. I wasn't prepared to see Patti. I didn't realize how she would affect me. I may call Ellen for the cottage key." She opened the door to her Subaru. "I'm sorry to have put you through all of this. This is mine to deal with."

Janet held onto the door. "Yes, it is yours to deal with, but you have help. Don't forget that. You're not alone or abandoned in this."

Beth nodded and waited for Janet to release her grip. "I just need to figure out what comes next. I'll let you know as soon as I do." She backed out of the parking space.

The last time Janet had felt this empty was when Edward

drove away with Melody after she told him she wanted a divorce. She knew the place Beth was in, and she knew Beth had to take the first step out of it.

Chapter Sixteen

Janet angled her ear toward the house. She thought she heard the telephone ringing. Of course, Ellen was in the den and oblivious to anything but the golf match. She would watch sports for hours on end if left alone long enough. Of course, she had earned her R-E-T-I-R-E-M-E-N-T, as she like to spell it as an obnoxious reminder. But it did grate on Janet's last nerve that Ellen would not answer the telephone. Ellen's reasoning was that it wasn't anyone calling for her because anyone who knew her knew she didn't answer the phone.

"Damn it. Do I have to do every friggin' thing?" As Janet started toward the house, the ringing stopped. "Fine." She returned to the flowerbed that she was halfway through weeding, determined to finish before darkness caught her. Why did it always come down to one more chore needing to be done on Sunday afternoon than there was time? Never mind that she'd spent the better part of the morning at the driving range. At least she had out-distanced Ellen.

Just as she knelt, the phone began ringing again. She threw her gloves down as she stood and hurried toward the door to the screened porch. "Damn you, Ellen. I hope whoever you're rooting for loses by one stroke in a sudden death playoff."

Janet kicked her shoes off before entering the house and was out of breath by the time she reached the kitchen extension.

"Hello." She held the handset away from her as she panted.

"Janet." The voice was that of a woman but so thick with tears that Janet didn't recognize who it was.

"Yes."

There was silence except for sobs.

"Let's both take a deep breath. Okay?" Janet struggled to slow her breathing. When did her old yard shorts shrink and become so tight. "Now who is this?"

"Janet...it's Lou...Lou Stephens." She lost her voice again. There was murmuring in the background.

Janet felt a sudden chill come over her. "Lou, what is it? Has something happened?" She held her breath.

"Janet, you have to come to the hospital. It's Beth. She's been in a terrible accident. She rolled the tractor yesterday." Lou spoke to others in the background. "It's bad, but she has stabilized. We're in the trauma unit."

"I'm on the way," she said to Lou and yelled toward the den as she hung up. "Ellen, Beth's in the hospital."

Janet heard the footrest on the recliner pop as it closed and the television was silenced. "Are you surprised?"

"She had a bad accident on the tractor."

"Shit."

For once, Janet didn't care what she looked like or who saw her; hell with makeup or hairspray. She straightened the baseball cap on her head, brushed off the worst of the grass clippings, and scrubbed her hands in the kitchen sink.

"Let me pee and I'm ready. I'll drive so you can call the boys." Ellen tossed her empty Coke can in the recycling bin.

"Good idea." Janet sensed that none of them had any time to waste. Ellen drove the limit plus seven miles per hour, her standard when in a hurry. She had as yet to be pulled over for speeding.

It took twenty minutes to get to the hospital. They parked in a spot reserved for clergy and dared anyone to say anything. The two women raced inside the building, stopping at the front desk only long enough to ask which floor the trauma unit was on. Once on the fourth floor, they stopped at the nurse's station.

"Beth Candler. Tractor accident. Serious." Ellen dared the nurse to ask if they were related.

The woman nodded and motioned her around the counter. She wore scrubs covered with Marilyn Monroe's face. If her hair was cut shorter, she could pass for the woman on the uniform. "They told us you were coming. Close enough to be counted as family. Follow me."

Janet and Ellen were led down a short corridor with rooms right and left separated by side walls and curtained entrances. They stopped at the last unit. Janet saw Will, Patti, and Lou huddled just inside the opening. "Get ready." She nudged Ellen.

Will approached Janet. "Thank you for coming. I know she'd want both of you here."

Janet stared at the motionless figure on the bed as Will spoke; this could not be her friend Beth.

"We're not sure of the extent of the injuries yet. She's on a ventilator. The worst is the closed head trauma. A CT scan was done soon after we got her here. The neurosurgeon relieved the pressure of the swelling of her brain late yesterday. Her vital signs have stabilized for now."

"She's on pain meds but can hear you." The Marilyn Monroe nurse gave Janet a nudge into the unit. "One at a time, please."

Janet slowly walked around the foot of the bed and stood on the far side, clear of the monitors and pumps and where she could also see the others. They eased closer to the curtained entrance. Ellen kept herself separated from them.

Beth lay still on the narrow bed, wrapped in an assortment of bandages and soft casts. Tubes providing various liquids fed into her body, the bag from the Foley catheter hung on the side rail. Her face was cut and swollen, the bruising heavy around her eyes. Her head was swathed in white. Her vitals were all shockingly low numbers.

Janet looked at Lou. "What...what happened?"

Lou stepped closer into the light from the head of the bed.

Janet gasped.

"She rolled the tractor down the hillside out from the house. I...I didn't even know she was mowing. It wasn't too long after lunch. I heard Buddy barking and went out on the porch to yell at him. I saw the tractor on its side, and Beth lying on the ground just uphill from it. I don't know how long she'd been there. Thank God she was clear of it, but it had to have rolled over her and not just thrown her off. By the time I got to her, she was out of her head and fighting me. She was hurt so badly I didn't know how to touch her. I tried to keep her still while Will called 911 and drove out to meet the ambulance to get it to the house." Lou touched her cheek below her black eye. "She beat the crap out of me."

A nurse entered the room silently. She wore solid brown and was of Janet and Ellen's generation. Reading glasses hung from a chain around her neck. Janet glanced at her and thought the woman looked familiar—Ruth, the nurse who had been with Keith also.

"She was combative when the crew brought her in. We tubed her and sent her for a CT scan." She spoke to Janet as she checked the drip in the IV, glanced at the blood pressure cuff and oxygen level clip, and held the catheter line up to empty. "Closed head trauma. Burr holes last night. Vitals finally stabilized early this morning. Now we wait." She frowned toward the others. "You can stand there, but leave us enough room to get in and out quickly."

Janet caught her by the arm. "What do you mean?"

"We monitor her vitals to know what the brain is doing. She can hear you." Ruth felt her pockets. "Here." She handed Janet a pad of paper and a drug company pen. "She may...*may*...be able to write. I wouldn't count on it making much sense."

Janet looked down at her friend. Beth stared at her. Janet leaned on the side rail to have her face as close to her as possible. "Hey, sweetie. Can you hear me? Blink."

Beth's eyes closed and opened.

"Very good. Well, you've really gotten yourself into a fine mess this time." Janet struggled not to give in to the sobs she felt inside. She looked for a place to touch and let her hand rest lightly on Beth's shoulder. She stared into the hazel eyes, trying to gauge how much thought was taking place in the mind she so admired. She looked across the room. "This happened when?"

"We think mid-morning yesterday." Will would not meet her gaze.

Janet watched the looks between Lou and Patti. Something

here was not right.

"Where were all of you, by the way?" Janet looked at them and saw a flash of collective guilt pass over each. "Why in the hell didn't you call me yesterday?"

"I was in the basement, shooting pool, with John Prine cranked up. Didn't hear or see a thing until Patti came to get me." Will looked away from Janet.

"And downing shots, as usual, no matter the time of day," Lou added.

"We were on the sofa in the living room watching a movie. I finally convinced Lou that the Lifetime Network is not trashy." Patti evenly met Janet's gaze.

"I thought she was at Keith's. She didn't come to the house for lunch, but that's not unusual these days." Lou's hands could not be still as she tried to decide what to do with them. "I didn't know she was getting the tractor out. I didn't know." She hit her hips with her fists. "The pastures didn't need mowing yet. I had the tractor ready, blade off the front end, oil changed, bush hog blades sharpened. I had to have something to do last weekend when you were at your parents." Lou reverted to her maintenance checklist and looked at Patti. "I didn't know. Why did she do it? It wasn't time yet. The timing was all wrong."

"You need to sit down and take deep breaths." Patti stared at Lou until she complied. "Get a fucking grip." Patti said the words slowly as a command.

"We...we waited to see how she was before we called anyone." Lou's face turned red. "There was so much going on. We had to make decisions to allow the surgery last night. They still don't know if she...if she's going to make it."

"Don't say that where she can hear you. Damn the three of you. Have you been talking to her or just staying in a group pity hug?" Janet was totally disgusted with the lot of them. She made herself calm down. She looked at Beth but could not read her eyes. "Honey, I want you to listen carefully and give this a try." Janet placed the pen in Beth's right hand and closed her fingers around the barrel. She held the pad beneath the pen. "What's the last thing you remember?"

Beth's hand moved falteringly.

"I can't read that. Can you try once more?" Janet patted her front pocket and felt no reading glasses.

Beth frowned. Her hand moved again. The letters were large, irregular, and required some imagination to read.

"Rolled." Janet held the paper at arm's length. "That's right. You were on the tractor." Janet tore off the sheet of paper and positioned the pad again.

"Burd know." Beth began writing and lost the thought.

Janet frowned. "Bird?"

Beth's frustration was clear if her writing was not.

"Burden of knowledge?" Janet thought of the phrase Beth had used so often.

Beth blinked.

Janet held the pad for her again.

Beth pointed to Ellen before she wrote.

"Arcanum?" Janet spelled the word aloud as she looked to Ellen for understanding.

"Is that really a word? You're the puzzle person." Ellen shrugged but jotted the word on her BlackBerry notepad.

Beth moved the pen again. It took all the concentration she could muster to write two words.

"Victor Victoria?" Janet stared at the paper.

Andy spoke from the doorway. He and Greg were dressed for tennis complete with sweaters tied around their shoulders. "Her favorite movie. *Victor/Victoria,* with Julie Andrews and Robert Preston. A woman pretending to be a man pretending to be a woman. She used to say she felt as though she had spent half her life pretending to be something she wasn't. I first thought she meant being a cut and dried accountant."

Beth's hand would no longer grip the pen. She was done writing.

Janet looked at Andy and Greg. "Thank goodness you two are here."

Ruth spoke from the laptop on the rolling cart in the hallway. "There's an empty family room just down the hall. There really should be no more than one or two of you with her at a time. We have to be able to maneuver, and this is getting out of hand."

"You boys go first. I want to talk to Will." Janet rested her hand on Beth's shoulder before leaving. She stopped beside Ruth. "Thank you so much for being here with her. She trusts you."

"I take an extra shift on the weekends, house payments." She shook her head. "Sweetie, it's not good. Be prepared."

Janet stared at the woman.

"The docs won't tell you. We missed the golden hour, the trauma team didn't see her until several hours after the accident. There's not much in her that's not broken or crushed. You can always pray for a miracle. Dr. Meadows is good. He's had two consults on her already. The team will put her back together, provided the brain swelling is under control. The next few hours will tell." She squeezed Janet's arm and closed the curtain behind her.

Janet caught up with the others. She closed the door of the small, comfortable room filled with overstuffed chairs and stared at them. "You may as well tell me what happened."

"Why did she run the tractor there? She knows damn well that I've been working on those downspouts." Lou paced the room. "Why now? Why?"

"Wasn't she just going around the house from back pasture to front?" Will scratched his head.

"It's as though she ran through that soft spot on purpose." Patti curled her legs under her in the largest chair in the room. "Will, I need coffee."

Will and Lou started toward the vending machines lining the short wall of the room.

"Wait a minute. What in the hell did you just say?" Janet stood directly in front of Patti.

Patti shrugged her shoulders. "She's been depressed ever since her mother died and worse since the blowup at the beach. You saw how she was in the restaurant that day. She was deteriorating mentally and physically and wouldn't let anyone help her. I think she deliberately ran the tractor through the soft spot in the ground, where she knew Lou had been digging, and intentionally flipped that tractor. Will, coffee."

Will walked over to stand beside Janet. "What? Lou, did you tell her you were digging there last weekend before the rains?"

"I don't remember." Lou was on the verge of a full panic attack. "I'm sure I told her, but she doesn't listen to anything I say anymore."

"Are you trying to tell me it wasn't an accident?" Janet stared from Patti to Lou and back.

"She wouldn't harm herself." Will folded his arms across his chest. "Of course it was a freak accident."

"Do you really care? Any of you? I don't believe…I don't want to believe what I'm seeing here. What in the hell was going on with the four of you?" Janet felt as though she was losing her mind. Ellen put her arms around her and held on tightly.

Will, Patti, and Lou stared at the couple wordlessly.

"Go home, go somewhere. You don't belong here. She only needs the people around her who love her. This isn't over." Janet opened the door and walked toward Beth's room. Andy and Greg looked pale as Ruth escorted them out. Greg held his arms out to comfort Janet.

"Her blood pressure is falling. You don't need to be in there. Wait where you just were. I'll let you know everything that's happening." Ruth turned Janet and guided the two couples back toward the family room. She hugged Janet. "I'm not saying this to you. Do you understand?"

Janet nodded.

"I think her brain is herniating. If that's true, there's nothing anyone can do for her."

Janet numbly returned to the waiting room. Will, Patti, and Lou stopped their conversation when Janet and Ellen walked in with Andy and Greg. It was as though a line divided the room diagonally with opposing factions in opposite corners.

Ruth proved right.

Chapter Seventeen

There was no stopping Janet from leaving the house a good thirty minutes before they really needed to. She insisted on driving since she didn't have the patience to be a passenger. "What are you doing with that thing?" She stared at Ellen using her BlackBerry.

"This 'thing' comes in very handy as you'll soon see. I was giving my e-mail a quick check and letting the boys know we were leaving, and I remembered…" Ellen waited a moment, then held the small screen toward Janet.

"Yeah, right, like I could see that even if I wasn't doing sixty miles an hour and had it in front of me."

"It's not my fault you won't wear glasses except when you're doing paperwork."

"I can see fine at a distance." Janet shook off the bickering. "So what does that say?"

Ellen angled her head so her bifocals were right. "Arcanum. It's a noun, meaning '1. A deep secret; a mystery. 2. Specialized knowledge or detail that is mysterious to the average person. 3. A secret essence or remedy; an elixir.' I looked it up on the The American Heritage Dictionary site."

Janet nodded. "From the Latin *arcanus,* meaning secret. I remember it now from school."

"Well, you have one hell of a memory if you can still recall high school Latin classes."

"It's a curse. I don't forget a damn thing even when I want to."

They were the first to enter the church. The dark walnut casket at the front of the sanctuary was closed. Janet and Ellen sat midway along the row of pews on the right side of the church in the middle of the seat to allow those arriving late a place without having to move.

"I can't believe she's gone," Janet leaned over and whispered to Ellen as she removed a handkerchief from her pocket. It didn't seem fitting to bring tissues.

"I can't believe I'm dressed up again so soon," Ellen whispered back and added because of Janet's expression, "You know what I mean."

They were in the small Baptist church that had embraced Keith when she moved to the country with her girls, as she had referred to Beth and Lou. People had listened to Keith's explanation and not asked questions; most of them understood the situation.

Will had wanted the funeral held at the large city church he and Patti joined after their return to Virginia. Surprisingly, Beth had attached to her will written instructions for her funeral. She made her own arrangements at the funeral home when she did the same for Keith. Janet remembered Beth telling her that the two of them actually giggled through pre-planning. The service would be held in the country Baptist church that had accepted Keith as though a lifelong member. The burial would be in the private cemetery on the original Candler farm.

Janet's mind wandered as the church filled to capacity. Beth's co-workers and colleagues mixed with the church members who came out of respect for Keith. Janet could hear folding metal chairs being opened in the vestibule.

"Damn." Ellen looked about at the packed sanctuary and received a frown from the woman beside her. "Pardon me."

The pallbearers were the last to file in and fill the front pew on the opposite side of Janet and Ellen. Andy and Greg held hands. Jerry and two of Beth's co-workers paid the gay men no mind. Will separated from the other pallbearers and sat with Patti and Lou on the front right pew.

The preacher had talked with Lou, Will, Patti, and Janet beforehand. Janet nodded as she listened to his comments.

"Crisis shows the measure of each of us. I came to know Beth Candler during her mother's illness. I came to respect her during her mother's last days on this Earth." His hands gripped either side of the pulpit as he wove his thoughts into the comments from the others.

Janet watched the front rows, glancing from the pallbearers to the family. Beth's first and second cousins, who Janet didn't know, filled the second rows of pews. Lou's shoulders shook with her tears. Will kept wiping his eyes and nose with his handkerchief. Patti kept glancing at her nails.

The service was brief and closed with the playing of "Blessed Assurance" as had been done for Keith. The cortege formed and was led by the white hearse and the family car. Most of the attendees stayed in line with their headlights and flashers on. The cemetery was on the way back to the side of town where most of Beth's associates lived.

The cemetery was just off the hard surfaced secondary road. Cars belonging to those already standing and waiting for the graveside service to begin lined the shoulders on both sides of the road.

Andy and Greg led the pallbearers in carrying Beth from the hearse to the family plot. They wore lavender shirts and ties in Beth's honor.

Beth's childhood pastor—retired from the Presbyterian Church near the farm—started the graveside service, gathering the crowd as close as possible to the grave so all would hear.

"Beth came to see me not long ago. As she was leaving, she teased me that if I should have this opportunity, I was not to take unfair advantage of it. It would be acceptable to speak of the softball games and all her questions during communicant's class, but not to mention that I caught them all smoking in the furnace room. Some of the parents still might not know. The last thing she wanted was to betray her old friends. Beth strove during her lifetime to serve her friends, and later her clients, well and to never betray anyone as she found out the details of their lives and businesses."

Janet glanced around the small clearing. She felt as though

she was burying Melody and shivered. She had watched Beth grow with her career, with finding acceptance in the community, with coming out, and with caring for Keith. There should have been so much more ahead for her.

The service ended with a prayer and the reading of "What A Friend We Have in Jesus," the favorite of Beth's father. The crowd milled about, catching up with one another and repeating their shock over Beth's death.

Lou's friends were present but not sure what to make of Patti. Will's friends from work introduced spouses. Patti kept a close watch on Lou.

Janet saw Andy and Greg approaching and waved them over to join her and Ellen. "You two look so distinguished. You did her proud."

Andy looked as though he had not slept since the hospital. He finally met Janet's gaze. Tears rolled down his cheeks.

"Bless your heart." Janet held out her arms to him. He leaned down and sobbed onto her shoulder.

"I think my heart is broken. She was my first love. She was all that was good about my youth." He struggled to collect himself. "I should have done something. I should have made her move in with Greg and me while she sorted things out after the beach. I shouldn't have trusted them near her." He wiped his cheeks with his handkerchief.

In an unheard-of breech of country etiquette, Patti, Will, and Lou left the grave before all mourners had expressed condolences. They walked toward the family car, forced to pass Janet and Ellen, Greg and Andy. Patti caught Janet's stare.

"Lou tried to tell you. Beth was clinically depressed. How surprised can any of us be that she did this to herself?" Patti waited for any of them to respond. "Come on, you two." She herded Will and Lou toward the funeral home's limousine. "Lou's staying with us for a few days. It's too difficult for her to be on the farm by herself."

Lou pulled away from Patti's touch and would make eye contact with no one. She walked away from the rest of them but toward the limo.

Ellen physically restrained Janet, knowing she was ready to let words, or worse, fly. Greg held on to Andy. "Think of Keith. Think how small this community truly is. This is neither the time nor place."

"This isn't over," Janet called just so they would hear.

None of the three paused or looked back.

"I'd say it's time for copious adult beverages, Auntie." Greg eased his hold on Andy as the doors to the car closed.

"I'm not going anywhere until they're done here," Andy said as he loosened his tie, always the engineer as he watched the backhoe.

"I don't want to see that," Janet said to Ellen. She shivered and had to remind herself that it was the second day of May.

Ellen looked at Greg. "We'll be waiting at Tudorville." She used her name for their house that usually brought a response of chuckles.

Greg only nodded. "You're welcome to stay the night."

Janet looked at the limo. "It's time to circle the wagons."

Chapter Eighteen

"Andy wasn't the only one who failed Beth," Janet said forlornly as she stared out the window of her home office, unable to distract herself with work as usual. Once again, she had not been able to sleep. She had tiptoed out of their bedroom shortly before five a.m., thinking she would knock out the work she'd brought home and have the rest of the day for Ellen. It was almost nine o'clock, and she had done nothing but stare.

"What did you say, sweetie?" Ellen stood in the kitchen, packing a cooler before their usual round of golf on Sunday morning. She knew they would both be off their game, but doing something mundane and routine seemed very necessary in the days following Beth's death and funeral.

"I failed Beth." Janet rocked slightly in her swivel chair. "I feel as though I lost Melody all over again, only this time it's permanent with no outside chance of reconciliation. I know I shouldn't process it that way, but it's how I feel." She looked toward the kitchen.

Ellen left the cooler on the floor and closed the door to the refrigerator.

"I'm guilty of the same as Andy." They talked to the boys throughout the night of the funeral, and it all came back to the same shared regrets. "I had a bad feeling about Lou from the start, and I didn't try hard enough to prevent Beth from getting in too deep too quick."

"Now wait a minute, sweetie. Don't do this to yourself again.

How old was Beth then?"

"Thirty-four." It took Janet only a moment to do the math—Beth had been twenty years younger than her, and Beth had met Lou the spring after the Dolly Parton party.

"She was old enough to make her own choices and old enough not to listen to any of us. You talked to Beth about going slow with any relationship. I talked to Lou about treating Beth right. Andy and I talked to Beth when they decided to move in together. What more could any of us have done?"

"You just had to invite Lou to that damn bonfire when you knew I wanted Beth there for her first party with all the girls."

Ellen walked over to the doorway. "Whoa, let's slow this runaway down."

The telephone rang, creating a much needed break in their conversation. Janet answered and listened. "No, I'm not interested in contributing to the Fraternal Order of Police. You shouldn't start this conversation by telling me you're a state trooper and trying to scare the crap out of me." She slammed the handset down, then looked at the telephone thoughtfully. "Have you checked for messages lately? We've been out or at the boys' most of this past week. So many of the girls are in town because of the funeral, I bet we've missed someone." She picked up the handset. "Yep, I hear clicks. We've probably pissed someone off without realizing it." She punched through to their mailbox.

Ellen couldn't care less, but she was grateful for the distraction. She was worried about Janet.

"Gayle wants to know if we stay in bed all the time. When we come up for air, give her a call if it's before Saturday. Oh, well." Janet cleared the message.

"The boys, calling to see if we made it home okay. Greg's on his way to e-mail, so you'll see it and let them know."

"I did."

Janet cleared the second message. "Only one more." Her face froze in horror as she listened. "Oh, no. It's Beth, on the day before her accident." Janet stared at the telephone as she heard the message. Her eyes widened and filled with tears. She looked at Ellen slack-jawed.

Ellen started to ask a question but was silenced by Janet holding up her shaking hand.

"What were you doing that Friday that was so damn important you couldn't answer the telephone?"

"Most likely mowing the yard...outside...where I wouldn't hear the telephone." Ellen felt her defenses rising and knew they were sidetracking themselves.

Janet's face had taken on a gray pallor that frankly scared Ellen. She'd never seen her this way and suddenly feared a heart attack or stroke.

Janet could not take her eyes off the telephone as though Beth was somehow inside with the message. She punched the speaker phone button that she normally used with the office and hit the asterisk and eight to replay the message. She rolled back from the desk as though distance from the speaker would make the message easier to hear.

Beth's voice came on the line, shaking with emotion.

"I guess you're not home yet, Janet, and Ellen is doing her usual ignoring the telephone. I heard them, Janet, I heard them talking about what it would take to be together. Lou and Patti. It's all been a sham. I don't care about me anymore, but oh, my God, Janet, they were trying to figure out how to be rid of Will and me so they wouldn't lose any of the cash or real estate. Both of us. Both of us. I promised Keith to look after Will."

The line went dead and the mechanical voice repeated itself. "One saved message from Friday, April 28, at 3:14 p.m."

The women stared at each other.

"I hate that goddamn message service. I'm buying an old-fashioned machine with a tape and a blinking light." Janet ripped the telephone loose from the cord and threw it across the room toward Ellen.

"Hold on just a minute. Don't direct this at me."

"Don't say it. Don't say anything. I don't want to hear you reason us out of this." Janet was, as Ellen's mother used to say, beside herself.

"Honey—"

"Don't, don't, don't." Janet put her hands over her ears. "I didn't make her understand that Lou was completely wrong for her. I made jokes about how horrible 'spineless Will' and 'snake Patti' were. I knew Beth was struggling with Keith's death. I heard Will torment her about Lou. My dumb ass sat there and told her that Lou seemed sincere, and she ought to give Lou and Will another chance. I let her keep going back to that damn house when I knew part of it was that she didn't have an agreement or contract to get herself out of that place solvent. She still loved Lou. How Lou used that. I know the signs. I've been trained to recognize abuse of all kinds. I knew Beth was in bad shape. I knew those women were capable of anything." Janet stared at Ellen. "You know what this means, don't you?"

Neither of them wanted to be the first to say it aloud.

"Don't cancel the service until you record that last message."

"We have a tape recorder at the office we use for conference call transcriptions. I'll do it from the office tomorrow."

"Let's run over there now. I can make duplicates here, but I want to be sure we have that message saved on tape and CD."

Janet nodded in agreement. Her voice sounded very far away when she spoke next. "They killed her. They killed her, and I have to figure out what to do about it." She reached for a fresh legal pad as a reflex.

"Beth said 'be rid of.'" Ellen reminded her. "And we have to figure this out."

"They killed her. You know it as well as me. Beth called me to save her. I missed her cry for help. I could have prevented what happened that Saturday. How in the hell do I live with that the rest of my life?"

Ellen shook her head slowly.

Chapter Nineteen

Janet's former boss, and the county's commonwealth attorney, Ben Richards, agreed with Ellen about the semantics of Beth's message. This did nothing to improve Janet's mood.

"The shelf is not crooked," Janet mumbled to herself. She straightened the row of handmade figurines that she had collected during jaunts into the surrounding counties exploring craft fairs. The small, delicate birds appeared to be listening for something as they listed to one side. They gradually moved forward on the shelf when she wasn't looking, from her footsteps across the floor.

"I'm telling you, the board is not level. All you had to do was wait for me to help you, and I would have put it on the wall correctly." Ellen's voice carried up the stairwell from the basement.

"How many GD years would I have had to wait for that effort to take place?" Janet clenched her hands at her sides, forcing herself not to take each bird from the shelf and hurl it across the room.

"Let's check it to be sure." Ellen walked into the room with a two-foot carpenter's level.

"What's that?" Janet felt the rage building within herself. She regretted saying anything about the shelf and the lack of Ellen's carpentry expertise after she became impatient and hung it herself. Whether it was hormones or schizophrenia, she didn't know, and at this point, didn't care. Her hands went to her hips as she began to formulate her defense for whatever Ellen said.

Ellen eased around her to the wall and placed the level along the front edge of the shelf, then back to front. "My eye is no good for something like this. The way the house has settled, I don't trust measuring from the ceiling or the floor." She nodded toward the bright yellow bar. "See, if the bubble was exactly in the middle it would be balanced and the shelf level. I'll fix it for you, sweetie, next time I'm here by myself. Don't want any of those slipping off and breaking." She kissed Janet's cheek and went to the den.

Janet looked about her office that had last been used as a teenager's bedroom before she and Ellen bought the house in 1983. She breathed in and released a deep sigh. Her mood was not Ellen's fault. She kept bringing work home and not doing any of it while more piled up at the office. She kept enough insurance in place to practice law from home as needed and as agreed to by her business partner. She liked being able to help friends with minor, but necessary, wills and powers of attorney without having to go through the overhead of the firm. It didn't help her workload that Beth's death had nudged several of the girls into finally wanting their last wishes in writing. "Where did all this crap come from?"

Janet began to shuffle piles around, straightening papers and adding more to stacks. She finally sat down at the Singer cabinet that held her computer and sighed again.

Ellen stopped in the hallway while en route from den to kitchen. "Sweetie, what in the world is wrong? Do you need to get out for a while? I'll drive you if you don't feel like it. I know you took something for your sinus headache and should be groggy by now," she said the last to herself. Ellen would drive Janet to the office and walk her to the front door if it would help her mood.

"It's not that. I can use a day here to catch up on things. My raccoon headache is better than it was early this morning." She rubbed her eyes and cheekbones.

"You can't get Beth off your mind, can you?" Ellen gauged Janet's reaction. "The last straw is being her executrix, isn't it?

Janet nodded. "I'm so sorry for being such a bitch to you lately. How do you put up with me?"

"Years of practice," Ellen said. She had known all along that

Janet wasn't angry with her. She was just a convenient punching bag, something they each had to do for the other at times. "May I come in?"

Janet nodded. "Damn Ben for not doing anything with that phone message."

"Sweetie, he didn't have much choice."

"I know. I'm the friggin' attorney, and you have a better grasp of the law about this than I do."

"Don't you hate it? I owe it all to Court TV." Ellen leaned over the chair and hugged her.

"If you pat my back, I'll slug you." Tears rolled down Janet's face. She was so damned frustrated with all of it. She knew—and she now had the burden of proof of that knowledge—that something was not right about Beth's death. It was as though Beth had forewarned her in the hospital; that in itself creeped Janet out. "You're being so nice about everything. Now I feel as though I've let you down as a partner. That damn Lou."

Ellen stood back and raised her eyebrows questioningly.

"She lied to me. You know how I detest that. She asked me to talk to Beth since Beth was so depressed. Lou was trying to set me up to be part of something. That's why she was in such a state of shock at the hospital." Janet paused to think.

"If Lou thought she could manipulate you, she was sadly mistaken." Ellen stood and looked at the shelf again. "I'll fix it for you now while we talk."

Janet slammed her fist against her desk. "Something went wrong with whatever Lou's plan was. I know it also involves that bitch Patti." Janet visibly fumed as she waited for Ellen to return with her toolbox.

"If anyone can figure out what happened and hold Lou and Patti answerable, it'll be you. Don't overthink it. Gather your evidence and think through it all as one of your puzzles. I'll help you and so will the boys. Between all of us, we'll nail those bitches." Ellen carefully set each bird away from the work area.

Janet reached for the mouse to bring the computer out of hibernation. "You're a dear to give up part of your baseball game, your precious Yankees. Finish that later, honey. I'm all right now. I'm going to revisit Beth's e-mails and check if I missed something between the lines. If there's more to know, Beth left me a map somewhere, I just have to find it." Janet reached for her rainbow frame reading glasses. "*Victor/Victoria* indeed."

Janet had to admit that she loved her computer and the Internet, not that she understood any but a small operational part of it. To think that all that information and ability to communicate was at her fingertips through a keyboard was amazing to her. She had caught herself at the grocery store reading the computer magazine covers instead of the celebrity tabloids. Ellen had a knack for computers and electronics that Janet envied.

Ellen had recently convinced Janet to bundle their Internet service in with their satellite dish provider. Getting rid of dial-up had been what really hooked Janet; she had barely been able to tolerate the interminable waiting of phone line access. All of it was now readily available in the blink of an eye. She hated to admit that she was as bad as Ellen about preferring e-mails to telephone calls. She couldn't remember the last time she wrote anyone a letter or even a note by hand. The worldwide research and shopping capabilities just blew her away. She found that once she logged on and started following the cyber trails of her thoughts, time lost all context. The difficulty was in pushing the chair back from the screen.

Janet signed in with her e-mail provider and began scanning her archived files. She thought about Beth's e-mails while she opened the one immediately following the talk in the clerk's office. Janet realized that Beth wrote to her to assure her that she was fine, not so much as what was on her mind but updates of all that she was doing. That in itself was not bad, but she should have recognized it was Beth's method of blowing smoke.

"*Hallooo, Auntie, what are you doing at home?*" Queen_of_ Denial, a.k.a. Greg Davis, popped up in her instant messenger text box.

"*Damn, I forgot that you can see when I'm online. How do I block that?*" Janet typed back.

"*Sick?*"

"*Sinus headache again.*"

"Pulease, it's stress. Try a warm compress and turn your brain off for a while. Do something non-productive. Surf aimlessly like the rest of us. Why are you really at home today?"

"Making myself start the paperwork on Beth's estate."

"Oh, bummer. Bless your heart."

"Something's bothering me."

The text block blinked as no immediate answer came back. Then came the message that Queen was composing.

"Andy too. Sit tight for a minute."

Janet looked at the screen and frowned. She made use of the time by grabbing a Diet Coke from the kitchen. Still no message.

"Greg, have to go."

"Wait."

She touched the Candler folder. It was not as though she really wanted to start the filing with the county. Beth's estate was only a little convoluted by the sale of the farm and moving Keith into the cottage at Lou's. Janet cringed at how Beth had insisted her will be written.

Beth and Lou had simplified things. Lou added Beth to her deed, giving her half interest in the property and keeping the mortgage in her name to hold the interest rate. Beth made improvements equal to the half interest from the equity in her city house and part of her inheritance. Their wills left the half interest to each other. Probate was not one of her favorite processes. At least Beth had taken time for the handwritten codicil to list specific bequests. Janet needed to review the list, yet had procrastinated unfolding the paper once she read the sticky note attached by Beth telling her what was in the envelope mailed to her.

"Andy has agreed to me forwarding an e-mail to you that Beth sent him. He's been worrying about what to do with it ever since the accident. He thought you already had too much on your mind. First impulse was Will, but we know how much Will enjoys our company—not. It will be to you in just a few minutes. Andy's forwarding it to me—can't find you in his address book—then me to you. Sorry in advance, Auntie, come over for dinner and drinks to talk."

Janet stared at the screen. Finally, the voice she wanted to hear. "You've got friggin' mail." Impatiently, she moved the cursor to the inbox item from Greg with the subject line "Auntie Em...Auntie Em...." He included no introduction to the message. She saw that Beth had sent Andy the message about six weeks after Keith's death, shortly before the horrendous beach trip.

I feel as though Jerry Springer's booking agent will be calling me any time to check my availability for a show. Andy, what the hell is wrong with me? I must be the crazy one. I'm seeing it in everything that happens between the four of us. And I feel them watching me. You know how a room goes quiet just as you walk in...that's how the four of us feel now.

I was just getting my brother back. Now he won't look me in the eye, and he refuses to talk about Lou and Patti. He will not entertain the notion of what I feel, with everything in me, is going on. He thinks I'm jealous because Lou spends so much time with Patti. Patti's nicer to me than ever before. She and Lou act so hurt if I question them about anything. Lou keeps saying it's all Patti's curiosity about our lifestyle, and that they're just friends.

Am I losing it? Do you see any of this when you're around them? I've tried talking individually with each one of them, and it only makes me doubt my own sanity. I even went to the company's referral psych service. They told me I seemed to be processing all of this reasonably. What the hell does that mean? You know I don't expect an answer from you on any of this. Just venting and leaving this behind in case I have gone over the deep end.

Why couldn't you and I have been right for each other, not that I would want to hurt Greg? God, I'm as bad as them thinking about someone else's partner. Love you, mean it. B.

Janet stared at the screen as she sent the message to the printer. Ellen yelled along with the crowd noise of the baseball game. Janet felt like joining in with a scream that no one would take notice of.

She picked up the list of bequests. Her eyes filled with tears at the sight of the neat block letters that she had always teased Beth must come from a human typewriter. "Okay, just do this. Stop being a wimp. Find out what was important to Beth." Janet felt her eyebrows rise as she read the handwritten document. "What in the hell? No friggin' way."

There was a neat list of bank account numbers, some from accounts her parents had set up when she was a child, some recent. Beth had established two trust funds—one for Will, in his name only, and one for their cousin in North Carolina. Lou was to receive a list of household items that she had paid part of the cost of, the rest of their furnishings, including the furniture Beth had restored, was to be sold with proceeds to the trust funds.

Janet read aloud. "As for you, dear friend, use the funds in this joint account as needed. You will know. If there's anything left, grab the old poop at home and take one of the golf trips you two have threatened to treat yourselves to for as long as I've known you. But be sure to cover the expenses I cause you, there should be enough. You know I love you as though I came from two mothers."

It was as though Janet felt the break in her heart widen.

Chapter Twenty

Ellen glanced about the cottage. She still couldn't believe that she had allowed Janet to talk her into taking a break from all that was going on at home. She loved Janet dearly, and she loved her time at the cottage. Janet knew and understood that; that was the true beauty of their long relationship.

By coming to Salvo on a Monday, Ellen could have a good rest, catch up with her friends along the Outer Banks, and be home by the weekend when Janet would really need her. It seemed the best of all worlds.

She went to the new Food Lion in Nags Head to stock the pantry, so to speak, and stayed in for the evening. On Tuesday morning, Ellen did the ritual sunrise walk, missing Janet, then napped that afternoon. By Tuesday night, she was ready for someone else's company other than her own.

Ellen found a parking space close to the door of the bar. She always loved coming to Lucky's. It hadn't changed any from the outside since she had lived at the beach—weathered clapboard with remnants of white paint deep in the exposed grains and a tin roof painted a bright red with LUCKY'S stenciled in bold black letters. What had started forty years ago as a place for fishermen to have an early breakfast was now a trendy nightspot. As Ellen walked in, she chuckled to herself about the fishermen who had been displaced by lesbians with a higher disposable income. The interior was dark paneling, dim lights, two pool tables, and an open area to dance, with the walls lined with booths for observers.

Food was basic, mostly fried, and definitely Southern.

Delores looked up and waved when Ellen sat down at the end of the bar. "What does my name rhyme with?"

"Thesaurus." Ellen pointed at the Bass tap.

Delores chuckled as she filled the glass. "You're the only one who ever says that." She kept her colored brown hair short in a shingle cut with bangs. Janet and Ellen teased her that she looked like a women's basketball coach. She definitely had the height and conditioning to play.

Ellen looked around. "I'm probably the only one here who remembers using one. Since when did the crowd become so young?"

"Since these girls are able to get the high-paying jobs out of college that we paved the way for. Since most of the women our age are too tired or too broke to sit around in a bar." Delores worked her way up with the state of Virginia's Department of Housing and Community Development. She had put her savings into buying the bar that she hired others to work during the week until she turned fifty-two and became eligible for early retirement. Five years before, she gave new definition to "take the money and run" by retiring and severing all ties with Virginia, including her partner. She had answered all questions by simply saying she was ready for a fresh start. "These girls walk in to the jobs we worked our asses off to have the last few years we worked to bump our pension. And you know what I say?"

Ellen raised her glass in anticipation.

"Damn right. Good for them." Delores tapped her bottle of water against Ellen's beer. "The first one is on me as usual, Toots."

"And you're the only one who calls me that."

"I know. You'd think I could make Janet a little bit jealous by using an endearment. How is our favorite attorney?" Delores watched her two waitresses and continuously poured or mixed drinks as she talked with Ellen.

Ellen hesitated.

"Uh-oh."

"She and I are fine. It's her friend, Beth. We brought her here over a year ago, mid-thirties, brunette, sweet personality."

Delores nodded. "I remember. That relationship didn't last long for her. Lou was all over me the first time she came here and brought a lipstick blonde in a few months ago."

Ellen stopped drinking and stared at Delores.

"I don't forget faces or dates, Toots. I remember the first time Lou came in very distinctly. She sat at the bar and flirted with me and everyone else who came in while you and Janet sat with Beth in a booth. That was October just over a year-and-a-half ago. Then October eight months ago, Lou rolled in here with the lipstick blonde."

"Patti."

"That's right. I wasn't young, cute, or rich enough for her to pay attention to, so I returned the favor...bitch." Delores concentrated on the mix of liquor and liqueur. "I'm sorry. I went off on a tangent. What about Janet's friend, Beth?"

"She died in an accident a little over a month ago."

Delores let go of the tap and stared. "No shit?"

"Serious as a heart attack."

Delores drank the half glass of beer herself, then pulled another and slid it to the opposite end of the bar from Ellen. "That's a damn shame. I thought about her after Lou was here with blondie. Why is it the decent sisters are treated like crap in a relationship?"

"That's the very reason I appreciate Janet so much. I know how lucky...no pun intended...I am."

"You know the rule. Dollar in the tip jar every time you get lucky at Lucky's."

Ellen smiled and dropped four quarters in the Mason jar. "So tell me about Lou and Patti last October."

Delores nodded. "They rolled in here about ten o'clock and appeared to have already had drinks with dinner. The booths were full, so they sat at the bar while they waited for one to clear out. I was back and forth, but I have good hearing and the longer they sat, the louder they talked. For a start, they were laughing their asses off about sneaking off while the rest of you slept. They were in here every night until last call. They giggled about how it reminded them of being in high school and staying out all night, each saying they fell asleep at the other's house, then partying all night."

Ellen handed over her empty glass for a refill.

"The worst part…and usually I don't pay any attention to this…was that they couldn't keep their hands off each other. You're telling me that Lou was still with Beth then?"

"It gets worse. Patti's married to Beth's brother."

"Jesus F'ing Christ."

"Why would anyone do that to Beth?" Ellen reached for the bowl of boiled peanuts.

"That's simple enough to figure out from the first time I met Lou. The conquest of Beth was over. She was reeled in. Lou was ready to move on to the next. Only I think she met her match in blondie."

"How so?"

Delores frowned as if double-checking her memory before she spoke. "The husband called while they were here that last night. Blondie actually choked as she tried not to laugh while imitating him and telling Lou what he said. He told her his sister knew everything and that blondie was going to have to choose between him and Lou. He'd already told his sister that blondie would not leave him, which they thought was hilarious. They settled down after that. I heard bits and pieces after they moved to a booth, had to be at the end of the bar closest to where they sat. What can I say, it was sort of like looking at a car wreck when you pass, wanting to look away but not being able to take your eyes off it."

Ellen nodded.

"They decided to apologize profusely…that was blondie's word. Make like they weren't making it anymore. They didn't want to pay for ditching spouses. And my personal favorite, it would make their love all the more special if they had to hide what they were doing."

Ellen covered her face with her hands. "Talk about burden of knowledge."

"What?"

"This is exactly what Janet needs to know, but how in the hell do I tell her?" Ellen thought it over. "Are you willing to jot down as much as you can remember about those nights last October, sign your statement in front of a notary, and mail it to me?"

Delores didn't hesitate. "Hell, yes. I'll even come back to Virginia if you guys need me to."

Ellen paid for her drinks and leaned over the bar and gave Delores a kiss on the cheek. "Janet won't mind this once."

"Because it's between friends, Toots. I joke around, but I don't fool around. I've been burned too many times myself." Delores was deep in her own thoughts. "Those women were crazy with the affair they were carrying on. They shouldn't have thought all of that shit, much less said it in public. It's as though they had a sense of entitlement about being with each other. That and all the alcohol, or whatever else they'd been ingesting."

Neither of them noticed that their conversation was very carefully eavesdropped upon. Addie had a knack for listening. She also had a tremendous respect for Delores and decided to wait for the right time to talk to her boss in private.

"Amen to that," she said as she picked up her drink order. "We have to look out for each other because no one else will." At twenty-two, Addie had already seen and heard enough drama to keep the curls in her blond hair tight.

Chapter Twenty-one

"Good God. They can't seriously think I'm going to wear something like this, much less buy it. It would make me look like a fifty-something woman wearing maternity clothes. Talk about lipstick on a pig." Janet held up what used to be called a peasant blouse made from a thin, gauzy material. "I'd look like I ought to be out on the beach providing shade for someone. Plus, what's the sense of buying something you have to wear something else under? Just wear what you'd have on under it." She quickly hung the top back on the rack.

"Are you done, Ms. Bitch and Moan? It's all about layering, sweetie. It's the thing this summer. You have to look flouncy. Not that it would look any better on me than on you, but they might buy the pregnancy thing. Think it would help me get a better seat at the movies? Come on, we need to at least try it on so we can say we did." Gloria Jarrett held the top against her. She was twenty-two years younger than Janet, had neither married nor borne children, and was about the same size as her friend. That was the beauty of their shopping together—they looked at the same size clothes and Gloria kept Janet from buying everything stodgy. She had almost talked Janet into a tattoo the last time they traveled north on Interstate 81 to shop. Gloria practiced law in Stanton, Janet in Roanoke. They enjoyed the retail that flocked around the university in Harrisonburg, even if they felt a bit of a traitor, and no one stopped either of them to talk about ongoing cases.

"You go first. I'm going to keep looking. Maybe I can find a compromise between blue-hair matron and hormonal teenager." Janet meandered through the store.

"Need any help, ma'am?" The salesgirl was just that, a girl in college, from the looks of her.

Janet glanced at her as she said, "I didn't wear these when they were popular the first time." She returned to the gauzy tops.

"I know, that's what my grandmother says every time she meets me for lunch. She finally pulled one of her old blouses out of the attic, and I wore it in here one day. Everyone wanted to know which rack it came off of. Gram thought that was hilarious, then listed it on eBay. She's now cleaning out the storage boxes in her attic. We do have something that might suit you better in the back of the store. That's where she usually buys her things and says they're so comfortable and easy to get spots out of." The girl pointed to a rack of plain cut suit separates in bland colors.

Gloria, standing slightly behind Janet, had listened to most of the salesgirl's comments and was doing her best not to burst out laughing. "Serves you right."

"Giggle and I'll leave you here to find a ride home on your own. I mean it." She snatched the top from Gloria and marched into the fitting room to try it on. She returned in a few minutes. "Looks fine. I'll buy the damn thing. Let's get the hell out of here."

Gloria snorted. "I haven't done that since the last time we were at a bar function together. What is it about you that makes me behave like a twelve-year-old?" She laughed uncontrollably as Janet looked at her and crossed her eyes. "That's quite all right about the top. You take it. It didn't hang right on me." She gave Janet a quick hug. "Make nice with the girl as she checks you out. She didn't mean anything by it. Most people don't think enough about what they say to come up with a really good insult."

Janet did as asked. She let out a deep sigh as they joined the crowd in the mall's common area. "I can't believe we spend hours on the road just to shop." She linked arms with Gloria.

"Oh, I can. When else do we get a break from all those social service cases that make us want to have a lobotomy?"

"Or drink too much."

"That no one else understands why we put ourselves in the middle of."

"Ellen saw some of it with the men who worked for her at the college. She's helped me on a few cases when I had to check out family situations and knew not to go alone. Still…"

"It makes us do what we do."

"What about your roommate?"

"He's still pushing for marriage. I'm still dodging a commitment. We'll see how long we both tolerate the situation. I don't think either of us is going to change. I can always get another dog."

"Based on my marriage, get a dog and a cat and call it even."

The women burst out laughing and slowed before the next chain restaurant.

"I think my blood sugar is low. I know my eyes are blurry. Let's grab a bite, or if nothing else, sit down for a bit."

Gloria nodded. "I'm starving. I skipped breakfast to be ready on time."

"Dope. Why didn't you say something earlier? I don't want you passing out on me." Janet led her into the restaurant and to a table in the very back corner. "I want to be able to talk without looking over my shoulder."

"Oh, yeah. Who about?" Gloria laughed and watched the humor fade from Janet's face. "So how are things really going?" She stirred the sweetener into her iced tea and watched her friend.

Janet sighed. "Okay." She glanced away for a moment. "I'll say it. I miss Beth, and I feel so damn guilty." It was that simple.

"I'm so sorry that I couldn't reschedule my court appearance the day of her funeral. It was a no-brainer case that I couldn't keep my mind on for thinking of all of you. I wanted to be there for Beth, and I feel badly that I wasn't."

Gloria took in and released a deep breath to hold off tears. Beth had been Gloria's assigned mentor when Gloria was a college freshman. Beth had actually enjoyed looking out for Gloria, and they'd become close friends. Beth helped Gloria decide on law school. Janet had taken Gloria under her wing when she passed the bar and practiced in Roanoke her first years. They often talked about the quirk of fate that made the three of them friends. "Any progress with the sheriff's investigation of what happened with the tractor?"

"Ongoing. I don't know what's taking them so long. Well, I do, too. They're enormously understaffed for the population they serve. She wasn't famous and most people try to ignore her lifestyle. Beth's accident is fairly routine, I guess, with no one really pushing them to conclude their report. I had no idea how many adults and children are victims of farm accidents until this happened. You know me, I had to research the stats. Still…"

"Accident?" Gloria's face said otherwise.

Janet stopped as she was reaching for her glass. "Yes, accident, what else?"

Gloria took a long swallow of tea. She shook her head. "Nothing."

"Don't say nothing. I see wheels turning. What are you keeping to yourself?" Janet watched her closely.

Gloria deliberated and chose her next words as carefully as a summary before a jury trial. "Janet, not yet. I can't say anything *yet*." She stressed her last word.

Janet frowned. She stared past her friend at the dead corner of the room. She trusted Gloria completely. The beauty of their friendship was that they watched each other's back and gave each other a heads-up when appropriate, and in such a manner as not to compromise either of their scruples. "I don't like it, but I'll let it drop for now. You owe me an explanation later." She leaned across the table. "I have to confess that I said accident to test your reaction."

Gloria nodded absently.

"Hellooooo." Janet had lost her attention.

"Holy crap. I don't believe it. I was hoping my eyes were playing tricks on me." Gloria stared past Janet's shoulder toward the entrance of the restaurant.

"Tricks are for kids." Janet couldn't help herself.

Gloria kicked her under the table.

"What?"

Gloria shook her head slowly. "You may as well look. Don't worry about being subtle. They aren't seeing anything past each other, and it's dark back here."

Janet turned in her seat, studying the faces behind her. She did a double take at the couple close to the front door—Lou and Patti—and they were very much a couple. Janet didn't take her eyes from them as she pivoted into the chair beside Gloria.

"Isn't that Beth's partner?" Gloria leaned over and whispered the question. "I only met her once at a party. Her hair is different, longer and more feminine. She hasn't lost any time, has she?"

"That's not the half of it. Do you know who the other woman is?"

Gloria studied the bottle blonde. "No."

Janet finally turned her head away from the women and looked at her friend. "She's the wife of Beth's brother and an antiques broker who loves the dealers along Route 11. I wonder who she's cheated out of family heirlooms that she needs to unload for a quick profit."

"What?"

"You heard me." Janet pushed her chair slightly back from the table. "God damn the two of them. They never stopped seeing each other. I knew it when Ellen told me what Delores said took place at the beach, but it's not the same as seeing it for yourself." Janet's hands tightened into fists.

"Slow down, buddy. You're losing me." Gloria openly stared. "They don't seem very grief stricken. Are they trying to put on a show for everyone?" She dropped her eyes as the women kissed.

Janet threw her cloth napkin down on the table.

Gloria put her hand on Janet's arm. "Don't do it. Not here, not now. Not before you have the sheriff's report. Don't tip your hand."

"What?" Janet couldn't take her eyes off the women. They touched with every word to each other, whispering and giggling as they leaned closer to each other for emphasis. "My God, is that what Beth had to put up with? Is that what she was watching, thinking she was losing her mind? Surely, it couldn't be happening right in front of her with a family member. Were they that obvious around her? Then the pretense of reconciling…those bitches."

Red crept up Janet's neck and cheeks. She felt as though the top of her head would blow off, hopefully as a mortar striking the two women. "Those goddamned bitches killed Beth. As much as I've tried to convince myself otherwise, they damn well did." She backed her chair away from the table so she had enough room to stand. "No wonder Delores heard so much. They're blatant with their infatuation."

"I'm begging you, don't do it. Don't break redneck on me." Gloria held onto Janet's arm.

"Beth knew. They were playing her grief for her mother and her love for her brother to get away with it. What kind of hell was Beth living through and not talking to us about?" Tears ran down Janet's cheeks.

Lou and Patti could not physically sit any closer. They traded quick kisses, not caring if anyone saw them. They smoothed each other's hair. When Patti wanted to know the time, she held Lou's wrist so she could see her watch.

"I'm going to be sick." Janet sagged in her chair.

The waitress brought their order to the table. They both stared at the food, making no motion toward tasting any of it. "Ladies, did I get your lunches confused?"

"No, no. We're fine. Could you bring the check, please?" Gloria encouraged the young woman to hurry. She relaxed her hold on Janet.

Janet blotted her cheeks with her napkin. She stared at Lou. "What did you do to our dear, dear friend?"

"Timing, Janet. Timing. Do your homework. Be ready to make a case." Gloria leaned closer and turned Janet's head toward hers with her pointer finger.

"What?" Janet found a tissue and squeezed her nose.

"Be ready to make a case. Beth stopped in to see me when she went to Harrisonburg for the spring Green Valley Book Fair. That's all I can say. That and let's get the hell out of here." She pushed her chair back. "We're going to walk around the far perimeter of the room, and they're not going to see us. You don't want them to see us. They're not going to know they've been seen out like this together. Do you understand?" Gloria tugged Janet in the direction she had just explained to her.

"No, I don't understand."

"Yes, you do. You're still processing all of this. Just trust me and follow me." Gloria placed a twenty and a five on the tray with the ticket. "Now."

Janet numbly walked out of the restaurant. Gloria was right—the loving couple did not seem to notice them.

"Lucy, you have some 'splainin to do," Janet said her favorite Ricky Ricardo line to Gloria as she tried to regain her composure. She was not accustomed to being unnerved.

"Later. Much later." Gloria encouraged her to walk slowly along the storefronts. Their drive home would be long and quiet. The bag with the top had been left beside the chair in the restaurant.

Chapter Twenty-two

"I just want to buy a loaf of bread," Janet said the words slowly to herself as she stood before the wall of bread bags and felt totally overwhelmed. Her brain had been on overdrive all day between gathering evidence to determine the fate of two abused children and thinking about Lou and Patti in Harrisonburg.

Her hands rested on the handle as she pushed the grocery cart slightly back and forth while skimming all the labels on the bags once again. Of course, the cart had one wheel that tried to roll perpendicular to the others.

A basket with a squeaky wheel rolled to a stop beside Janet. "When I can't decide which healthy grain to congratulate myself for buying, I go with the thick sliced white bread…it's comfort food."

"There's no earthly need to have more than the basic choices, white, wheat, or rye. How in the hell am I supposed to know which one of these blends to buy? I don't read the frou-frou magazines to know what the latest fad is."

"I know. Mike always tells me he can gauge my mood by how I grocery shop. I seem to need something every day. It's on the way home from the hospital."

"If you spend the money a little at a time, it's not nearly as life-threatening as a three-figure grocery ticket."

"Exactly."

Janet finally tore her gaze away from the bread bags and looked at the woman she was carrying on a conversation with.

"Ruth! How long were you going to let me rattle on before I looked at you?"

The woman laughed. "Sounded as though you needed to vent. I don't think bread is what's really bothering you, though."

"Can you believe it's been almost three months?" Janet felt her eyes filling up. "Crap."

Ruth reached over and gently squeezed her arm. "It's okay. Our jobs suck, don't you think? We meet people during the most stressful times in their lives when they're dealing with life and death, or with something serious going on with children. We're thrown in the middle of what they usually wouldn't tell anyone and know more than they do about it. We have very short, intense relationships. Then most of the time, people want to forget us because we're associated with trauma, mental or physical, as a bad memory." Ruth reached for a bag of cinnamon raisin bagels.

"How about a cup of coffee?" Janet inclined her head toward the grouping of small round tables at the bank of coffee carafes.

Ruth nodded.

They parked their carts along the side wall.

"Oh, Christ. Now I have to decide on which flavored coffee." Janet stared at the row of eight carafes brewed from as many different types of beans.

Ruth laughed. "I just stay with plain and caffeinated, no sweetener, no flavored creamer. It simplifies things considerably."

"Okay, I too can make a decision this late in the day. French vanilla." She pulled back a chair at the closest table and sank into it. "It's been a long week."

"Tell me about it. We do three twelve-hour days. By the end of the third day, I'm ready to be a patient." Ruth sat opposite Janet and sipped the coffee. She raised her cup. "Here's to simple pleasures."

"Amen."

"And to decent women."

Janet nodded.

"Keith and Beth Candler were very special. I'm glad to have known them."

Janet nodded again. She felt her eyes filling with tears. "Beth was a good friend."

"She certainly loved her mother even with the expectations Keith had of her. Keith reminded Beth almost daily that she was responsible for her brother."

"Keith thought the sun rose and set with Beth," Janet smiled fondly, "and knew how weak Will was."

"The conversations they had. They included me since I was in the room so much." Ruth stared at her coffee.

Janet could understand why patients and family members alike trusted this woman. There was a genuine no-nonsense empathy about her. Her brown hair was short and spiked. Her makeup suited her age and complexion. She carried extra weight comfortably. Her scrubs were slightly wrinkled and always a solid color, brown today—no cutesy animals or cartoon characters. She had a look of perpetual weariness that came with her profession, slightly dark half moons under her eyes and a sag to her face that spoke greatly to the seriousness of what she dealt with day in and day out. Reading glasses hung around her neck, the kind bought at the drugstore and replaced frequently from breaking or losing. Her badge showed her years at the hospital evidenced by annual service pins.

"You were the one who advised Beth about the non-resuscitation order and the morphine pump for Keith, the withdrawal of life." Janet remembered how fondly Beth had spoken of this woman. "She appreciated that advice more than you'll ever know. I know she was glad you were one of the nurses with both of them."

Ruth stared past Janet and carefully considered her next words. "They used to talk about it…that there are worse things than death. They must have been through a hell of a time looking after the father." She lowered her voice.

Janet nodded. "Beth once told me that after watching her father waste away, her one wish was a quick death. She didn't care at what age."

"That's why she wanted her mother to decide about another surgery, but she had no doubts about making the decision for her." Ruth's voice remained low.

"Both of them were very pragmatic about death. It was inevitable. Beth told me her father died slowly over nine years. First the body failed, then the mind. She told me she'd thought about ending her father's life, about ending his suffering. Keith tried to dismiss it by saying that Beth would never have actually done it. But you know, I think she would have if her mother hadn't been holding onto her father so tightly. Beth had a tough streak that most people never saw. She tried to reason through everything, see all the sides of something, and some people misinterpreted that for being meek. She just wanted to think things through all the way. Once she decided on something, that was it. I used to tease her about quick decisions, that on the surface she would buy a car on a whim, before explaining to me that she'd been thinking about it for months but not discussing it. Then she'd just do it. No big deal." Janet raised and lowered her shoulders.

"Once Beth made up her mind about something..." Ruth drained the last of her coffee. "Family meant everything to her. She had a fierce loyalty to her mother and father. She adored her brother, despite some of his choices."

"Staying with Patti?" Janet frowned. "Sorry, that wasn't a question for you."

Ruth nodded. "She told me a story that she said only she and her mother knew. She tried to make it funny, but it was easy to tell how much it bothered her. It happened when she was still living on the farm looking after her father. She was awakened one morning by dogs baying and a cat screeching for all it was worth. She loved all the animals, farm and pet. She rolled out of bed and ran outside to find that a pack of hunting dogs were trying to take down one of the farm cats. The cat was trapped in one of the sheds. She didn't miss a beat, grabbed a shovel and beat her way through six dogs. She was mortified that she killed one of them. She knew the farmer whose pack it was and loaded the dead dog on a cattle truck and drove it home. The rest of the pack was already there but scattered when they saw her. She laid that man out from the sound of it. She laughed and said she never saw that pack of dogs, or any other, loose on their property again. And the cat survived."

146

"She was tough when she needed to be."

Ruth nodded. "You know she'd made up her mind that she was dying by the time she reached the hospital that day?"

Janet stared at the woman.

"She was barely lucid by the time she reached the ER, but she knew and accepted that she was dying without a complaint or a whimper. It was as though she just wanted it over and done with. Those women..." Ruth stopped herself, trying to control her anger.

Janet nodded. "I know."

"Her partner at least had the decency to feel guilty and be sorry to lose her. That other one, she didn't care one way or the other, despised the husband, and was toying with Beth's partner. He might as well have been dying as far as that blonde was concerned, and the novelty of sex with a woman was wearing off. Sick, twisted people."

"Was it an accident?" Janet held her breath.

"The EMTs couldn't stop talking about the circumstances when they brought her in. They kept checking on her and talking about it every time they came in during the rest of my shift." Ruth looked at her hands. "My father is a cattle farmer. I grew up hearing horror stories about farm accidents. From everything the guys told me, it was a clean roll, no blown tire, no fence, no guy wire involved. It sounds deliberate, almost planned. You have to roll over a soft spot just the right way on an incline to flip a tractor that size. Why didn't she see fresh dirt? Why didn't she know where her partner had been digging? Why was she mowing so early in the season on a farm tractor that close to the house?"

"What are you saying?"

"Who wanted her dead?"

Janet was absolutely stunned. Finally, someone said it all aloud and as a matter of fact. It made sense. The answer was very obvious.

"She should have tied that damn blonde to the tractor seat and sent her down the hillside," Ruth said as she placed her hand over Janet's.

Janet left the store without a loaf of bread.

Chapter Twenty-three

Janet sat behind the wheel of her car and stared at the house. It had lost all its charm and warmth. She made herself move her hand to the door handle only because of the July heat building within the sedan. "This should be a laugh-packed afternoon."

She opened the back door and removed her briefcase and the plastic bag with all the tags. She stood beside the car and took a deep breath. "You can do this. Just remember…don't tip your hand, observe."

It didn't help to walk past Lou's battered truck—sans the rainbow windsock—and the Cadillac SUV that bore the vanity plates "PrincessP." She resisted the urge to key the Cadillac's shiny silver paint. "Princess Patti indeed." She reminded herself, "Don't tip your hand, observe."

"Hey, boy, how are you?" Janet stopped on the porch beside the tri-colored Australian shepherd. "You're not even going to try to jump up on me? No kisses? What's wrong, boy?" She set her briefcase and bag down as she knelt beside the dog.

"He doesn't have much interest in things these days." Lou stepped onto the porch. She was immaculate in crisp new khakis and a polo shirt. Her hair had almost grown out to shoulder length. Patti had not yet convinced her about makeup. "I don't let him in the house anymore. Patti only likes small dogs. He smells from roaming around outside all the time. If he doesn't go back to the neighbors soon, I'm calling the animal warden. We don't need a stinky dog camped out on the front porch." She leaned down and looked the dog in the eyes with the last sentence.

Only Buddy's eyebrows moved.

"Go on." Lou gestured toward the yard. "Go make your rounds looking for her again."

Janet flinched and repeated her mantra in silence. She slowly stood. Lou picked up the briefcase and bag for her.

"Hope you don't mind, but we're all here. Thought it would make settling things easier. If no one contests anything, maybe we can just go ahead and divvy it all up and be done with it." Lou sounded hopeful. "I need to clear out some space for Patti."

"Really?" Janet felt a chill settle over her. She was glad she remembered to bring her cell phone and that Ellen knew where she was—but that was foolish.

"Patti and Will have been looking for a weekend place in the mountains. I told them it would be stupid as hell for them to buy something else, just help with the payments on this place and we can all share. We even have a guesthouse so we can invite others out or that we can put Will in." Lou laughed awkwardly as Janet remained stone-faced. "He likes the idea and has almost figured out how to stretch their budget enough to make it work. He only has to give up a few more luxuries like his club memberships. God knows I can't afford this place on my own. I should have thought about that when we did the renovation. I ended up holding the bag on that extra twenty thousand dollars we needed for the basement, and I need to trade my truck in. Oh, well." Lou held the front door open for her.

Janet blinked as she walked into the house. The curtains were drawn. The air conditioning was turned up enough to allow meat outside of the refrigerator. Gone was the sense of the country home that Beth had designed the renovation plans for; there was no evidence of being in the mountains or surrounded by woods.

Lou leaned close to Janet. "Patti gets migraines and is allergic to just about everything."

Janet took a deep breath and made no response to Lou. "Will, how are you?"

Will sat on the couch and didn't look up. He had two fingers of what appeared to be scotch in a glass beside a photograph album. He stared at each square black and white snapshot held to the page by its corners before turning to the next set.

Janet glimpsed two small children in each of the photos that had the look of being snapped by a Kodak Brownie Hawkeye camera that had been popular in the 1950s. She had similar collections of Melody—she too had preferred her old Hawkeye received on her tenth birthday to the newer color cameras that flooded the stores later. "All righty then."

Patti was in the downstairs bedroom. Janet could see her moving between the closet and the pile of business suits on the bed. There were two large matching suitcases with Patti's monogram on the floor that she was clearly making room to unpack. She glanced over her shoulder and caught sight of Janet and quickly dropped the armload of silk blouses that went with the suits. "We've contacted a women's shelter that helps single mothers back into the work force. I thought they could use these if you don't have to do something else with them." Patti walked to Janet, stopped within a foot of her, and leaned close without touching for an attempt at a friendly buss.

Janet stiffened, inadvertently pulled away from the woman, and glanced about the room. Now she knew what was so different about the house—all the furniture had been rearranged into different groupings. What had been a guest bedroom was now clearly the master. There was a black plastic bag next to the doorway. Janet glanced down and saw framed photographs tossed haphazardly with no regard for the glass. She spied Beth and Lou on the beach and Beth and Buddy walking through the woods. "Trash?"

Lou blushed.

"You don't mind then." Janet removed the photo of Beth and Buddy and slid it into the briefcase she took from Lou's hand. Her jaw clenched so tightly it was difficult to speak. "Let's get this done, shall we?" She removed a three-page list from the folder. "Beth recently added a handwritten list to her will. She designated things to be sold for the trusts she had set up and things to go to friends." Janet rummaged through the bag she had taken from Lou for a gel pen and removed the first packet of tags. "This would have been easier if you hadn't moved the furniture." She looked over her reading glasses at the two women who feigned innocence.

"Well, they couldn't exactly leave it looking as it was when Beth was here." Will spoke from the living room.

"Nineteen thirties walnut secretary bought in Stanton." Janet glanced around the living room.

"It's in the den." Lou inclined her head toward the back of the house.

Janet walked through the kitchen, noticing the long row of liquor bottles on the end of the counter. Beth had been strictly a beer drinker.

Janet tied a tag to the small knob on the upper doors of the secretary. "Auction."

"But I use that." Lou looked from the tag to Janet and back again.

"Did Beth buy it?"

"Yes."

"Did you contribute to the purchase?"

"No."

"She made a very specific list. Family pieces go to Will if he signs a statement that they stay in his home. Purchased pieces she had before you two met are to be sold. Beth started a trust for her cousin's child in North Carolina who is set on medical school. Pieces you bought together stay here. Clothing to charity. Family papers and Bibles to the cousin in North Carolina who does all the genealogy research. Luke's uniform and flight jacket, things he had during World War II, to the county museum. Kitchen things to you, Lou. That's pretty much it." Janet held up the sheaf of papers. "It's all in her handwriting, signed and notarized. I brought a copy for you and for Will." Janet handed the papers to Lou and started to hand the other copy to Patti, then stopped.

"William, get in here now!" Patti's voice carried through the house.

Buddy barked from the front porch.

Moments later, Will stood in the doorway from the kitchen to den. His clothes were wrinkled as though worn for several days—

the jeans and cotton shirt were uncharacteristically casual for him. His hair looked shaggy and in need of a trip to the stylist he and Patti went to. His eyes were dark, giving him a haunted look that was accentuated by his whiskers. "I heard all of it. It was Beth's to do with as she chose. She was the one who looked after our parents. God knows she earned all of it." He took the handful of papers and glanced only at the front page. "That's her writing. Put all of the furniture up for auction. I don't want any of it. Don't start, Patti." He turned, reached for the unopened bottle of scotch on the counter, and walked back to the living room in a not quite straight line.

"Damn him. He doesn't care about anything. He has no backbone whatsoever." Patti stopped herself from saying anything more.

Lou swallowed. "That's the majority of the furniture, what she restored before she met me and what came from Keith's."

Janet looked over her glasses. "Well, let's tag it and see how it works out. Remember, if you bought something together, it's yours." Janet caught the look that Lou gave Patti that seemed to say "fat chance."

"Surely, we could settle on some of the pieces that are just perfect for the house. Couldn't we make an offer to 'buy' them?" Patti smiled.

Janet removed her glasses. "That's the thing of being an executrix for someone like Beth. She was a detail person. I have to follow her instructions to the letter. There's no room or need for interpretation."

Patti visibly regrouped. "I know this must be hard on you. Losing such a close friend and having to go through all of this for her estate. Surely, we can help you make it as simple and painless as possible."

"What don't you understand? I have a list of instructions, and I must follow them. These are Beth's last wishes. They will be followed exactly as written, and I will see that every item is handled as she specified." Janet wished her mother had not instilled her with manners. Again, the mantra in silence—don't tip your hand, observe. As Gloria had glimpsed, Janet had a redneck side buried deep within her that badly wanted to break loose at times such as this. She would not compromise her executrix duties or give any reason to have the dispensation questioned. This had to be done calmly and professionally.

Patti looked at Lou. "Don't you need to check something outside?"

Stunned, Lou left the house through the back door.

Patti closed the distance to Janet. "Don't play games or favorites with me. This all needs to be settled. Will needs the money. I know there's to be a trust for him also, and we'll find a way into it. So go ahead with your tags. Make your stand today. You don't control a damn thing. If I were you, I'd not look too closely at things in this house. We were four consenting adults. You may not like what you find out about your dear, sweet friend who was so damned perfect. It's none of your business unless you just get off on it." Patti grabbed Janet's arm as she tried to back away from her. "Oh, yes. I saw you and your chubby friend in Harrisonburg watching Lou and me. So what? We're close. Beth and Will knew what was going on and didn't try to stop us. Put your tags on, and get the hell out of here and leave us to our arrangement. We'll make sure that all the tags are right, you can count on that."

The rest of the afternoon was spent in silence. Will remained on the sofa drinking steadily until he finally fell asleep holding the photo album. Lou and Patti followed Janet through the house and cottage. By the time every piece of furniture was photographed, tagged and marked, Janet was exhausted. "Are you going with me to the tractor shed?" She looked at the women who had stayed on her heels all afternoon.

Patti's complexion lightened beneath her makeup. "I am not. Will—"

Janet went out the back door.

Lou tried to bounce along like her former self who managed to cultivate flirtation with whomever she was with. "Sorry about the tall grass. I'm letting the fescue grow this summer. Old Man Burnett is going to pay me for the bales he makes off it."

Janet made no comment.

Lou nudged Janet's shoulder with hers. "I've better things to do with my time than bump along on a tractor. I refuse to try to use that antique of Beth's. I don't have her touch, can't get it to start half the time. Whoever changed the magneto for a distributor didn't do a very good job."

Janet stopped and stared at her.

Lou shrugged. "Okay, here's the deal. I can't afford to have the John Deere repaired. The fat-ass sheriff's dragging out completing his report. It's July already. Until I have the sheriff's report, I can't get my insurance carrier off dead center, plus the Deere dealer is saying the damage is not under warranty. I haven't been able to do a damn thing with my tractor since it was towed under roof right after the accident. At the least, I know the engine mounts sheared."

Janet checked the setting of the digital camera for outdoors and made herself walk to the open shed and look inside. Seeing the John Deere tractor that had crushed Beth made all the breath exit her body. How could Lou tolerate the machine being on her property much less use it again? Janet felt as though she raised the camera in slow motion. "She wants the county museum to have the old wooden wheelbarrow that her great-grandfather made and Andy to have her father's old McCormick Cub tractor. Her estate will pay for moving both."

"Bessie." Lou patted the cowl of the small red Farmall. "Beth named the tractor after the postmistress assigned to the community that the Candler farm was part of, said they were both contrary to deal with sometimes. She called Bessie her training tractor, learned to drive it as a kid as soon as her legs were long enough to tap the brakes." Lou's voice was subdued.

Janet took the photographs without looking at the saved images. She felt as though she was wearing leg weights as she walked back to the house. Something tickled her memory. She didn't know if she had the concentration for the drive home or not, but she was surely going to try.

"You know where the door is." Lou and Patti stood side by side in the kitchen examining the Bourgeat copper cookware that would stay with Lou, as Janet checked it off the list. Beth had bought the French set at the beach as a surprise she never gave to Lou.

"I can't wait for the door to close behind me. All of you are absolutely despicable. There will be reckoning." Janet stared at Lou. "She loved you so much."

Janet stopped in the living room to glare at Will but had no reaction from the man. "And you, too." If he was feigning unconsciousness, he was doing an excellent imitation.

Janet left the house. She stopped on the front porch and looked down at the dejected shepherd. "I can see why she loved you the best of anyone here." She scratched the dog's head. "I know you miss her as much as I do. Come on, Buddy, we're going home." The dog followed her to the car and hopped onto the front seat as though an old hand at riding with her. She rolled the window halfway down for him. She knew that Ellen would welcome him.

"We'll both try to make this ride without throwing up." She rubbed his head and saw a glimmer of the sparkle that used to be in the dog's hazel eyes for Beth.

Chapter Twenty-four

Janet's pen stopped, poised over the sheet of paper. She was using the fountain pen she had splurged on when she passed the bar exam. She delighted in keeping it filled with bright red ink. She refused to draft anything but a hard copy; she still didn't quite trust not losing her work if only in the computer.

She thought she heard a noise from the front of the building. She angled her head and closed her eyes slightly. "Damn it. I purposely stayed late tonight so I could lock myself in and get caught up on work."

It was Ellen's ceramic class night—Janet had a bet with herself on how many of the classes Ellen would actually attend. She glanced at what Ellen had started as a coffee cup and ended as a pencil holder that Janet actually liked having on her desk. She had tried to convince Ellen that if she had seen it in a store, she would have paid money for it. Ellen told her she was always wasting her money on foolishness.

There it was again. Someone was knocking on the front door of the small office building that had once been a brick ranch on the fringe of downtown.

"Damn it." She pushed away from her desk reluctantly and started out of the room. She went back to her tote bag for her cell phone just in case. Some of their clients were not always pleased with the case outcomes, regardless of whether they had violated the law or not.

She crossed the open file room, then the reception area and

pulled the narrow curtain aside to look out of the side light at the door.

"Shit." It was Will Candler. He looked worse than the last time she'd seen him.

The hand held up to her in greeting shook slightly.

Janet turned the deadbolt and opened the door.

Tears ran down his unshaven cheeks. "Mrs. Evans."

"You need to talk. Come inside. I'll fix us a cup of tea." One deep breath told her he'd already put quite enough alcohol in his body. She ushered him into the conference room off of the lobby. She went into the kitchen entered directly from the conference room. Conveniently, a second door from the kitchen led to the back hall—just in case. She filled two cups with water from the sink and dropped in tea bags, then set the mugs inside the microwave.

Janet turned and looked at Will as the water was nuked. He wore a ragged T-shirt over cargo shorts. His hair almost reached the back neck of his shirt. He had not shaved for several days. She smelled the alcohol coming through the pores of his skin. His eyes had progressed from haunted to dead. Red streaks were almost solid across the whites of his eyes. She returned to the conference room and led him to her back corner office, each with mug in hand.

"I just wanted to make sure you had enough working capital to cover expenses as you settle Beth's estate." He perched on the very edge of the sofa. His gaze darted about the room, looking anywhere except into Janet's. His leg bounced in a fast, unconscious rhythm.

"Yes. It's all coming along, it's just a slow process. Beth had a fair amount of cash in an interest-earning account that she had already put me on as a second." Janet watched Will's face.

"What?"

Janet nodded. "You heard me. I had no idea, either." She blew on the tea before taking a sip.

Will looked down at the floor. His leg stilled. "She was right, wasn't she?"

"About what?"

Will finally met Janet's gaze. "She tried to talk to me. I wouldn't let her. I couldn't. I was awful to her. I have become an awful person." He stopped, unable to say more.

"I heard your conversation with Beth at the beach last October. I'll never forget what was said or how much you hurt her that night." Janet sipped the tea.

"Yet she gave me another chance."

"And Lou and Patti continued their affair, enjoying it all the more because of the subterfuge. They thought they were fooling you and Beth, or were they?" Janet watched Will's shoulders sag and his entire body slump.

Will's voice was broken. "I knew they wouldn't stop. Beth believed them for a while. Beth wanted to believe them. I didn't care. What they did didn't matter to me. I was stuck with Patti until she was willing to let me go. That damn Lou. It was all her doing. I hate that woman." He struck his thigh with his fist.

Janet waited for him to calm down and continue.

"Beth knew I couldn't face how horrible Patti is, and I'm no better."

He had finally said what Janet needed to hear.

"Did Beth ever come to you before about Patti?"

"Only when she tried to figure out what was going on about a year after we married." He stared at the floor. His tone was flat when he spoke. "I mishandled a client's funds, and Patti took money out of her trust to keep it from being found out. I was so sure of the quick return that I went way over my authorized limit, and it was a six-figure bust. I could have asked Beth for help, but I went to my wife."

"And ever since?"

Will nodded. "Ever since, she owns me. Worse still, she's bored by me and unsatisfied. She decided to make me suffer as I tried to maintain her standard of living while attempting to pay her back. At the rate I'm going, it will only take another twenty years or so. She never lets me forget that she can take away my client base like that." He snapped his fingers.

"Did Beth ever exaggerate anything or come to you for help without reason?"

Will stared at Janet. "No, not even when we were kids."

"What about after the trip to the beach?"

"I don't remember much. I've been drinking rather heavily."

"What do you remember?"

"That Patti and Lou were inseparable. That I had never seen my baby sister so miserable. That I couldn't do anything about any of it." He whispered the last.

"It was easier for you to pretend it wasn't happening." It was not a question.

"Yes, may God forgive me."

Janet felt nothing for the man—neither pity nor anger. He was in his own personal hell.

"I know," Will took a deep breath, "Beth told the truth. Beth always told the truth. She looked out for everyone's interest except her own, looked out for me. It's just that the last time she brought up Patti and Lou, she went too far."

Janet looked at him and raised her eyebrows.

"She said they were planning to kill me after killing her so neither of them would lose money when they lost their spouses. I told her she was crazy as hell and I never wanted to see her again." Will stared at his hands. "It's all I can do not to choke the life out of Patti every night when she comes to bed when she's not staying out in the country with Lou. I know Patti has documented my faux pas with her attorney. Patti leaves nothing to chance. She comes home just enough for appearance's sake with the neighbors. They think she has some sort of job where she travels during the week."

Janet was speechless.

Will held out his hands, palms up. He imitated weighing something. "My wife...my sister...my wife...my sister. I made the wrong choice again, and it cost me the one person left in this world who truly loved me. I thought Beth would eventually tolerate Lou as I did Patti. Beth honestly loved Lou." Will's hands slowly dropped to his side.

"And you," Janet said quietly.

"And me. Mom and Beth were right." He waited for Janet to look at him. "They learned with my dad. There are worse things than dying. There's having to live with seeing things you wish you'd never known and seeing yourself as you never thought you'd be." He stood and walked to the door and didn't turn when he spoke.

"I'm sorry. I'm so very sorry." He shuddered. "I just needed to say that out loud to someone. Do what you have to with all of this...with all of us." He left the building.

Janet pressed the speed dial button for home. "Don't ask questions, just please come get me." She didn't trust herself to drive.

Chapter Twenty-five

"What is it about being out of town at a conference that makes us think there's no limit on how many of these that we may drink?" Janet stared at the pile of tiny umbrellas in the middle of the table.

"And that there are no calorie consequences." Gloria raised her glass to her friend and smiled contentedly.

"Just what do these coconut shell glasses have to do with Colonial Williamsburg, by the way? Doesn't everything else around here have pineapples on it?" Janet had to admit, if only to herself, that this was the most relaxed she'd been in months.

"Not a damn thing, historically speaking." Gloria belched gently and giggled. "I think we're too far north to have been part of the rum runners. Pineapples signify hospitality."

"Couldn't be any more hospitable than this." She raised her glass in return. "To be able to drink these secret concoctions, we must have salty quesadillas." Janet caught the waiter's eye and held up the empty appetizer plate. "You don't want to spoil our buzz with a heavy dinner, do you?"

Gloria shook her head and mouthed, "No."

Janet glanced at her watch and tried to read the dial. "Ellen is supposed to meet us. She couldn't wait to get her laptop out and try the free wireless connection in the room. She said she had an idea she needed to follow up on." Janet shrugged.

"Whatever." Both women giggled as though Gloria had told a hilarious joke.

They had ducked out of the opening session of the conference as soon as they gathered all the registration information. The trick with any conference was to decide early on what was mandatory and skip the rest. They had to accrue hours each year to stay current and maintain their bar standing.

"Well, I'm glad to see I'm not the only one playing hooky." The voice boomed across the bar.

Janet and Gloria reacted identically—their eyes closed as though trying to keep the sound out, then opened as their heads turned to follow the voice to its source.

"Ben Richards." Janet waved at him to join them. "Don't take his tone personally. Tank duty in Iraq during Desert Storm, hearing's not worth a damn, and he hates wearing his hearing aids."

The man made his way across the room. Gloria stared. He was a fortyish Richard Gere lookalike with brilliant white hair and round black eyeglasses. Green eyes sparkled at her. He leaned into the booth and hugged Janet. She scooted over so he could sit beside her.

"These conferences are never worth how far behind it puts me at the office, yet I can't afford not to have occasional face time with my counterparts from other jurisdictions." He drained the last from his mug.

Janet did the honors. "Gloria Jarrett…Ben Richards. Ben… Gloria." She spoke to Gloria as though Ben was not there, "My first boss when I left law school, commonwealth attorney for the county. Scared the bejesus out of me the way he would just hand off cases to me as though I'd been in practice for years and knew what I was doing."

"Well, that's the only way to learn. Just do it." He signaled the waitress for another beer. "Where do you practice, Gloria?"

"Staunton. Janet and I are both alumnae of Washington and Lee. She was a legend whispered about on campus by the time I was admitted."

"Uh-huh. I bet you could tell stories." He tried to clean his glasses on his necktie.

"Well, there is one story I've been trying to catch up with you about." Janet knocked her shoulder into his.

Ben rolled his eyes. "It was an accident. Nothing you've told me makes me think otherwise. Relax and enjoy your weekend off, for Christ's sake."

Janet didn't miss a beat. "The brother is suspicious."

"The same brother who has not made any type of complaint, statement, or even questioned the sheriff's office?"

"Yes."

"Give it a rest, Janet. Your friend is gone. I know it's difficult for you, but you must accept it. Hell, I knew Beth. I thought the world of her. I'd like to have married her and don't think I didn't try. If I had even a shred of proof of foul play, I'd light up this case in a heartbeat."

Janet nodded. "Fair enough. I'll hold you to that."

Ben looked over his shoulder. "What do I have to do for another beer?" He caught Gloria looking at him. "Don't answer that question." With a blazing grin, he was out of the booth and taking a beer from the bartender.

Gloria studied Janet before speaking again. "Are you doing any better about Beth?" She asked the question gently. All it had taken was mention of Beth Candler to sober both of them up.

Janet stopped the glass en route to her lips and returned the drink to the table. "Some, until two weeks ago when Beth's brother came to see me. About the time I calm down, something else happens. I can see Beth writing 'burden of knowledge' now."

"How is the brother?"

"Not good. I keep trying to tell myself that alcohol had much to do with the conversation we had. Before, on his part, after, on mine." She leaned back from the table as the platter was set between them. She motioned Gloria to go first.

Gloria selected the smallest slice and heaped salsa and sour cream on the tortilla. "I've been thinking about our lunch in Harrisonburg quite a bit." She licked a small spot of sour cream off her finger.

"Those two." Janet shivered. "Patti did see us."

Gloria frowned. "I've also been thinking about attorney-client privilege." She took the first bite of the quesadilla.

Janet nodded. She knew how deliberate her colleague was. She needed to build slowly to her point whether in a meeting or a courtroom.

"I think you need to know that Beth came to see me several weeks before her death." Gloria folded her napkin and pushed her plate to the side.

Janet stared.

"She had very well-thought-out questions that she wanted to ask me after she made me take a twenty-dollar bill." Gloria pulled a small notebook from her bag. She habitually jotted notes about everything.

"I have debated confidentiality with myself. I've taken a hard look at my own ethics. I've researched time limitations. But it all comes down to the plain fact that you need to know what was on her mind."

"Such as?"

"Such as, if someone inherits, then is convicted of a major crime against the deceased, what is the impact upon that inheritance?"

Janet blinked in rapid succession.

"Such as, if the bulk of an estate ends up in probate entangled with a criminal or civil case, what are the statutes? Who then decides the dispensation of the estate and what is it based on?

"Such as, if she set up a trust for her brother, is that enough to keep him out of the rest of her estate if he contests the will?

"Such as, exactly what rights did the woman she was living in a lesbian relationship with have if she recanted any verbal agreement with a legal will?"

Janet drank the entire glass of water that she had avoided so far for fear of diluting the piña coladas.

"And the kicker. Could she file a lawsuit against her sister-in-law for alienation of a same-sex partner's affection and have it taken seriously?"

"You are friggin' kidding."

Gloria shook her head. "She was strongly considering it. I hated to tell her that type of suit was no longer allowed in the commonwealth. She bounced between estate questions and wanting to know what was considered a frivolous case in her type of relationship. She was torn out of the frame over what Patti and Lou were doing to her and to Will."

Janet stared across the room. She had to think.

"I still can't believe what a mess her life had turned into. She went from being so happy with having a true relationship to sounding like she was the sociopath with her questions. Yet I knew her well enough to know if anyone had just cause, she did. But I couldn't understand why she wasn't talking to you."

Janet briefly covered her face with her napkin. "That's easy. Our friendship went too deep. I would have realized what a nightmare her life had turned into and dragged her ass out of there. I would have hurt those two women and that sorry-ass brother of hers."

"The things we do to each other are incomprehensible."

"Gloria, what did you advise her?"

"The joint bank account with your name on it. The trust for Will. The trusts and personal items to the cousins in North Carolina, establishing them as family she had interest in leaving part of her estate to. Leaving Lou only what Lou had participated in the purchase of. Basically, the handwritten codicil to the will that you had done for her. Someone," Gloria looked pointedly at Janet, "needs to bring them to trial for what they did."

Janet looked about the room. "I shouldn't tell you this. I'm being very careful before I do with this what I'm going to." She leaned across the table. "Beth told Will that she knew Patti and Lou were making plans to kill both of them."

"I feel sick."

"Welcome to my world."

"I'll transcribe my meeting notes, have them notarized, and overnight a packet to you as soon as I can next week."

Janet nodded.

"I don't know what happened, but her death was not a routine farm accident on a tractor." Gloria's face was as red as if she'd been out in the sun all day.

"Hell, no."

"Count on me if you need any help."

"Can we make this a threesome?" Ellen slid into the booth beside Janet. "Nice perfume. You're looking particularly lovely tonight, Mrs. Cleaver." She leaned into Janet.

"Behave yourself. What took you so long?" She punched Ellen solidly on the arm. "And stop making fun of me because I was a traditional housewife in my youth. You won't believe what Gloria just told me."

"What a mean right hook. You won't believe what I got into by myself in our room." She grinned at Janet.

Janet elbowed her. "Not in front of Gloria."

"With this, knucklehead. I can tell where your mind is." Ellen set her laptop on the table. "Gloria, I'm going to open this file, and I'd like you as a witness. This booth seat is long enough for all of us on one side. Do you mind?"

Gloria moved beside Ellen.

Ellen began. Janet knew it was important because Ellen waved off the waitress who would have taken her drink order. "I had a thought, and I know that always surprises you."

Janet threatened another punch.

"Hotmail, it's a free Internet e-mail provider. Remember Beth's e-mails with her initials and birthday as the account name?"

Both women nodded.

"My thought was that I wondered if Beth's e-mail was still sitting out in cyberspace."

Janet's eyes widened.

"I had her address saved in my AOL contact list. So I went to Hotmail and decided to give it a try. The stumbling block was her password. I tried her childhood nickname, the dog's name, her parents' first names, none worked. I didn't want to throw up a red flag to freeze the account. Then it hit me as though she whispered it in my ear." Ellen waited, looking from blank face to blank face.

"Remember at the hospital when she looked at me and wrote that word that neither of us knew was a word?"

"Arcanum," Janet whispered.

"Secret," Gloria said, immediately thinking of the Latin origin as Janet had, "from *arcanus*."

"Sheesh, you two and your high school Latin." Ellen typed in Beth's e-mail address and arcanum. Beth's e-mail account opened. "I hit the mother lode."

Their eyes followed the cursor to a file named Betrayal. Ellen began opening one e-mail after another written by Patti and sent to Lou—explicit paragraphs filled with her declaration of love for Lou and her absolute joy with the physical side of their relationship and how she was experiencing so many firsts with Lou.

Ellen made herself be quiet as the women skimmed the screen.

"I can't read any more right now." Janet rubbed her eyes and returned her glasses to the case.

Gloria pursed her lips and blew air. "Sheesh, she was laying it on a bit thick, don't you think?"

Janet looked at them. "Reeling Lou in to do her bidding and every damn one I read reminds Lou to hit delete."

"Exactly," Ellen said. "But do you realize what this means?" Ellen glanced at the number of tiny umbrellas on the tabletop. "Beth cracked Lou's e-mail and forwarded these to herself to have absolute proof of what she suspected. Look at the dates. She picked ones for each month from August when Keith was dying to October when they had the blowup at the beach until February eight weeks or so before the accident. She knew for sure what was going on between those two."

Janet stared at the list of e-mails. "Oh, my God, it goes one step further than that." She looked at the other two women. "I recognize some of these phrases. The lunch in February when I was to meet Beth and she brought Lou who in turn asked Patti to be there."

Ellen nodded.

"Beth acted so strange that day. No wonder. She was quoting from these e-mails to let Lou and Patti know they were busted. She cracked Lou's e-mail and threw down the gauntlet. No wonder Patti was so pissed. Lou was to have deleted these, not saved them."

"And look where it got her," Gloria whispered. "She's up shit creek. Both of them are. I'm going to give you two Nancy Drews a little advice you need to listen to because this mess is only going to become worse. Play this thing very closely. Those two are a force to be reckoned with. Be sure, or they'll sue you and ruin everything you've worked for. Do you have proof or instinct?"

Janet and Ellen looked at each other.

"Do you have real physical evidence?"

Janet shook her head. "It's circumstantial or hearsay."

"How in the hell are we to prove it if the cops haven't?" Ellen said.

"All I'm saying is be damn sure. Have a string of evidence, connected and leading to only one possible outcome, or you're committing professional suicide. I know damn well that they killed her. Just as I knew they were cheating on her. But I know it here." Gloria pointed to her heart. "I don't know it as hard fact that I could put before a judge. Read those e-mails carefully. My instinct screams that Patti just may have written something she shouldn't have, besides the love crap."

"At the very least, enough pieces of circumstantial evidence will have to be put together so that a jury will draw the same conclusions we have." Janet swirled the alcohol mix in the glass.

"Is that all?" Ellen took the glass from Janet's hand and drained it.

"All for Beth, damn it." Janet hit the tabletop with her fist.

"Beth," Gloria echoed.

Gloria looked at Janet and Ellen. "I need to lie down. Janet, I'll see you in the morning."

Ellen signaled the waitress to come back for her order. "Gloria, it's always a pleasure. Come to the beach for a weekend sometime soon. We have a spare room at the cottage you would be most welcome to use when this mess is resolved."

"I would love to." Gloria waved over her shoulder to them as she walked away.

"We have scintillating meetings tomorrow. Something tells me we'll be text messaging most of the day." Janet looked at the laptop again. "Let's bribe someone to connect us to a printer."

Ellen nodded. "I've already forwarded the e-mails to my account, but a hard copy is a good idea."

Janet studied her. "Have I told you lately, or often enough, just how much I love you?"

"I'd rather you show me."

"Elevator or room?"

Ellen laughed so loud that all in the bar looked their way. "Surprise me." She knew this would be their last unbridled fun for some time.

Chapter Twenty-six

Lou Stephens slid into the booth across from Janet and looked at her as though she had no idea why she'd been invited to lunch. "Mrs. Evans."

"Don't even try that." Janet spoke quietly and deliberately. She had called Lou and purposely asked her to meet at the neighborhood diner on the fringe of the Fletcher campus. It was basically one big room with a half wall separating the kitchen behind the bar from the customer area.

Janet wanted Lou to be able to walk so that she couldn't deny that she had time, and Janet wanted the meeting in a public place. Normally, students packed the stools along the bar and waited turns for the six booths. Janet had timed it just right to arrive after the grilled cheese at noon crowd, even if it meant tolerating soap operas playing on the television in the corner.

Lou stared at the tabletop, tracing the years of whittling with her index finger. Each class was encouraged to leave their marks behind.

"You're wearing makeup. Unreal. Princess Patti wins yet another round." Janet made herself focus. "We need to talk. I'm only giving you this chance because Beth did love you."

The color drained from Lou's face. She stared at Janet.

"Six months since Beth's death, another October. Do you ever think about Beth? Which was your favorite fall beach trip, with Beth or Patti?" Janet was deliberately cruel.

Lou started to answer and stopped herself.

"I know you lied to me." Janet waited. In her mind, it was that simple.

Lou looked as though she wanted to bolt and run. Her entire body sagged against the hard bench as though she had been carrying a heavy load too long. "What gave it away?"

Janet slowly shook her head. "That's not what's important."

"Okay. She wasn't depressed. I made all of that up. That's how Patti thought we could control her so we could be together and not have to go through a big property split. Patti and I never stopped seeing each other. Is that what you wanted to hear me say?"

Janet maintained her silence.

"Don't you think I know that I ruined Beth's life? I feel horrible about what happened. I should have just told her I wanted to be with Patti, but Patti wasn't ready to free Will, so we had to try it another way." Lou aged before Janet's eyes.

The cuteness that Lou cultivated as a means to flirt with everyone and be liked by all slid off of her like a gauze veil. "I thought she would stay with me as a roommate, dividing the house and sharing expenses and not make a big deal out of it so she wouldn't lose Will."

Janet raised one eyebrow.

Lou leaned across the table. "You want me to say it?" She took a deep breath. "We lied. We tried to manipulate her. Beth would have none of it. She could think circles around the rest of us. Okay? The one rule was to deny, deny, deny and twist everything back on Beth and blame it on the loss of her mother. Most of the time, it worked the first time she questioned something. Patti is brilliant, she can plan anything. We had Beth doubting everything she thought she saw until she went over and over it. It almost worked." A slight smile passed across Lou's face. "Will wouldn't listen to any of it from her because he already knew and didn't care. I know she didn't talk to you about most of it."

"So you manipulated Beth because of how much she loved you and Will. You and Will were the family she thought she could count on, the family she had to be able to count on."

"That's right." Lou met her stare unflinchingly.

"Did Patti plan the tractor accident for you or did you think of it yourself?"

Lou jumped back as though slapped. "What?"

"You heard me."

Lou shook her head. "I don't know what you're talking about." Her voice was suddenly without inflection.

"Just how did you get her on the tractor and driving over such a big soft spot? Did you have to dig that trench out a little wider and looser? Did the spring rains have the ground wet enough, or did you have to hose the spot down?" Janet shook with rage she barely contained inside of herself while asking the questions.

Lou shook her head again and started to slide out of the booth.

Janet grabbed her arm just as Patti slid onto the bench beside Lou.

"Have you ordered yet? I'm starved." Patti glanced at both women as she reached for the envelope-size menu. "Can you say 'carb haven'?" Patti frowned as she glanced first at the menu, then at Janet. "I take it you didn't come here for the food." She looked Janet up and down. "Maybe you did. How about letting go of her before everyone in here sees what a grip you have on her?"

Janet released Lou's arm and stared at Patti.

"What have you two been talking about? Let me guess, how depressed Will is? We are all worried about his mental health what with the untimely death of his sister and losing his mother to such a degenerative illness that he'll likely inherit. I'm so concerned about him I'm seriously considering sending him off for a little rehab time. He's such a sloppy drunk. A little break would do him good. He can't afford to lose any more clients. We're almost on food stamps as it is if it weren't for help from my parents. His heart is no longer in his work. This type of midlife crisis must run in his family."

Lou stared at the woman beside her.

"I just don't think permanently taking on Beth's share of the expenses in the house would be the best for us. We're stretching our finances awfully thin. You know how that is, don't you, love?" She bumped shoulders with Lou.

"We may just sell the house here and move in with my parents for a while to give Will time to get back to his usual workaholic self. Besides, they really shouldn't be by themselves. They have a house much too big for just two people in their seventies. Will can make a boatload of money when he puts his mind to it, not like working for a private college with endowment issues.

"No, this won't do at all." Patti smoothed the menu on the table. "I need to go where I can find food that I'm actually able to digest. Louise, I was looking for you to drop this off from Will." She handed her an envelope. "Our share of the utilities for the past month in the country, we've been there so much, what with sorting out Beth's things and going through the slow process of all the sales." She dug at Janet. "Must run. You two enjoy your lunch. Think long and hard about being seen here too long. Wouldn't want to fuel any gossip, would we?"

Patti stood and moved closer to Janet's bench and leaned down. "I'm hearing rumors of questions being asked that had best be put to rest. There are all types of lawsuits that may be filed and counter-filed. My attorney just loves messy litigations, and she'll do anything I ask of her. Don't push me. I won't tolerate it." She stood and straightened her suit jacket.

"Louise, later. William and I will let you know how much longer we'll be staying with you." She strolled out of the bar, turning heads as usual.

Janet stared across the table—she had just been threatened. Lou was clearly stunned—she'd been financially dumped.

"You didn't realize their leaving would be part of 'Will's depression,' did you?" Janet reached for the menu. "She's right. The food selection is not that great unless you're nineteen years old. Of course, at my age..." She signaled the waiter and imitated pulling a beer tap. "Sam, please. Two?" She looked at Lou.

"I can't drink during the day, no matter how much I want to," Lou said.

"Make that one." Janet straightened the salt and pepper shakers and organized the artificial sweeteners.

"She's a piece of work, don't you think?" Janet watched the full glass of beer make its way to her. "Thank you." She smiled at the owner, who was also the only waiter during the afternoon. She raised the glass a few inches from the table. "To Beth." Janet took a long swallow.

Lou didn't move.

"First Beth was losing her mind, now Will. If Patti stays in whatever type of relationship you think you two have, how long before it's you who is losing her grasp of reality so that the country place would be totally hers? Have you changed your deed or will? I wouldn't advise it." She held her free hand up. "Don't answer. I really don't want to know."

Janet appeared to ponder more than the beer dwindling from her glass. "Was that the plan? Eliminate Beth, then Will, so it would all come to you two without messy separations? It really hadn't occurred to you that Patti would tire of you? You've been a break in a stale marriage. Beth was the means of that break. Now Will is a minor inconvenience. He's not providing, and he's not staying busy so you two can do whatever. How long before she wants her so-called respectability back? How long before she starts leaving you at home to do things on her own while scoping out the next target—her next male target? Ah, the thrill of the chase." Janet drained the glass. "I wouldn't want to be you for so many reasons…the things that must be going through your mind."

Lou stood and left the diner as though sleepwalking.

"Hmm." Janet shrugged and decided on the signature grilled cheese sandwich and another Sam Adams from the keg. She was going home after this to show Ellen well-deserved appreciation for being a good woman and loyal partner.

Chapter Twenty-seven

"Damn it," Janet whispered the curse and slammed her fist against the countertop. Even subdued, her temper drew nervous glances from others standing at the row of oversized books. "Sorry."

Janet could not concentrate. Here she was in the clerk's office at the courthouse, amid the deed and plat books that she loved to puzzle through, and she couldn't concentrate. She was only trying to trace back the ownership of undeveloped land before her client closed on an offer to build a new subdivision.

Of course, her mind was on Beth and the last time they'd crossed paths here amid the old records. Beth had been in a manic whirlwind of grieving for Keith and over-booking everything else to stay too busy to think about anything but the task at hand.

"Why didn't she tell me how bad it was and how much she knew?" Janet whispered the words to herself and again drew stares.

"Sorry. Bad day." Janet made herself focus on the grantor list and the search for the family name of the original owner of the land that had been given by the King of England to one of Virginia's first families.

She glanced at the briefcase beside her feet and forced herself not to reach for it until she found the conveyance record she was looking for. She jotted down the number of the deed book and page, then pulled the thickest file from her briefcase. She pushed the index book aside and began to leaf through the documents she knew by heart—the death certificate, the will, the handwritten codicil, the estate listings, the e-mails, the statements from Delores and Gloria, and the sheriff's accident report. She flipped through the pages of photographs taken the day of the accident and wished the copier quality was better. What was she missing?

"Damn it to hell." Janet didn't look up this time. She was old enough that her colleagues should be used to her eccentricities by now, or at least allow her a few. She had earned the right to talk to herself.

"Mrs. Evans, don't make me escort you out of here." The deputy stood at her elbow and held his chuckle in for a full thirty seconds.

Janet elbowed him in the rib cage. "Very funny, Bo."

"How's Melody?" He had gone to high school with Janet's daughter. Due to the imaginary districting line, Beth had attended the other high school in the county.

"Melody is in Chicago and loving it, from what little I hear." She turned and faced the young man. Clearly, he had barely known her daughter, but he meant well by asking after her.

"How are you?" The man's shirt was stretched tight over the muscles that he obviously worked out to maintain.

Janet sighed. "Troubled."

Bo Watson looked past her shoulder and read the name on the document. "Beth Candler." He shook his head and looked about the room. "Can I buy you a soda or cup of coffee out of the machine?" He inclined his head toward the employee lounge.

"I don't know, can you?" She smiled at him and waited.

He grimaced. "You know I hate it when you do that. You're worse than my former high school English teacher about correcting me. Okay. *May* I buy you a soda or cup of coffee?" He rolled his eyes.

"You bet. You know it's my duty to give you a hard time. Most of you uniformed boys are young enough to be my children."

"You would have had to become pregnant awfully early." He picked up the briefcase for her as she gathered the file. "I ought to do this more often. I wouldn't have to lift at night."

She punched him in the arm and watched him feign a grimace.

"Looks can be deceiving. My upper body strength is good even if my knees are shot."

"Do you still play golf?"

"Every chance I get. Not enough lately. I'm obsessed."

He closed the lounge door behind them. "Beth Candler." He said the name again as he sorted through the change from his pocket.

"Diet Coke, please. Can't help it if it is mid-November, damn hot flashes. And, yes, Beth."

He fed the machine enough coins for two drinks before joining her at the round table in the corner. "I worked on that accident report you have a copy of with several of the other guys. I was first on the scene the day it happened." He drank half the contents of the can in one swallow and excused himself for a muffled burp.

"You have grown up."

"Try telling that to my wife." He grinned. "Beer burps are still the best."

She shook her head. "Beth?"

He frowned. "We classified it as an accidental death due to operator error."

"I know."

"But it doesn't make any sense." He stared at her.

"What do you mean, Bo?"

The young man looked about the room already knowing they were alone.

"The guys I work with are townies and don't understand. Mrs. E., you know me. I lived and worked on a farm all during my school years. I still go out on weekends and help my dad. I tried to buy some of the Candler land, but it went for too much and was in tracts too large for me to afford what with house payments and a baby."

Janet nodded her understanding.

He stared at his hands, rough from years of manual labor. "There was nothing wrong with the tractor, no broken axle, no burst tire, no sheared lynchpins. The only damage I saw came from the roll down the hillside."

"That's not conclusive."

"No, ma'am, but I also knew Beth. I used to watch her work about the farm. I had a huge crush on her when I was a kid. I thought it was so cool that she was president of her chapter of the Future Farmers of America when I was a freshman and she was a senior. I tried to talk my dad into letting me switch high schools because of her." He grinned at the memory of seventeen-year-old Beth. "That girl knew her way around a tractor."

"I know."

He shook his head. "With all due respect, no, you don't know what I'm saying. She knew to back up and drive down a steep slope. She knew not to follow a contour around a hillside and put herself at better than a forty-five-degree angle sideways. She knew not to let two tires rest on a soft spot at the same time. Even if the soft spot was covered with grass clippings, that was exactly the type of conditions we were all taught to watch out for. Edges of holes have a way of breaking. The ditch was not compacted, the dirt was not packed tight in the trench."

"What…what exactly are you saying?" Janet gripped the can until the sides compressed.

"She knew better. Something had to distract her or someone had to cover something up. My mind is not comfortable with what happened to her being an accident, even though I was overruled and it went on record that way. There was no hard evidence to prove it wasn't an accident but also none to prove it was. Understand? It's nothing I could explain so anyone else would go along with me. Half the force has never sat on anything but a riding lawnmower and consider that a tractor. Hell, if your feet can drag the ground while riding it, it's not a tractor."

Janet studied the young man. He knew the same as she did, even if neither of them could quite piece it together. "Would you testify and repeat that before a judge?"

"Yes, ma'am. Even if it costs me this fancy shirt and badge that lets me just stand around and watch people most of the time. Yes, ma'am. I owe her that."

Janet nodded and reached across the table to squeeze his hand—one more person willing to express reasonable doubt.

Bo's expression was puzzled. "I can't help noticing when I

make my rounds that the tractor hasn't moved since the accident. I was the one steering when the wrecker towed it. Lou must not have time, or she's waiting until all the holidays are over, to deal with the insurance company. Until the last several weeks, that big Cadillac SUV was always in the driveway."

Chapter Twenty-eight

"Hey, Cupcake, call me back soon, please. I need to see you and that handsome husband of yours." Janet snapped her cell phone shut and concentrated on driving. She normally would not use the phone while operating the car, but she was unable to slow her mind down long enough to pull over. She could not continue to stew about all that was churning through her head. She knew she was very close to something that had been staring her in the face all along.

Her phone vibrated and startled her. "Shit."

"Most people say 'hello,' Auntie." Greg's tone was teasing.

"Sorry, Cupcake, the phone scared me. Jittery nerves from too many Cokes this afternoon."

"Well, didn't you want me to call you right back?"

"Yes, I did. Thank you for listening to me for a change."

"Don't make me hang up on you, Auntie." He chuckled.

"Don't you dare. Hey."

"Hey, yourself. Why is it that you call me cupcake, anyway?"

"Because I had to bake so many of the damn things when you were in school because you wanted all the cute boys to like you."

Greg burst out laughing.

"That's okay, I have another eardrum."

"Bitch, bitch, bitch. You called me first, remember?"

"Of course I do. Are you and Andy at home for a while? Hold

on a minute." She pinched the cell phone between her ear and shoulder and put both hands on the wheel to negotiate the sharp turn onto the subdivision street. "I'm back."

"Yes, we're in for our usual exciting Friday night of DVD critiquing."

"Good, I'm pulling into your neighborhood. I need to talk to both of you."

"Front door's open. Come on in. I'll have my honey mix up some drinks."

"Thank you, sweetie. You may be sorry. You know what I need to talk about."

"I know. I loved her, too. Come on in."

Janet hit the speed dial number saved on two.

"Hey, cutie." Ellen actually answered her BlackBerry. She had promised to do better.

"Hey, yourself. Can you meet me at the boys and bring your laptop?"

"Give me fifteen minutes."

"I'll give you anything I have."

"Promises, promises." Ellen disconnected.

Janet parked behind the bright red Ford F-150 4x4 that Andy had recently bought with twenty-three thousand miles on it, barely broken in, according to him. He swore that based on how and where he was raised, it was his only choice for a vehicle. Janet believed him. Greg had a silver Lexus coupe that he insisted on leasing new with an option to trade every other year.

"How in the hell do they afford all of this?" Janet said the same to herself every time she came to the house. "Twenty-eight hundred square feet for two grown men." She looked at the mock Tudor house complete with small turrets on each front corner that served as storage rooms and shook her head.

"We work our cute little butts off all day and bring more work home at night." Greg answered the question. "We love spending our money on our home."

"And each other." Andy joined them in the front hall, holding an extra margarita glass.

"I'm assuming the Great White is on her way? The guest

room is prepared." Greg giggled. "I love saying that."

"And I know you call her that because of her disposition and hair color. Yes, she is." Janet sipped the drink and didn't set her briefcase down until she reached the large walnut partners' desk in the middle of the boys' den. "I know I shouldn't, but I enjoy the salt on the rim of the glass." She sighed, contented for the moment. Janet could think in this room. She loved the rich paneling and all the books she teased the boys about not reading. Best of all were the logs blazing in the fireplace. Christmas was only a few weeks away, and she knew what she wanted.

"Live large while we can, Auntie. It can all change in the blink of an eye." Greg stood beside her and toasted her glass. Andy returned to the kitchen.

"He put shrimp in to marinate, always a good appetizer." Greg cleared a place on the desk. "Okay, what do we have?" He pulled a chair over beside hers.

Janet began emptying her briefcase of the Candler files for Keith and Beth. The estate work, the probate photo proof sheets, the statements, the e-mails, and the sheriff's report were spread out on the large surface of the desk in short order.

"Keep those vile things away from me." Greg moved the e-mails to the bottom of the stack. "Enough to give porn a bad rep."

"Greg, be serious." She took one more sip from the glass and smacked her lips. "I know the evidence is here. You must help me see it. You know how just saying things aloud to someone else oftentimes helps the answer pop into your mind."

"Let's do it. Walk me through it. Just a sec. Andy, you need to hear all of this, too."

"I'm on the way with the shrimp, and I don't mean this fine figure of a woman I found on the doorstep." He walked into the room with a platter of shrimp surrounded by chips and salsa, and Ellen on his arm. "I know us. We'll get started, forget all about dinner, and three hours from now wonder why we're ravenous."

"I'm already hungry." Ellen munched from the tray before it was set down and added her laptop to the pile on the desk. She tossed her coat over the recliner near the fireplace and warmed her hands by the crackling flames.

They settled around the desk with files, food, and the margarita pitcher all in easy reach, and waited for Janet to tell them a story.

Janet began with Keith and the creation of documents for Beth to handle her mother's estate and caretaking. She explained Beth's investment in Lou's property and what she knew of Will's use of his share of the farm and estate. She touched lightly on the e-mails and Delores's statement. She took the most time explaining Beth's handwritten codicil, including her notes from Gloria. Then she walked them through Beth's estate, using the contact sheets with the postage stamp-size photos of everything Beth owned keyed to a written list.

"I keep thinking about my conversation with Bo Watson in the clerk's office a week or so ago."

"Lucky you." Greg dodged a punch from Andy. "Seriously, he's a nice guy even if he was clueless why I schlepped along as manager on the football team."

"He explained to me what was wrong with the accident report on Beth's death." Janet held the bound copy and riffled the pages. "The sheriff's photographs make me crazy because of the poor copy quality."

Janet refilled her glass, realizing that the alcohol was taking the edge off her thought process, but recognizing that sometimes— like that night—that was a good thing. "Up and down versus sideways on the tractor, compaction of ditches." She waved her hand knowing Ellen and Andy were familiar with both.

"She would not have mowed around a steep hillside unless she was used to knowing she could." Andy expanded the thought for her.

Janet and Greg stared at him.

"That's bothered me ever since the accident was first explained to me as operator error. Beth knew better." He drained his glass.

"Exactly. That's what Bo said and is willing to testify to."

Andy nodded.

"But is that enough for me to go to a judge? I don't think so. Most people 'know better' than to have the accidents that kill them." She leaned back in the chair to straighten her spine. She had that nagging feeling again—same as when she left Lou's the last time feeling as though wearing leg weights. Weights.

Janet suddenly sat forward. "Ellen, were you standing near me the first time we went to Beth and Lou's to see Keith when Beth drove up on the tractor?"

"Briefly. I went to find Lou after speaking to Beth to give you time alone with her."

Janet nodded. Her eyes were not focused on the room. "I teased Beth about the makeup box on the front of the tractor."

Andy frowned.

"It was an old toolbox that Lou had rigged to add weight over the front axle. When the girls renovated, they saved all the old cast iron window weights. Lou collected more and filled the box with over two hundred pounds." Janet hit herself on the forehead with the palm of her hand. "Beth used the added weight for traction so she could make loops around the house when mowing so that she didn't have to waste time backing up and down the steep slope out from the house. I'm an idiot!"

"Meaning less chance of rolling down a hillside with the tractor coming after you," Greg whispered.

"Enough compensation to make you think you could do a quick mow with the contour instead of taking the time to go up and down a slope." Ellen understood exactly.

Andy picked up the contact sheet. "Do you have these any larger?"

Janet glanced at the files. "The prints are at home. We can look at them online. You-know-who set me up on a Web-based service for back-up storage."

Ellen used her laptop to quickly access the Web site.

Janet logged into her account at the digital upload site that she had gigs of storage on, even though she had no clue what a gig was except when it was up. She found the index and opened the folder of photos taken the day of the estate listing. She slid the laptop over to Andy.

Andy navigated through the images, zooming in and out, finally concentrating on the ones taken at the tractor shed. "She knew tractors, grew up on them. One would not have gotten the best of her," he said to himself as he went back and forth through the images. He held his hand out to Janet. "Accident report." He motioned to Greg. "Magnifying glass." Andy held the report next to the computer screen.

Greg shook his head slowly when he caught his aunt's eye. He whispered, "He's processing. Let him work through it."

Andy settled on the shot taken looking into the shed that had caught the front of Lou's John Deere and Beth's McCormick Cub. He stared. "Bessie."

Greg leaned closer to Janet. "He keeps that old tractor in the garage instead of his truck. He disappears, and I find him tinkering with the motor or wiping down the body. The neighbors can't believe he'll mow the vacant areas of their lots and push snow out of their driveways for nothing. I know he's thinking about Beth any time he's near Bessie."

Janet felt foolish as tears filled her eyes.

Greg squeezed her arm. "I do the same."

Andy spoke, more to himself than to the others in the room. "The front blade is off the Deere. Lou said at the hospital that she had prepped the tractor for mowing. They kept the bush hog on the back because it was so cumbersome to take off and put back on, and it gave them more traction in the rear when they did use the blade. The blade is off. Beth hated having to adjust the pitch of the blade so it didn't hit ground on sharp turns when she was mowing." His face froze and his mouth dropped slightly open. "What a dumbass I am. How do we know the weights were in the box? How did Beth know?"

"She trusted Lou," Ellen stated simply. "Look, hanging on the wall of the shed, a clipboard and a maintenance checklist same as Lou uses at work. Lou did all the maintenance on the tractors. Beth did all the mowing."

Greg and Janet stared at each other.

Andy spoke deliberately. "What's different between the sheriff's photo of the Deere and yours?" He didn't look at Janet.

They clustered behind Andy.

Greg spoke first. "Grass is taller. Lawnmower is positioned farther back and at a different angle."

"What's different is not important. What's the same?" Ellen took a wooden pencil from the can on the desk and pointed to the bottom horizontal log of the shed that the exterior siding was nailed to. "Enlarge that." Her voice was barely audible when she spoke. "Look what's on the log in the shed in both photos…a socket wrench. How is the lid attached to the box the weights go in?"

"Bolts," Janet remembered.

"Want to make a bet what that socket fits and who left it there?"

"No," Janet and Greg said together.

"I wonder if your friend Bo looked inside the box on the front," Ellen said.

"I know how to find out. Where's your telephone book?"

Greg found the latest in a bottom drawer and held the book for Janet as she turned to the Ws.

Janet drew her cell phone from her pocket as though a gun from a holster. She called Bo and began with an apology for disturbing him at home before asking the question. Her eyes widened as she listened. She lowered her phone and looked at the others.

"The lid was bolted tight after the tractor rolled. They looked inside and assumed it was just an empty toolbox."

She dialed the next number from memory.

"Ben, it's Janet Evans."

Andy and Greg grimaced as they heard the volume of the man's barely muffled voice from the cell phone several feet away.

"Yes, I know what time it is…Yes, I know you have young children…No, I'm not going to apologize. You told me when I had proof…" She let him rant until he ran down.

"Calm down, Ben. Yes, it's about Beth. I don't appreciate that kind of language." She put her hand over the phone and whispered to the boys, "Unless I'm using it."

Janet spoke deliberately when she could get a word in. "You told me when I had proof, you would initiate a case. I need items from Beth's home to be impounded and fingerprinted. Well, they belong to Lou Stephens now. I've seen something as Beth's executrix." She waited on him again.

"Damn it, Ben. Listen to me. Lou took the weights out of the box on the front of the tractor, causing it to flip. Bo Watson told me that the box was empty when they examined the tractor after the accident. Lou tampered with the tractor knowing that Beth would be the next to use it. The damn wrench is still in the shed, there's no difference in position between the May and July photographs. Someone needs to look for a pile of old window weights." She nodded as his volume decreased.

"How in the hell should I know what one looks like?" Janet raised her eyebrows at the boys.

"Yes, you can prove it. Take my word. Promise me you'll do this first thing on Monday."

They were both quiet for a moment.

"Because you owe me, Ben, and we all owe Beth."

"Excellent. Assign it to Howard. He'll have it put together in no time. I'm talking murder of the first degree. It's going to be nasty. I'm betting the partner did it, and the sister-in-law directed it. The brother knew some of what was going on."

Janet waited through a brief silence, allowing him time to digest it all.

"Yes. Impound the John Deere farm tractor, the socket wrench that I'll e-mail a photo of, and look for the weights. Fingerprint all of it. I'll bet you a new laptop that the fingerprints are all from one person, and I don't mean Beth."

He didn't take Janet up on the bet, either.

"Thank you, Ben. Thank you."

Greg divided the last of the drink mix between the four glasses. "You have your case."

They emptied their glasses in stunned silence.

Chapter Twenty-nine

"What have you done to us?" The man's voice was on the verge of hysterics.

"What?" Janet bobbled the handset of the phone and fumbled for the switch on the stem of the lamp beside her bed. Buddy whimpered from his bedding beneath the window and watched her to know whether to bark. Ellen hit a knot in the log she was cutting through—Janet often teased her that her snoring sounded like a chain saw under water.

"You've ruined us. Patti and I did nothing to hurt Beth that day. It was that damn Lou. You've had them both charged with first-degree murder. Both of them. It was supposed to be just Lou."

It was Will Candler.

"That day." Janet felt the blood rise in her face as she struggled with the bedclothes, and it wasn't a hot flash. Her T-shirt was tangled with the sheet. She motioned the dog to stay in his bed as she carried the phone into the living room. She struggled to keep her balance as she pulled on sweatpants; the house was chilly.

"You don't deny that you did this? You're the reason I've had to use all the equity in our home to retain a goddamned lawyer. My wife's been indicted for murder, and my home is my only real asset. I can't afford the bail to get her out. You know what Patti is holding over me if I don't get her off. Patti is in fucking jail!" Will screamed the last into the phone. "Patti has flipped out and won't even talk to me other than to threaten me. You've made my life hell. Everyone looks at me like something they would scrape off the bottom of their shoes."

"At least you still have your life. I'm not at fault. Think about what the three of you did to set all of this in motion." Janet knew she shouldn't be having this conversation, but her temper momentarily overcame her professionalism. "You told me to do what I had to."

"To Lou, for Christ's sake. Did I have to spell that out? Don't forget that there were four of us involved. Have you ever thought about it that way? You're not going to like what you'll hear or what will come out. Call this trial off now," Will yelled into the telephone. "I'm telling you neither Patti nor I did anything to that tractor or Beth. Patti is right. Beth was the one who had given up on everything."

"It's not possible to stop the trial unless Lou and Patti confess their guilt. Otherwise, it's up to a jury to hear both sides and make a decision." Janet paced along the back of the sofa. Her voice was cold as the February night outside. "We shouldn't be having this or any conversation. I'm hanging up. Don't call back. I'll have to notify the commonwealth attorney of this."

"You've destroyed all of us, yourself included, you judgmental bitch. You still don't understand. Patti has already brought in one of her crazy-ass friends from college who just happens to be one of the best criminal lawyers in the Southeast and has been carrying a torch for Patti ever since their sorority days. Ashley Tate will do anything and everything to save Patti, and I'll go broke paying for it!"

"You destroyed yourselves." Janet hit the end call button on her phone. She held onto the handset as she stared into the dying embers of the corner fireplace. Each day gave new meaning to the word "irony." She knew Ms. Tate by reputation only.

Ellen walked out of the bedroom in sweatpants and T-shirt, rubbing her head. "Is everyone okay?"

"Just the usual harassment before a big trial." Janet looked to her for reassurance.

"Beth's case?"

Janet nodded. "It was Will."

"Holy crap. He knows better."

"He will tomorrow. I have to call Ben and Howard first thing." She looked at the clock. "Three a.m. Great."

"I know. I haven't been asleep long. You were tossing and turning, mumbling to yourself when I came to bed. Showtime was running 'The L Word' again. I love that show even if the girls are too young and too California." Ellen frowned slightly and hesitated before speaking. "Do you have any idea how difficult the next few months are going to be on you?"

Janet nodded. A tear rolled down her cheek. "On both of us. I didn't know if you did."

Ellen shrugged. "I had a pretty good idea when this started that it would turn into a three-ring circus with a lot of elephant shit to dodge."

"Everything will come out. Beth will be judged in absentia for her lifestyle. How can a client ever trust Will again? I have no doubt that Lou and Patti will be convicted felons." Janet took a deep breath. "They're all three ruined…reputations and finances…regardless of the verdict. Will is right about that. The attorney costs in a trial like this will be astronomical."

"Boo-fucking-hoo. Let me feel sorry for any of the three of them, or not. It's you I'm concerned about. I hate to think what this may do to your practice. These are the years we've worked so hard to enjoy. It's never easy being a whistleblower. You knew that when you started the proceedings. It's that damnable burden of knowledge. You had no choice." Ellen motioned Janet to follow her back to the bedroom. She climbed in and held the covers up until Janet was settled. She pulled her close and held onto her.

"I didn't have a choice once I had a doubt. My only regret will always be Beth and the fallout on us." Janet nestled against Ellen and felt better. "Beth won't be able to tell her side or clarify any of it. It will come out as the prosecution and defense spin it for the case."

"We're tough old birds, we can handle it. It's not going to be a pretty story any way you look at it."

"No. There were still so many that didn't know her lifestyle, just her professional side. But I don't think it makes as much difference anymore." Janet sighed. "It's just that Beth was so private. She would be the last person to want headlines. I can identify with that."

"I keep thinking about Keith. You know how I mean this, but thank God she's not here to know all of this…to lose Beth and see Will's true nature. Good Lord."

"What a mother's nightmare." Janet surprised them both by chuckling. "I bet Keith would have kicked Patti's butt at the thought of her hurting Beth by taking up with Lou and Will's for allowing his wife to run rampant."

"And yet," Ellen thought aloud, "Keith knew to make Beth promise to look out for Will. Who else would have taken on Patti?"

"I keep thinking back to what I could have said or done differently. Then I catch myself…what foolishness. I know it was the way Beth's life had to play out, none of us could have changed any of it to amount to anything. What a harsh ending to such happiness. She had finally come into her own. That's what bothers me so much, what drives me."

"You became her second mother."

Janet finally allowed the tears. All the frustration of Beth's death, of the nagging questions, and of the months it had taken to figure it all out eased down her cheeks. "I would just as soon not have known it was anything other than a tragic accident. Maybe I should have…"

"That's early morning gibberish. Don't even try to go there. It was a wrongful death. It's up to the system now."

"I wish you hadn't put it that way."

"The law is your constant." Ellen looked at her questioningly.

"But remember the blindfold. 'Justice is blind' can have more than one meaning." Janet pulled away from Ellen. "I'm going to start coffee. Want a late dinner while I have an early breakfast?"

Buddy's tail thumped on the floor next to his bed at the prospect of food.

"Yes, you too. Come on, my loves." She pulled on the robe she had decided not to save for a hospital stay. "Let's break bad and do waffles." They beat her to the kitchen.

Chapter Thirty

Janet closed her eyes against the dull pain along her jaw from grinding her teeth together. She would be down to her gums and soft food by the time this trial was over. As always, Ellen sensed her mood and reached for her hand. Ellen had not left her side since Lou's trial began a week earlier. Janet felt as though she was giving birth to this verdict. She knew Ellen's hand was bruised by now as much as she squeezed it.

Once again, Janet checked the players—Judge Daphne Henderson at the bench, Howard Mills at the prosecutor's table, and Richard Tyler at the defendant's table. She and Ellen sat on the first bench—made by a local church pew manufacturer—behind the railing separating them from the prosecutor's table midway on the right side of the courtroom. Janet could almost read Howard's notes, depending on how he left the file on the table. Will sat directly behind Rich and Lou.

They were in the main gallery of the courthouse constructed in 1855 that was gradually being phased out of use due to accessibility issues. The ceiling was twenty feet high and tied into the understructure of the domed roof. The walls were painted an off white to highlight the details of the handcrafted plaster. The room had the smell of over a hundred and fifty years of trials—that slightly musty smell of stored paper, human nervousness, and too many humid summers with no central air conditioning. Luckily, the cross-ventilation and early April temperatures made the room comfortable.

Judge Henderson had exercised her ability to bifurcate the trial, separating the proceedings into guilt and sentencing phases.

To the initial shock of all involved, Patti Candler had admitted her guilt and entered into plea bargaining.

Jury selection had taken twice as long as usual—Beth was too well-known in the community. The group of twelve sat crowded in the tight grouping of chairs on a platform to the far right front of the room. It was a good mix of age, race, and sex. Their faces remained neutral as they listened to the whittling down of the jury pool.

Janet watched Judge Henderson observing Lou and Will. Lou appeared subdued, her hair bobbed neatly and clothing in neutral colors. Her face registered no emotion. Will appeared a shadow of himself, slumping in the pew and unable to sit still. A haircut and shave only made Will look worse for wear. Janet had silently given thanks when she found out which judge the case was to be tried before. Daphne Henderson was a force to be reckoned with—a practitioner of family law until appointed to the bench. Daphne had made a career out of helping decent people out of untenable situations.

Howard Mills bowed slightly to the bench and introduced himself to the jury. He was a compact black man of extreme intelligence and minimum ego, who dressed sharply yet understated. Fully clothed, he might weigh in at 125 pounds. Janet knew that Howard's opening statement would be true to his character—not one word extra or the court's time wasted.

"Ladies and gentlemen, my job is relatively simple. I'm responsible for what is called the burden of proof…to establish the guilt of Louise Stephens for the first-degree murder of Elizabeth Candler." Howard carefully explained the primary elements of the crime that he was going to prove. The jury members listened intently. He concluded with, "Beth Candler died after a farm tractor rolled over her and crushed her. Her death was caused by the woman before you on trial." He finished his statement beside his table and with a slight nod to the judge, took his seat.

Rich Tyler looked at his opposing counsel as though waiting for more and smiled as though he had the best car on the lot for the lowest price. He easily weighed close to four hundred pounds and was slightly less than six feet tall. His round face was topped by combed over, thinning hair that clung to his scalp. "If only it was that simple or easy. Mr. Mills neglected to tell you that he must prove his case beyond a reasonable doubt. It's my job to refute the so-called evidence that the state has gathered at the urging of Ms. Candler's friends." His implication clearly reflected the unavoidable headlines when the indictment was announced— that this was a matter of dirty laundry being aired in the gay community and what else could be expected. "My argument is very straightforward." He paused for the groans. Rich countered each element Howard had mentioned, while managing to include negative overtones about Beth. "Beth Candler was killed in a tragic accident. Beth Candler had family problems the same as everyone else. This woman," he pointed to Lou, "is not guilty of any criminal act." He smiled at the jury and returned to his table, leaning sideways to listen attentively to his client.

Howard began the painstaking process of calling experts and witnesses and introducing physical evidence.

The county sheriff explained the initial accident report filed by his office that detailed the layout of the small farm, contained photographs of the tractor and the accident scene, and concluded while no mechanical failure was apparent, there was carelessness on the part of the operator.

Rich Tyler saw no need for cross-examination.

Experts from the local community college, as well as the John Deere dealership, were called in to explain farming techniques and the particular John Deere tractor used.

At the end of the third day of actual testimony, Deputy Bo Watson was called to the stand.

"So the report was filed stating death by operator carelessness and the matter closed?" Howard asked.

"Yes, sir. Until we received a call from the commonwealth attorney with regard to additional evidence."

"You returned to the scene of the accident?"

"Yes, sir. We tagged and bagged a socket wrench located in the tractor shed as noted on the exhibit photograph taken on

December 5. The photographs from May and July corroborate the wrench in the same location and position."

"What size was the socket on the wrench?"

"One-half inch."

"What size are the bolts on the box on the front frame of the tractor?" Howard aimed the laser pointer at the bottom front of the large green tractor in the photograph on the projection screen.

"One-half inch."

"The box," Howard pointed again, "was opened and noted as empty during the initial investigation?"

"Yes, sir."

"What else did you find during your follow-up investigation?"

"We established a grid out from the house and searched until we found thirty-six cast iron window weights partially buried in the original property owner's trash dump in a hollow approximately eight hundred feet northwest of the back corner of the house and as shown on the site drawing." Bo nodded toward the screen.

"Window weights."

"Yes, sir. In older homes, wooden casement windows were hung using sash cord and pulleys with a weight on either side for raising and lowering each section. Each weight is thirteen inches long, one-and-one-half inch in diameter, and is solid cast iron weighing six pounds."

"So thirty-six of them are a fair amount of weight?"

"Yes, sir. Two hundred and sixteen pounds, not including the weight of the box itself."

"Forensically speaking?"

Bo smiled. "Yes, sir. I was getting to that. According to the lab work, the wrench had fingerprints from Louise Stephens as did the window weights and the box on the front of the tractor. There was residue in the box on the front of the tractor that matched the scaling from the weights. The thirty-six weights fill the box."

Howard nodded to Bo. "Thank you, Deputy Watson."

Rich Tyler stood and approached Bo. "You found a socket wrench in a tractor shed?"

"Yes, sir."

Rich shrugged. "And you found old window weights in a private trash dump?"

"Yes, sir."

"Covered with the fingerprints of one of the owners of the property?"

"Yes, sir."

"And that changed your report how?"

Bo did not blink. "With additional evidence that requires us to further examine the cause of Beth Candler's death."

Rich quickly said, "That's all, Your Honor," and sat down.

They began the next morning on a grim note. Dr. Jordan Meadows, the trauma doctor who attended Beth after the accident, summarized her injuries. He appeared too young and too fresh to be an experienced doctor but spoke with the mannerisms of an old soul. He followed Howard's technique and kept his testimony in layman's terms.

"On Saturday morning, Beth Candler suffered a severe closed head injury and numerous crush injuries to the head, chest, and pelvis. She had borne the full weight of the tractor rolling over her body and lain unattended for several hours. We conducted tests and performed surgery for burr holes to relieve the pressure on the brain. By Sunday afternoon, her vital signs stabilized, then became erratic before plummeting as the brain herniated. There was nothing we could do to save her considering the extent of her injuries and the time before we initiated treatment. She was pronounced dead at 5:15 p.m."

Howard guided Dr. Meadows through a series of questions that detailed each stage of Beth's injuries to ensure that the jury fully comprehended the extent of the damage done to Beth Candler by the tractor.

A compassionate silence settled over the courtroom.

Rich reluctantly approached the doctor. Even he was subdued when he asked his questions. "Was Beth Candler's family in attendance at the hospital?"

The doctor nodded. "Her partner, Lou Stephens, her brother, Will Candler, and sister-in-law, Patti Candler, as well as several of her friends were in attendance."

"As a physician, what was the family's medical state?"

"Shock, disbelief, and grief."

Howard did not redirect. Nothing had been said that damaged his case.

Chapter Thirty-one

Ellen leaned against Janet. This was the day they had dreaded.

"The state calls Janet Evans."

Janet looked at Greg and Andy in the row behind her and Ellen. The boys wore dark suits with purple ribbons for Beth on their lapel. Greg briefly touched Janet's hand as she passed in front of him on her way to the aisle.

This was Janet's first stint as a witness in a criminal trial. She would much rather be in Howard's place. Howard caught her attention and winked at her with his right eye so Judge Henderson wouldn't see.

Janet glanced at Daphne and knew her friend would remain stoic throughout her testimony. Janet took a calming deep breath and focused on Howard.

In as unemotional a voice as she could manage, Janet described her duties as Beth's executrix and the terms of Beth's will and codicil, entering the documentation as evidence.

"How do you manage all the items in an estate such as Beth's?"

Janet smiled. "With painstaking detail, greatly enhanced by the use of a digital camera. Before I tag items for distribution, as directed by the client, I take a photograph."

"As part of Beth's estate, you went to the tractor shed with Ms. Stephens accompanying you?"

"Yes. I prefer having family members present to witness the

process after they have been notified of the contents of the will. Ms. Stephens and I went to the tractor shed to document a wooden wheelbarrow that Beth Candler's great-grandfather made by hand and the Farmall Cub tractor that had belonged to Beth's father."

Howard nodded his understanding. "Taking photographs of those items, as well as anything else in their proximity?"

"That's correct. Two items came to my attention upon later examination of the photographs...a socket wrench left lying exposed in the shed and the box on the front axle of the John Deere tractor. These items were previously mentioned by Deputy Watson."

"I take it you knew Beth Candler well?"

"Yes, indeed. She was one of my closest friends. I was at the hospital when she passed."

"You actually saw Beth operate the John Deere tractor on one of your visits to her home?"

"Objection. Mrs. Evans is not a tractor expert."

"But she observed the operation which is in question." Howard waited.

"Overruled."

"That's correct. I teased Beth about the makeup box so handily located on the front of the tractor." Janet paused for the brief laughter that passed through the crowd. Judge Henderson silenced the audience with a single look. "Beth explained that Lou had designed a system of using window weights in the box to add weight and improve the performance of the tractor, allowing her to loop around the pastures instead of backing up and driving down the steep slopes."

"Beth's words?"

"As exact as I am able to remember."

Howard checked his notes more to give Janet a breather than refresh his memory.

"You received a telephone message from Beth Candler on Friday, April 28, before she died on Sunday, April 30?"

"Yes."

"With the court's permission?"

The judge nodded and the taped message was played.

Beth's rich contralto voice floated across the courtroom. "I guess you're not home yet, Janet, and Ellen is doing her usual ignoring the telephone. I heard them, Janet, I heard them talking about what it would take to be together. Lou and Patti. It's all been a sham. I don't care about me anymore, but oh, my God, Janet, they were trying to figure out how to be rid of Will and me so they wouldn't lose any of the cash or real estate. Both of us. Both of us. I promised Keith to look after Will." Beth's last sentence was whispered in agony.

Shock registered on all faces in the courtroom, including the defendant.

"It was a week before you heard the message?"

"Yes." Janet explained her previous message system and her difficulty with using it, accepting the entire fault for not hearing the recording promptly. No one laughed about her earrings.

"Thank you, Mrs. Evans." Howard returned to his table and waited for the cross-examination to begin.

Janet watched Rich Tyler stand and idly wondered if the chair was coming up with him stuck to his wide hips. She realized that she was grabbing at any comic relief available because she knew Rich was coming after her as advised by Patti's legal counsel.

"My goodness, Mrs. Evans, you seem to know everything about Beth Candler and have such wonderful recall."

"Beth was a dear friend."

"Where do you live, Mrs. Evans?"

"I am co-owner of ten acres with a nineteen hundred-square-foot brick ranch in western Bedford County."

"No close neighbors?"

"Not to mention."

Rich nodded. "I understand the need for that. In fact, was not Beth Candler introduced to Lou Stephens at one of your parties?" Rich's insinuation when he said "parties" was clear.

"Yes, she was."

"A bonfire party at your home attended by all women?"

"Yes."

"The home you co-own and share with Ellen Harris, your partner for more than twenty years, who we are to hear from later?" He asked the question so casually that it took everyone a moment to realize that Janet Evans had finally been outed as a lesbian.

Howard started to object and Janet caught his eye and shook her head.

"That is absolutely correct."

Rich seemed disappointed with Janet's lack of emotion. "You never approved of Lou's relationship with Beth, did you?"

Howard ignored Janet. "Objection."

"Sustained."

"I'm done." Rich nodded to the judge and squeezed into his chair.

"You're excused, Mrs. Evans."

Janet returned to her seat. She felt oddly relieved. There had been enough secretiveness in her life.

Ellen was livid. "That fat son-of-a-bitch had no call—"

Janet silenced her with a look. "He was very slick. I'm glad it came from me and was not badgered from you. Calm down, you'll have your chance."

Ellen nodded as she was called to the stand. She was all business, looking Howard and faces in the crowd in the eye as she was led through explaining how she opened Beth's personal e-mail and found the correspondence Beth had forwarded to her account.

"So at the time the last of these e-mails was written, Beth Candler and Lou Stephens were attempting to reconcile the problems they were having in their relationship?"

"Yes, they were, from October to mid-February."

"I see." Howard deviated from the script he had rehearsed with Janet and Ellen.

"And would you read an e-mail from the month of November in Beth's file labeled Betrayal?"

"Objection. Hard copies have been introduced into evidence."

"Overruled. This will assist in summarizing the exhibits given to the jurors."

Ellen almost kept the corners of her mouth from twitching

as she adjusted her bifocals and referred to the e-mail Howard requested. She made sure she was aligned with the microphone and proceeded in a clear voice.

"'Good morning, my sweet L-baby. How I wish I was there with you in our country home to gently awaken you with kisses all over and so much more. I cannot bear being separated from you so much of the time. You have suffered through so much with Beth and Will as have I. We only have to hide our love a little longer as we figure out how to be together for the rest of our lives, no matter what it takes to be rid of the obstacles standing in our way. We have had enough pain being apart and enduring life with the wrong partners. What a difference it makes to find your soul mate. I could not love you more, and if you love me, don't forget to remove this from your inbox permanently.'"

"It is signed 'PrincessP." Ellen did not wait to be asked. "That's the same as her personalized license plate—Princess Patti."

The courtroom was absolutely silent.

"And the e-mails were sent from Patti Candler's account to Lou Stephens's account?"

"Yes, sir."

"Discovered by Beth Candler and forwarded by Beth to her own account?"

"Yes, sir."

"All password protected?"

"Yes, sir."

"And the other e-mails are similar in content?"

"Some are more sexually explicit."

"Would you read the e-mail from the Betrayal file dated February 3?"

Ellen remembered that one well. She read without embellishment—none was needed.

"'It is early morning, L-baby. Will snores contentedly in the bed as I slip away with my laptop. You must promise to delete this as soon as you read it, as I know you have all the others. I've given our last conversation much thought and have decided now is the time for you to proceed with my plan. More when I see you next. PrincessP.'"

Howard nodded and sat down, daring Rich to open the can of worms of cross-examination.

Rich moved as though to stand and changed his mind, restraining Lou instead.

Greg leaned forward and whispered in Janet's ear. "That's the one Howard used to bait Patti, isn't it?"

Janet nodded.

Chapter Thirty-two

"I'm sorry, because I hate using the word on a man for all the obvious reasons, but the expression fits. Will Candler is a pussy." Ellen slammed her mug of Folgers on the kitchen table to accentuate her point.

Buddy raised his head and issued a deep-throated growl.

"Yeah, that's exactly how I feel." Ellen rubbed the dog's head. "Sorry, Bud, I didn't mean to disturb your breakfast nap."

The Australian shepherd settled back onto the braided rug under the table and chairs and sighed.

Janet repeated the sigh and gave up on working the crossword puzzle. She had looked at nothing else in the newspaper, and the small televisions in the kitchen and office were silent. Ellen was at the table with her because Janet had requested the set in the den also remain off. "Okay, Ms. Court TV aficionado, what do you not understand?"

Ellen made her voice stay at its normal volume. "Well, it's really pretty simple, they killed his sister. Why wouldn't he tell everything he knows against them?"

Janet looked out the kitchen window. The male finches had turned a brilliant yellow with their spring coats. They covered the feeder filled with thistle seed. "He agreed to cooperate with Howard, but he feels obligated to protect his wife. He's a man clearly torn by the few emotions he will allow himself to feel. He blames Lou for all of it." Janet had told only Howard what little she knew of Will's mishandling of client funds that Patti held him in tow with—that it happened ten years ago in another state with no formal charges filed.

"Bullshit. He knows. He's just a damn pussy. He should hate those two women." Ellen stormed out of the kitchen to dress for court.

"It's never that simple." Janet finished her coffee and followed to suit up.

Janet and Ellen settled in on the bench immediately behind Howard. It was now their designated seating that others stayed clear of. Janet found it to be a dubious honor. She felt a hand on her shoulder and knew it belonged to Greg before she looked.

"Are you girls okay?" Greg leaned forward and whispered.

"We were worried about you after yesterday," Andy added. "Every time I called last night, your line was busy."

"We're as well as we can be. She's thrilled that I'm out." Janet nodded at Ellen. "It still has not sunk in with me, even if Mother has decided her life is ruined." Janet rolled her eyes. "I figure we're the least of anyone's worries at this point."

Ellen took Janet's hand in hers. "It'll be okay."

"That's easy for someone who's R-E-T-I-R-E-D to say. Tom was certainly gracious enough about it." Her law partner, Tom Langhorne, had been the first to call her at home the previous night. She explained to Greg, "He's decided that whatever clients we lose, we'll pick up more from the publicity, and we didn't really want the ones lost anyway, wheat from chaff." She shrugged. "At least I don't have to live with what's on his mind." She stared at Will.

Will Candler approached the witness stand. The expensive suit that had once made him appear so dapper now hung loosely on his body. His complexion had taken on an unhealthy gray cast. He looked as though he was taking his place before the executioner's chopping block as he was sworn in and settled into the wooden chair. He had to be reminded twice to speak up as he went through the process of stating basic facts about himself and his relationship to Beth.

"Were you and your sister close while she was helping your

mother care for your father?"

Will shifted on the hard bottom chair. "We talked on the phone and we e-mailed."

"Daily?"

"No."

"Weekly?"

"No."

"Monthly?"

"Yes."

"And you were given an equal share of your father's estate?"

"Yes."

Howard glanced at the judge. "Same with your mother's worsening health?"

"Excuse me?"

"Monthly e-mail or telephone call?"

"Yes. Until the last time she was in the hospital. Patti and I were here when Mother died. We helped divide the household when Mother sold the farm and moved to Beth and Lou's. We moved back to Virginia after Mother's death."

"To be close to Beth and Lou?"

"Yes."

"And you inherited an equal share of your mother's estate?"

"Yes."

"Beth treated you fairly in the settlement?"

"Yes. Beth was Mother's executrix. Mother left everything to Beth to do with as she saw fit."

"Beth looked out for your interests?"

"Yes. Beth was always fair." Will's hands gripped the arms of the chair as though the only way for him not to fidget.

Janet nodded to herself. Howard Mills was an excellent trial attorney. She had given thanks many times since being told the case was on his list. Anyone who didn't realize that every nuance of a trial he was involved with was scripted and in his head soon came to regret taking the slight black man for granted. Howard's small stature was no reflection of his intelligence. Quite the opposite.

Howard rubbed his cheek as though checking for whiskers.

"How long have you been married, Mr. Candler?"

"Not quite twelve years."

"And what does your wife do?"

"Patti is an antiques broker, buying estates and selling to dealers. She also volunteers for the United Way and the Cancer Society…at least she did when we lived in Tennessee."

"Have you ever considered divorce?"

"No. I am committed to my marriage." Will's voice was flat.

Howard nodded as though in sympathy. "Where were you when the accident occurred?"

"In the basement at Beth and Lou's, shooting pool."

"Drinking alcohol?"

"Yes."

"Heavily?"

"Yes."

"Did you know where your sister was or what she was doing?"

"No, I hadn't seen her since breakfast."

"Did you know where your wife was or what she was doing?"

Will stared at Lou.

"Mr. Candler?"

"Patti was with Lou on the sofa in the living room, watching television. Patti was also by my side at the hospital as we prayed for Beth to live. Lou was the one who aggravated Beth the morning of the accident. Lou taunted Beth that the tractor was the only thing that made Beth happy anymore. Beth agreed with Lou and left the house headed toward the tractor shed."

"Did you and Patti and Lou usually stay inside the house during the day?"

"Patti had to because of allergies. I did because I have never done manual labor. Lou was usually in and out, tinkering with the tractors or lawnmower or working on outbuildings or the house, always trying to be the man of the house. Lou never could sit still very long, even for Patti. Beth either worked in her office or at Mother's or was on the tractor."

"Beth had operated a tractor since childhood?"

"Yes, since her feet reached the brake pedal." Will's face paled.

Howard nodded and seemed to hesitate before asking his next question. "The last time you talked to your sister, did you tell Beth that you never wanted to see her again?"

Janet held her breath. She had prompted Howard to ask this without forewarning Will.

"Yes." Will's expression and voice were anguished.

"Thank you, Mr. Candler. I reserve the right to redirect later if needed." Howard sat in front of Janet and Ellen and reached for the glass and pitcher of water.

It was all Janet could do not to lean over the railing and hug him.

"Damn, he's good." Ellen whispered to Janet with her eyes on the defendant's table.

Janet nodded and felt a hand on her shoulder. She looked behind her, then covered Gloria's hand with her own. Gloria sat between Andy and Greg. Janet saw Ruth Dunn in burgundy scrubs two rows behind Gloria. They both must have used vacation hours to observe the proceedings.

They watched and listened as Rich Tyler unsuccessfully tried to defuse Will's testimony. He only emphasized a man miserable with his life. Janet thought of one of Keith's sayings—when you dig yourself into a hole, remember whose hands were on the shovel.

Howard had subpoenaed Delores Clowdis from North Carolina and kept her in a motel room until ready to bring her to the stand.

Delores approached the front of the courtroom, keeping her eyes on the judge and moving with a grace that belied her height. Like Ellen, she had pulled her former office clothes from the depths of her closet and applied base makeup to her tan and weathered complexion. She looked like one of the new, older models for L.L. Bean.

Howard guided her through introducing herself and explaining her past and present occupations. There was an incredible air of genuineness about the woman, just as Howard had banked on.

She answered Howard's questions calmly and rationally without embellishment. Howard stood so that as she looked him in the eye with her responses, she made eye contact with the jury. She told of the first time that Lou Stephens came to Lucky's with Beth.

"And the last time that you saw Ms. Stephens, was she alone?"

"No. She came in with Patti Candler last October, a year after she was there with Beth Candler."

"As friends?"

"Extremely intimate friends." Delores put the emphasis on "friends" that closet lesbians used.

There was a low rumble of nervous laughter across the courtroom. Judge Henderson rapped her gavel.

"The women were romantic in public?"

"Very much so."

"Were they planning the rest of their vacation?"

"They discussed how to continue their affair while they found a way to be free of their spouses without suffering financially. They joked about deceiving their spouses and friends. When the husband called and told Patti Candler to choose between him and Lou, they decided to hide what they were doing. They thought secrecy would make the affair even more special." Delores was unable to contain her disgust.

"Hot damn," Ellen whispered to Janet as Howard thanked Delores and returned to his table.

Rich tried to rattle Delores's memory. "Ms. Clowdis, you're absolutely sure that Patti Candler was in your establishment with Lou Stephens?"

"Oh, yes. Faces and dates are two things I have absolute recall of after years of working with the public on behalf of the commonwealth."

"And just what type is your establishment," Rich glanced at his notes, "Lucky's?" He looked puzzled.

"It's the most popular lesbian bar in the Outer Banks. All the girls come there to be seen and hook up where they can be open about their sexuality. We're even used to the women who are only experimenting while leaving husbands at home."

Ellen elbowed Janet. "He asked for that one."

Rich backpedaled. His tactical error was in thinking he would discredit Delores because of her clientele. Instead the courtroom was nodding in understanding. "Where were Lou and Patti seated?"

"They took stools at the bar while waiting for a booth to become available."

"And you heard every word of their conversation?"

"I was back and forth serving customers at the bar and mixing drinks for the waitresses. I heard enough of their conversation. The more they drank, the louder they talked."

Rich Tyler returned to his seat.

Next, Howard called Addie Tomlinson, one of Delores's waitresses.

She took a deep breath and shook her blond curls as she walked along the center aisle of the courtroom toward the judge. Addie sat on the edge of the witness chair. No amount of coaching by Delores would keep the nervous timbre out of the girl's voice. This was the most exciting thing she had done in her twenty-two years. She explained who she was and where she worked.

"Were you working the night that Lou Stephens came into the bar with Patti Candler?" Howard asked.

"Yes, sir."

"How can you be so sure?"

"I didn't know who they were at the time, but I noticed that they were the only customers that Delores, Ms. Clowdis, paid any attention to that night, so I did the same after they moved from the bar to one of my booths."

"And did you hear them discuss how to continue their affair while they found a way to be free of their spouses without suffering financially?" Howard trusted his memory and Rich's objection if he strayed.

"I didn't hear as much as Ms. Clowdis because I was back and forth between booths while Ms. Clowdis stood at the bar. But Ms. Clowdis missed the last of it after them two moved."

"The last of it?"

"Yes, sir. I'll never forget because they were trying to act like they were carrying on foolishness like most of the customers, but they were serious."

Howard waited.

"The fancy blonde asked the little dyke," she pointed at Lou, "if she would kill for her." Addie said it so simply that it took a moment for the answer to sink in with the jury and the audience.

Howard stopped in front of the defense's table. "If I may, for the record. Patti Candler asked Lou Stephens," he gestured at her, "if she would kill for her?"

"Yes, sir." Addie nodded emphatically, curls shaking in all directions.

"And Lou Stephens's answer?"

Addie closed her eyes briefly, as though revisiting the scene. "Anything for you, baby."

"Thank you, Ms. Tomlinson." Howard nodded first to the judge, then to Rich.

Rich Tyler stood at his place at the table. "And you remember this verbatim, word for word?"

"Yes, sir. I'd never forget those two. They tried to tip me enough to take them back to my place, but I wasn't interested. I could tell they were two fucked-up bitches."

The judge rapped her gavel and stared at the jury. "Disregard the witness's last sentence. Miss Tomlinson, use that language again in my courtroom and you will be severely fined."

"Ms. Tomlinson, did Patti Candler ask my client if she would kill Beth Candler for her?"

"No, sir."

"Did Patti Candler and my client have their physical relationship on their minds that night?"

"Were they hot for each other? Oh, yes, sir." Addie glanced at Judge Henderson, afraid that she had blundered again.

"And they were drinking heavily?"

Addie mentally counted trips to the booth. "Yes, sir, at least four drinks each, maybe more."

"Thank you, Miss Tomlinson." Rich sat down, looking pleased with himself as he forced his body between the arms of the chair.

Janet looked over her shoulder at Greg. "Badabing badaboom."

Greg leaned forward. "That's why Patti pleaded guilty and cut a deal to rat."

Janet closed her eyes and nodded.

The hole was deepening.

When they returned from lunch, Janet knew that the afternoon would wrap up Howard's portion of the "case-in-chief." She silently prayed that the string of evidence was compelling enough to make up the jury's collective mind.

Janet studied the woman at Rich's elbow. So this was Patti Candler's attorney and besotted sorority sister. Her legal reputation preceded her. Ashley Tate's name was whispered often at bar functions, and not in a good way. She was as ruthless in her client's defense as she was obsessed in maintaining her college looks and figure. She could easily pass for Cindy Crawford's mid-forties sister. She routinely decimated opponents. Today her caramel hair was swept up on the back of her head and her blouse unbuttoned to her sternum. She was giving Rich Tyler last-minute instructions that he would be well advised to follow.

"This should be interesting. Howard has been in the negotiation of his career already to make this happen, gambling with years off of Patti's sentence. It all depends on how damaging Patti's testimony is to Lou." Janet whispered so that only Ellen heard her.

Ellen nodded, unable to take her eyes off of Patti being escorted into the courtroom. "How in the hell did they manage to make her look like she just came from the salon rather than the cell?"

Janet shrugged.

"Is that wise?"

"They must think so."

Patti Candler had just been called to the stand by Howard. She stated her name, address, and relationship to Beth. Her eyes bore into Janet's.

Lou was stock-still in her seat.

"Were you and your sister-in-law close?" Howard hesitated

with the last word as he looked at the jury members.

"Fairly."

Howard nodded. "Did you consider her a friend?"

Patti thought the question over. "More an acquaintance." She smiled.

"Didn't have much in common?"

"Not really."

"Have you worked, Mrs. Candler?"

"I have my own business, brokering antiques."

"I see." Howard was too casual. "What is your source of income?"

"Trusts and stocks from my family. My husband," she added as an afterthought.

Howard nodded again. "Do you volunteer?"

"I have. The usual, United Way, Cancer Society, MS."

"But not for extended periods of time?"

"No. It becomes too tedious."

"I see." Howard rubbed his cheek. "Did you enter into a carnal relationship with Lou Stephens after you met her as your sister-in-law's partner?"

"Yes." She answered as casually as about her volunteer work.

"Did you and Ms. Stephens discuss leaving your respective partners?"

"I was dabbling. I never intended leaving a good marriage, but Lou was over her involvement with Beth."

"I see." Howard clearly did not. "So your husband and your sister-in-law were to just allow this 'dabbling' to run its course?"

"Yes. Will and I have always had an open marriage."

"I see. Open, as in free to pursue sex with other people?"

"Yes."

"So you participated in extramarital affairs prior to Ms. Stephens?"

"Oh, yes."

Janet heard the gasp that escaped Lou.

"Were you the author of the e-mails to Lou Stephens?" Howard asked the question innocently.

"Yes, I wrote e-mails to Lou." Patti's face was expressionless.

"The e-mails that were explicit about participating in a physical relationship with another woman, wanting to be with that woman, and being rid of obstacles? The e-mails that referred to a plan for Lou Stephens to carry out?"

"Yes. I wrote in the heat of the moment."

"And you had no qualms about relations with Lou Stephens and your husband at the same time?"

"No."

"You wanted a residence with both your husband and your sister-in-law's partner?"

"We all enjoyed going back and forth between the city and the country."

"Did you and Ms. Stephens discuss what it would take for her to be free of Beth Candler?"

"Yes. Beth was never going to be as open-minded as Will, but Lou had put Beth on the deed to her property."

Howard looked at Will as he asked the next question. "Did you plan the tractor accident that would have Lou Stephens free of Beth Candler without buying her out of Ms. Stephen's property?"

"Lou and I discussed the possibility of something happening to Beth while on the tractor."

"Do you know how to operate a farm tractor?"

"With these nails?" Patti waited for laughter from a silent courtroom. "No."

"But you watched Lou and Beth?"

"Yes."

"And you understood the basics?"

"Yes, Lou explained it to me."

"Do you know what a window weight is?"

"Not until Lou showed one to me."

"Do you know what a power take-off is?"

"Not until Lou demonstrated one for me."

"Did you encourage Lou Stephens to free herself of Beth by harming her?"

"Objection!" Rich Tyler finally knocked his chair over.

Judge Henderson did not hesitate. "Overruled."

"Only if she wanted to. Lou had been through so much with Beth about her career and her mother."

"Yet you asked Lou if she would kill for you?"

"After four mixed drinks, yes, I did. And, yes, she was willing."

"Were you willing to buy Beth out since you wanted her share of the farm?"

"It would have drawn too much from my portfolio."

"That's a no?"

"Yes."

Howard stared at the members of the jury, then turned to Patti. "Did you take Lou Stephens up on her willingness to remove all the weights from the tractor knowing Beth would use the tractor on a steep slope?"

"I came up with the plan as more of a mind challenge, never really believing Lou would carry it out, even after I suggested it was time to set things in motion. It was so simple. Lou should have thought of it herself."

Judge Henderson stared at Patti Candler with no sympathy.

Ellen gripped Janet's arm as though readying to saw it off. Neither woman could take their eyes from Lou as she whispered furiously in Rich Tyler's ear while gesturing at Patti. He repeatedly shook his head in response to her ranting.

Chapter Thirty-three

Janet felt Ellen's eyes on her. She leaned closer as the crowded courtroom settled down for a new day of testimony. Proceedings would begin in fifteen minutes.

"That bitch," Ellen muttered. She leaned forward and looked across the aisle as Ashley Tate wordlessly took a seat behind Rich Tyler, completely ignoring Will Candler. Ellen had seethed all night about Patti's testimony against Lou.

Janet squeezed her hand. "Don't start that again."

"She's a conniving bitch." Ellen hissed the words. "Patti reeled Lou in and has now ratted her out to save herself. Conspiracy my ass, Patti is the damn mastermind of all of it. Lou is going to take the fall because Rich Tyler's fat ass didn't think of ratting first."

Howard Mills looked over his shoulder and pressed his index finger across his lips.

"Sorry." Ellen folded her arms over her chest as though to hold her frustration in check.

Janet was truly ashamed that she snickered as Rich Tyler tried to stand and the chair he was sitting in came several inches off the floor with him. The fact that Janet could not keep her mind off Rich and his chair told her she was seriously torn out of the frame over the trial.

Ellen smacked Janet's forearm. "Be serious."

Greg leaned forward and whispered. "We don't need a judge, we need an interrogator."

"You guys behave." Janet looked first at Ellen, then over her shoulder at Greg. Andy raised his eyebrows as though innocent of thinking the same. "It's all part of due process. Now is the hard part. The prosecution's facts have been presented to the jury. It's Rich's turn to cross-examine and challenge the evidence on Lou's behalf."

"Patti should have just been made to testify, no deal, no plea bargain, no high-dollar bitch pressuring everyone, no twisting the truth to benefit her." Ellen sat on her hands, attempting to calm herself down.

"*Nemo tenetur se detegere,*" Janet said clearly. She saw Howard nod.

"You do and you'll clean it up," Ellen said, and Greg giggled.

Janet patted Ellen's thigh. "Latin for 'nobody has to reveal oneself.'"

Ellen frowned. "Fifth Amendment?"

"Very good. Look, we know Lou and Patti are equally guilty, but they have the right against self-incrimination. They can't be forced to be a witness against themselves. We're damn lucky for the e-mails and waitresses' hearing what allowed Howard to leverage Patti into testifying, or they both would have been much more certain of getting off scot-free."

"Entire process sucks, doesn't it?" Greg leaned forward with his face between the two women.

"Well, no. But it does create a boundary that the prosecutor may not cross unless the witness so chooses," Janet explained.

"Who in the hell would do that?" Ellen spoke before Greg beat her to the question.

"Someone who, in their mind, is sure of their innocence and needs the rest of us to believe them to restore their reputation and popularity enough to risk taking the stand."

Ellen and Greg spoke simultaneously. "Lou."

Janet nodded in agreement. "I'd bet money on it and that's what worries me."

Lou's appearance had changed drastically during the weekend break. Her hair was cropped close to her head—shorter than she had ever worn it—and there was no softening of her features with makeup. She had the appearance of not sleeping and a deep set wariness in her expression. Lou finally understood being betrayed by someone she was completely in love with.

In response to Rich's questions, Lou stated her full name, address, and relationship to Beth. "We were lesbian partners for over two years."

The packed courtroom was silent. The jurors stared at the woman seated beside the judge.

Rich stopped midway in his approach to the witness chair. "How was Keith Candler with that relationship?"

"Uncomfortable at first. It was hard for her to accept Beth's coming out, but she came to consider me as her adopted daughter."

"You helped with her care after she moved into the cottage on your property?"

"Yes, sir."

"You had a good relationship with her?"

"Yes, sir."

"Was caring for her mother hard on Beth?"

"Yes, sir. She handled everything, wouldn't let anyone else help with grocery shopping or taking Keith to the doctor, even though it tore her to pieces."

"Was losing her mother hard on Beth?"

"Yes, sir. They were very close. More like friends most of the time than mother and daughter. Beth was devastated by her mother's death. There was nothing any of us could do to help her deal with it."

"Beth was a strong, independent woman?"

Lou almost smiled. "Yes, sir."

Greg leaned over to Janet. "Should he be going there?"

"I knew he would." Janet concentrated on observing Lou.

"Was she strong and independent the entire time you knew her?" Rich folded his hands together.

"The last several months, we were all worried about the changes in Beth."

"You and her brother?"

"And Patti."

"What changes?"

"She lost interest in work, in her friends, and in her family. We couldn't convince her to see a doctor, but she appeared very depressed."

Rich nodded. "Over the loss of her mother?"

"Yes, sir."

"What was your arrangement with Beth Candler?" Rich tried to cross his arms over his chest, but they didn't quite reach. He slid his hands into his tight pockets. "Did you two have an open relationship?"

Lou frowned.

"Did both of you date and have sex with other women?"

"No, sir."

"Just you?"

"Yes, sir." Lou's body slumped in the chair. "Only once while we were together, though."

"You had a sexual relationship with only one other woman while you were with Beth Candler?"

"Yes, sir. Patti Candler."

"Was it just sex? Was it merely 'dabbling' on Mrs. Candler's part?" Rich asked the question, knowing Ashley Tate would make him pay dearly.

"I didn't think so at the time, and that wasn't what Patti told me. We both felt we had found our soul mates for the first time in our lives, that we had known each other in previous lives." Lou glanced at the jury members.

"So you were in love with Patti Candler?"

Lou did not hesitate. "Yes, sir."

"Were you still in love with Beth?" Rich's voice was incredibly gentle, as intended.

"Yes, sir. I cared for her very much. She had become more of a lifelong best friend."

"You weren't over the involvement with Beth, as Mrs. Candler stated yesterday?"

"No, sir. The passion was gone, but I could see us growing old together as roommates."

"It wasn't fun or exciting anymore?"

219

"Beth didn't need me. Patti said she did. Patti said she would have died without the love I brought to her. I believed her." Lou said it simply.

"Beth Candler had just experienced a grievous personal loss and was self-sufficient in dealing with it. Patti Candler was bored with her marriage and you were her savior?"

"Yes, sir." Lou wiped her eyes.

"Would Beth have shared you with Patti Candler?"

"No, sir. Beth made it clear to me in the very beginning that she was strictly monogamous. It was also her brother's wife. That's what made all of it become so jumbled and crazy. I was so caught up in what Patti wanted."

Ashley Tate earned the judge's glare with the loud sigh she released.

"What about your financial arrangements?"

"We had made the commitment to live together as partners. I gave her half interest in my home. Beth made improvements to it. We were equal partners in everything."

"You both worked on projects inside and outside of the house?"

"Yes, sir, together and separately. We both liked tinkering about the farm...Beth was raised on a large one...and manual labor."

"Did you tamper with the tractor before Beth used it on April 29?" Again, Rich's voice was deliberately gentle.

"No, sir." There was no hesitation on Lou's part.

"Did you take the weights out of the box on the front frame of the tractor so that the bush hog would not be counterbalanced?"

"No, sir."

"Did you carry thirty-six weights to the trash pile on your property?"

"No, sir, I did not remove the weights from the box."

"Did you explain the tractor and weights to Patti?"

"Yes, sir. She was very curious about all that Beth did. She played games with different scenarios of how Beth might die. It became an obsession with her."

"Refresh my memory. Each weight was approximately how

heavy?"

"Six pounds, a little more than a bag of sugar."

"Easy enough for anyone to lift," Rich said. "Tell me again how the tractor was used."

"In winter, a blade stayed on the front to push snow. The weights over the front axle helped so that the blade would break through ice or frozen slush. If it was a light, powdery snow, I took the weights out so that the gravel wasn't scraped into the ditches, stacking the weights right beside the tractor. The bush hog stayed on the back for balance and traction, it was too much trouble to remove. Rest of the year, blade was off and weights on the front with bush hog on the back for mowing grass."

"You sound as though you know your way around the mechanics of tractors."

"Yes, sir, that's part of my job at Fletcher Women's College as grounds manager."

"You maintained the tractors at home?"

"Yes, sir."

"But Beth did all the mowing?"

"At least ninety-five percent of it. I used the riding mower immediately around the house. She used the tractors for the fields and paths through the woods. I did nothing to tamper with the tractor, ever. The last time I worked on it, I changed fluids, checked tire pressures, sharpened bush hog blades, and readied the tractor for mowing grass."

"In April?"

"Yes, sir. It was an early spring. I made sure the tractor was safe for Beth and ready whenever she wanted to use it. She loved being outside after spending the week inside at the office." Lou's genuine affection for Beth showed clearly on her face.

Rich returned to the defense table with his shoulders drooping, knowing Lou's insistence on testifying was an error he had not been able to dissuade her from making—she accepted and understood that it was her call.

Howard referred to his notes jotted during Lou's testimony. He approached the witness stand still processing the questions he could ask so that they might actually be answered. He knew exactly what Lou Stephens was trying to accomplish.

"Would you have been able to buy Ms. Candler out of your partnership?"

Lou looked at her lap. "I exercise my right to silence."

"Wasn't Beth Candler's distress during the last months of her life due to your affair with her sister-in-law and the deterioration of her relationship with her brother?"

Rich quickly objected and Judge Henderson just as quickly sustained.

"Are the front weights on the tractor something to check as routinely as say gas and oil levels?"

"No, sir. Most of the time, you don't even think about the weights being there."

"Easy off and on?"

"Yes, sir. That's why I improvised using old window weights in a toolbox instead of the ones that attach to the wheels or the liquid that goes in the tires."

"Do you recognize this socket wrench?" Howard handed her the tool to examine.

Lou glanced at the wrench. "It belonged to Beth's father. Most of his tools are stamped with his initials to make sure borrowers didn't keep any of his by mistake. Beth said he would loan anything he owned, but he wanted his tools back." She pointed to the three letters.

"You left the wrench in the shed the last time you worked on the tractor?"

"No, sir. Beth gave me hell for leaving her father's tools lying about."

Howard nodded. A photograph of Lou's shop area at the college appeared on the projector screen. "This is the work area at Fletcher Women's College that you are responsible for?"

"Yes, sir." Lou's face turned a bright red.

"There are tools scattered on every surface."

"Yes, sir."

Howard walked toward his table, then stopped and faced Lou.

"The trench down the hillside...one of your projects?"

"Yes, sir. Taking the roof and foundation water away from the house."

"How did you leave the trench?"

"So I could find where I stopped." Lou looked puzzled.

"Backfill compacted?"

"No, sir. That would have been a waste of time since I would have to dig it out again."

"How long have you been working on this project?"

"Since Beth moved in. She always gave me a hard time about not finishing things."

"Over time, with rains and with normal freeze and thaw, wouldn't letting an underdrain just cause a sink hole?"

"It would depend on the soil and amount of water."

"But you are employed as a grounds manager of three thousand acres?"

"Yes, sir."

"So it just looked like another red clay bare spot?"

"Yes, sir."

"Were there other spots like that in the pasture?"

"Oh, yes, sir. If the dog peed on the same spot twice, it killed the grass."

There was nervous laughter among the jurors.

"So Beth didn't always know the progress of your digging?"

"We used to joke about it." Lou frowned. "She knew it was an ongoing project."

"And you didn't always know when she used the tractor. How did you know which red spot marked the end of the trench?"

"By finding the one out from the corner of the house."

"Easy enough to do on foot?"

"Yes, sir."

"Not so easy if riding on a tractor?"

"I don't know."

"You didn't mow there on the lawnmower?"

"No, sir. Beth did all the pastures using the Deere. I did the yard with the riding mower."

"And you dug the trench by hand?"

"Yes, sir. Small pipe. Didn't want to disturb any more of the grass than I had to. Beth said I was too cheap to rent a ditch witch and hardheaded enough to dig it a little at a time with a shovel and mattock."

"One last question about the tractor itself, Ms. Stephens." Howard leaned against the railing of the jury box.

Lou waited.

"Did you ever consider putting a roll bar and seat belt on the tractor?"

Lou's face remained blank. "It…it didn't come with those."

"But both could have been added fairly easily?"

Lou's head dropped. "Yes, sir."

"Twenty/twenty hindsight."

"Mr. Mills," the judge warned Howard.

"I swear that I did nothing to the tractor that day," Lou volunteered.

"That day?" Howard pounced on the very words that Lou should not have spoken.

"I did nothing to the tractor that would have caused Beth's accident. I swear to God and anyone else you want me to. I did not hurt Beth." Lou was adamant, too much so.

"Did you encourage Beth to leave the house, to leave you and Patti alone on the sofa, watching a movie?"

"Beth hated those damsel-in-distress movies…that's what she called them."

"Really?"

"She never understood why they didn't just do something to resolve the problem, that it was like her father used to tell her, do something even if it's wrong. She said she could solve their problems in far less than two hours."

"And is that what you and Patti decided, to do something to get rid of someone standing in the way of what Patti wanted?"

Lou looked evenly at Howard. "No, sir."

"Beth Candler could not be manipulated by you and Patti Candler, so a more drastic solution was needed?"

Lou appeared rigid in the chair. "No, sir."

"Patti wanted you to execute her plan for Beth's death?"

"Yes, sir, but I didn't do it."

"So you removed the weights and urged Beth onto the tractor?"

"No, sir."

"But you said you would kill for Patti Candler." Howard's voice cut through the entire room.

"I would have done anything for her." Lou's voice was as wistful as a child making a wish on the first star in a dark sky. It took Lou a moment to realize she had spoken aloud.

It took Judge Henderson a full thirty seconds of sharply rapping her gavel to quiet the courtroom. She then stopped the proceedings for the day.

The days that followed brought a repetition and reinforcement of what had already been said. The closing arguments were an exercise in dramatic rhetoric—short on Howard's part, long on Rich's. Three weeks after the commencement of the guilt phase of the trial, it ended. The judge and both attorneys spent the next morning instructing the jury, emphasizing that invoking the Fifth Amendment was not an admission of guilt. The diverse group of men and women deliberated for three hours.

Judge Henderson stared at the packed courtroom. "I will only caution you once. The jury has reached their verdict. They will return in a few minutes. I will read their statement as prepared by their foreman. I will then announce the jury's verdict. I will not tolerate any outbursts or interruptions." She stared the crowd into silence and the defendant into immobility.

Gloria anchored the end of the first bench. She held Ellen's hand, Ellen held Janet's, Janet held Greg's, Greg held Andy's, and Andy held Ruth's. They were split fifty-fifty with heads down and eyes closed or eyes locked on the judge's. Janet stared at Daphne and willed her to speak true to Janet's own heart.

Lou stood, visibly shaking.

It was not until Daphne was silent and the courtroom erupting that the verdict sank in with Janet. Her mind replayed it several times.

"The jury has unanimously determined that the defendant, Louise Stephens, is guilty of murder of the first degree in the death of Elizabeth Candler. The sentencing phase of the trial will follow. Dismissed."

A lone blow of the gavel ended the day. There was little sense of leniency among the jurors or the judge. Lou Stephens faced the consequences of a class two felony with possible sentencing of twenty years to life and a fine up to $100,000.

Patti Candler while successful in reducing her charge from murder of the first degree to conspiracy to commit murder faced the consequences of a class five felony with possible sentencing of one to ten years in prison.

Press coverage in the days to follow regarded Ashley Tate's finesse with the prosecution. Speculation focused on how few years Patti Candler would spend incarcerated. Lou Stephens was a done deal.

Epilogue

Janet Evans stared at the ceiling of the bedroom. There was just enough light from the dusk-to-dawn light outside to make out vague images of their furniture. Once again, she was wide awake at two a.m. and unable to go back to sleep. She had done this every night for the past two weeks—every night since the end of the guilt phase of the trial. She listened to Ellen snoring and wondered that her partner had any sinus linings remaining in her head. Buddy eased across the room and raised his front paws to the edge of the bed.

"Come on up, boy. I could use the company." Janet patted the king-sized bed.

Buddy clamored up on the bed, turned around in a circle twice, and dropped beside her hip. She let her hand rest on his chest, idly rubbing his stomach.

"Good boy." She patted his head. "Do you still think about her, Buddy? Do you remember her?" Something nagged at Janet.

Janet and Ellen had hosted a party the Saturday following the end of the initial portion of the trial—neither of them had the heart to suggest a bonfire, even though it was still cool enough to enjoy one. It was a bittersweet celebration of Janet's coming out to the community at-large.

Although the girls at the party felt vindicated, how could there be any measure of satisfaction or victory? Beth was dead. Now everyone knew her lifestyle and the details of the privacy she had so diligently protected. It was not Beth's complete outing or even her own that bothered Janet. The phone had rung continuously at work with clients using any excuse to let her know their opinion of her was no different than it had been before the trial.

Janet adjusted the sheet as Buddy settled beside her. "Don't hog the covers, boy." She tried to convince herself that if she lay still, she would go back to sleep. "Something is just not right." If she had thought and said it to herself once in the past two weeks, she had done so a hundred times. Janet kept seeing her friend Beth—her calm, deliberate friend, who thought through every action, who saw all sides of any issue, and who explored every possible way to consider options. Next was the worst. As much as Janet hated to allow the thought in her head, she found herself believing Lou's testimony.

Janet eased out of bed and went to her office waiting for Buddy to follow before closing the door behind her. She moved the mouse enough to activate the operating system of the computer. She checked her e-mail.

"*Auntie Em...*" The instant messenger popup waited for her to type after letting her know Queen_of_Denial was online.

"*What are you doing awake, Cupcake?*"

"*It's me, Andy.*"

"*Did his snoring force you to the computer like my partner's did?*"

Janet stared at the pulsating prompt. Neither of them was typing.

"*What's wrong, Andy?*"

The blinking continued.

"*What's wrong, Andy?*"

"*I don't want to think or write this.*"

"*What? Don't make me come over there in my housecoat.*"

She waited with growing impatience until he began typing.

"*Beth would have felt the difference in steering without the extra weight on the front end.*"

Janet frowned. "*I don't understand.*"

"*Why didn't Beth check for the weights when the tractor was not as stable as she was used to?*"

"*She didn't notice the difference until too late.*"

"She chose to mow over a fresh trench covered with dead grass clippings, the one soft spot in that field on enough of a slope to flip a tractor."

"She was on her way to the front pasture and decided to ride around the low side of the house. She just wanted to get out on the tractor and clear her head. She was in a hurry to be alone, or she felt a little reckless."

"The tractor was always her escape. She killed herself to expose Lou and Patti."

Janet stared at the dialogue box. She saw Beth's determination in the hospital as she lay dying to write a few last words—the phrase 'burden of knowledge,' reference to a character whose livelihood was based on pretending, and the clue needed to access her e-mail.

"Janet, you and I both know that Lou, Patti, and Will killed something very precious in Beth before she ever sat on that tractor the last time. Her spirit was gone long before her body."

Janet cut the power strip off so that everything about the computer died at once. Why had she come into her office? Andy's words reverberated through her mind. Janet agreed that the tractor was always Beth's escape even as a child. Had Beth killed herself? Surely not.

Janet leaned back in her chair. What did she know? Buddy nudged her hand and whimpered.

"I know you're the best dog ever." She leaned down and kissed his head. He licked her knee.

But what did she know? Beth had loved Lou. Beth had finally found happiness in a relationship. Beth had lost Keith after helping her mother face her sexuality and leave the family homeplace. Beth could put a guilt trip on herself like no one else. Beth had tried to talk with Lou and Will, only to have her logic twisted back on her or ignored or worse—find out that Will didn't care. Beth had lost interest in her work. Beth knew that Patti was turning Lou against her and that Will was lost to her. Beth had promised Keith to help Will free himself of Patti. Beth had watched Keith choose death rather than suffer with uncertain surgery and dialysis.

Beth had lost faith in everything and everyone. Yet she could not bring herself to harm Lou or Patti, and she knew they were planning to harm her and Will. Beth must have been fairly certain the women would get away with their plan based on all else she had witnessed.

Patti and Lou had discussed an accident of some sort to get Beth off of Lou's property. Lou could not afford the renovated farm on her own. Beth knew all that they were plotting. Once Beth was out of the way, they would go after Will.

"Beth gave up on life." Janet didn't like the sound of her words. "She wanted her own kind of revenge. She had to help her brother." Tears ran down Janet's cheeks.

Janet would never know for sure—none of them would. But what if Beth was so devastated by the combination of her mother's death, Lou and Patti's scheming, and Will's complete rejection of her that she decided to go through with her version of the plan? What if Beth committed suicide so that it would look like the murder being planned for her? What if Beth counted on her friends not resting until Lou and Patti were brought to some sort of reckoning? What if she reasoned the tractor roll to be her only way out that would ensure Patti's exposure? What if she decided that the tractor roll was the only way to save Will? Who but Beth could turn a murder planned to look like suicide into a suicide that would be judged as murder—a suicide pretending to be a murder pretending to be a suicide?

Janet spoke to Buddy. "Beth did throw her body on the grenade of Lou and Patti to save Will." Suicide was Beth's revenge and solution—the arcanum of Beth.

Buddy placed his front paws on her thigh and rose up to lick her cheek. Janet held the dog close, as close as she would keep her suspicions about Beth Candler's ultimate revenge. She turned the computer on to check if Andy was still there.

There was a new message in her inbox from "melwindcit." She opened the single line message. "About damn time you came out."

About the author

Mary Jane Russell is a native Virginian—the sixth generation to be raised on the family farm. She recently retired from local government after thirty-one years of service, during which she set a series of firsts—first female draftsman, staff engineer, project manager, and first female director of economic development.

Her lifelong love has been books and reading; her dream since a teenager was to be a published writer. This made her second career an easy choice. She is encouraged by her Cardigan Corgi, Winnie, and ignored by her cats. She lives with her partner in Roanoke, Virginia, and is discovering the joys of being an honorary grandmother.

The Arcanum of Beth is her first published novel.

Intaglio titles you may also enjoy

Deception
by Erin O'Reilly
ISBN: 978-1-933113-87-6
Price: $16.95

Lane Cuthbert knew exactly where she wanted to go and what she had to do to get there. Her goal was to challenge the network legal gurus for their positions, but first, she needed a juicy scandal or murder. What she found was a beautiful woman with a secret in need of a lawyer.

When the sheriff charges beautiful and wealthy Bryce Clayton with the murder of her nemesis Preston Garrett, Lane sees her chance at fame. The only problem is, Bryce won't say where she was at the time of the murder. Although Lane is able to discredit many of the district attorney's witnesses, she still has a problem — the alleged murder weapon belongs to Bryce.

Picking Up The Pace
by Kimberly LaFontaine
ISBN: 1-933113-41-3
Price: $16.95

Who would have thought a 25-year-old budding journalist could stumble across a story worth dying for in quiet Fort Worth, Texas? Angie Mitchell certainly doesn't and neither do her bosses. While following an investigative lead for the Tribune, she heads into the seediest part of the city to discover why homeless people are showing up dead with no suspects for the police to chase.

Coming Soon

Echo's Crusade by JM Dragon
ISBN: 978-1-935216-02-5
Price: $16.95
April 2009

Echo is now on a quest, and with the help of Detective Roan Keating, searching for justice becomes *Echo's crusade.*

Clinical Distance by Maria Ciletti
ISBN: 978-1-935216-03-2
Price: $16.95
May 2009

Will Mina sacrifice her heart for another chance at love, or will she keep a *clinical distance*?

Prairie Fire by LJ Maas
ISBN: 978-933113-47-0
Price: $16.95
June 2009

In this sequel to Tumbleweed Fever, the story of Devlin Brown, an ex-outlaw, and Sarah Tolliver, the woman of her heart, continues.

Survive the Dawn by Kate Sweeney
ISBN: 978-1-935216-04-9
Price: $16.95
July 2009

Alex and Sebastian are back in this sequel to *Away from the Dawn,* and must keep one step ahead of Nicholae the elder of the hierarchy.

The Very Thought of You by S. Anne Gardner
ISBN: 978-1-935216-05-6
Price: $16.95
August 2009

When Alex and Reese's worlds collide, they discover an attraction too strong to deny. A love that binds overcomes a past colored with heartbreak and becomes the hope of a little girl who dreams of a happy ending.

You can purchase other Intaglio
Publications books online at
www.bellabooks.com, www.scp-inc.biz, or at
your local book store.

Published by
Intaglio Publications
Walker, LA

Visit us on the web
www.intagliopub.com